The Ugly Truck and Dog Contest and Other Tales of Northern Life

Cathy Jewison

Published by Borealis Press Ltd., 2009

Canada

The Publishers acknowledge the financial assistance of the Government of Canada through the Book Publishing Industry Development Program (BPIDP) for our publishing activities.

Many thanks to Mike Kalnay for granting permission to use *The Ugly Truck and Dog Contest* as the title of this book, and to Terry Woolf for granting permission to use "The Dog Island Floating Film Festival" as the title of one of the stories.

Library and Archives Canada Cataloguing in Publication

Jewison, Cathy, 1961-
The ugly truck and dog contest, and other tales of Northern life / Cathy Jewison.

ISBN 978-0-88887-374-3

1. Yellowknife (N.W.T.)--Fiction. I. Title.

PS8619.E95U45 2009 C813'.6 C2009-901699-0

Cover design: drt, 2009
Cover image: Cathy Jewison
Author photo: Pierre LeBel
Printed and bound in Canada on acid free paper.

The Ugly Truck and Dog Contest and Other Tales of Northern Life

Cathy Jewison

BOREALIS
BOOK PUBLISHERS

Borealis Press
Ottawa, Canada
2009

For my grandmothers

Grace Stewart

who shared her love of Canadian literature

and

Violet Jewison

who showed me how much fun it can be
to cultivate a rich inner life

Table of Contents

Acknowledgements

Many, many thanks to the people who have helped me over the years. Dave Miller of CBC Mackenzie and playwright Tom Lackey provided early encouragement. My top-notch writing instructors have each helped in her own way: Mary Nilsen of the University of Iowa taught me essential techniques; Annabel Lyon of the Sage Hill Writing Experience provided solid advice; Rachel Wyatt of the Banff Centre nudged me out of the nest at the right time. Critiquers Charlotte Babicki, Fran Kimmel and Anita Daher have slogged through many an early draft and provided valuable suggestions for improvement. Anita gets bonus points for helping me navigate the business side of things, and for ongoing moral support. A great big thank-you also goes to Terry Tyo and Melanie Fogel of *Storyteller, Canada's Short Story Magazine*, who have published many of these tales and have played an invaluable role in my development as a writer.

Preface

Although these stories are works of fiction, they are based on some of the quirky and unique aspects of actual life in Yellowknife, Northwest Territories. The Ugly Dog and Truck Contest was invented by Mike Kalnay and friends, while passing the time at a local watering hole. Mike organizes this venerable and much-anticipated event, which takes place each spring during Caribou Carnival. Likewise, the Dog Island Floating Film Society, brainchild of Terry Woolf and Andrew Spaulding, holds occasional screenings on Yellowknife Bay during the fall. As the northern nights lengthen, all eyes in the Old Town turn toward Dog Island—when we see a torch flame, we know the films will be shown that evening. Other realities of life in Yellowknife: the golf course really is composed of sand, and the ravens really do have a predilection for stealing golf balls; people from all walks of life scavenge at the dump; Yellowknifers frequently leave "for good," only to find themselves back in town in no time flat. And we have dogs—lots and lots of dogs.

I've used our collective eccentricities as a starting point, and employed a good deal of literary licence in developing this collection. The characters are all products of my imagination. The names of some community events have been rearranged. Those of you who know Yellowknife will notice that I have played fast and loose with the geography of the Old Town when it suited me.

In the years since I wrote these stories, many things have changed in Yellowknife. The Black Knight Pub and bingo nights at the Elks Hall are now smoke-free. The junkyard in Peace River Flats that inspired the "installation piece" in one story has long since been cleared away. And Highway 3, the road that leads from the Alberta–Northwest Territories border to Yellowknife, was completely paved as of 2006.

Despite any creeping gentrification, life in northern Canada is still considerably different from life "down south." Ours is a unique environment, and we have our own way of approaching things. Even if some details have changed, the northern spirit that inspired these tales lives on.

Cathy Jewison
Yellowknife, N.W.T.
2008

The Ugly Truck and Dog Contest

The day the gods spoke to Marge, their voices reverberated with the roar and rumble of thunder. Actually, it was the crunch and crumple of her passenger-side door collapsing, but they spoke nonetheless. Marge sat stunned. Then she rolled down her window and stuck out her head, motioning to the driver who had hit her truck to do the same. He reluctantly complied.

"Way to go, Freddy!"

Freddy shook his head sadly.

"Really messed up, haven't you?"

Freddy closed his eyes in anguish.

"Because you've just guaranteed me first place in this year's Ugly Truck and Dog Contest, and you know it." She cackled.

Freddy rallied.

"Since when you got a dog?" he shouted.

Marge smiled mysteriously and drove off, leaving her neighbour in a haze of greasy fumes.

Yes, this was a sign. The sign. The one she'd been waiting for. This was going to be her year.

It was Marge's great passion to win Yellowknife's annual Ugly Truck and Dog Contest, that ultimate expression of individuality and character in a frontier town that was losing more of its individuality and character with each passing year. Every March during Caribou Carnival, Marge strolled out on the ice of Frame Lake to check out the competition. The trucks were "decorated" with all sorts of junk—fish nets, old tires, gas cans—which were often just window-dressing on a somewhat bedraggled, but still respectable vehicle.

Freddy, who lived across the road from Marge in the run-down heart of Yellowknife's Old Town, also coveted the title. He entered each year, without fail and without success. An autobody worker, he'd find the roughest-looking junker he could, then weld on pieces of metal that stuck out at odd angles. Sometimes he'd also take a sledge hammer to the selected vehicle, but this was sheer thuggery—there was no poetry in it, and the judges knew it.

Not so with Marge's truck, a battered baby-blue half-ton she called "Delilah" because it was not to be trusted, frequently conking out miles from anywhere. Marge loved to claim that Delilah was almost as old and experienced as she was, winking broadly as she uttered the word "experienced." This usually made listeners wince as they tried to block out any mental pictures of Marge gaining said experience.

No one really knew how old Marge was, but it was safe to bet that Delilah dated from the late '50s. Time and experience had indeed chiselled their mark on the truck with a graceful hand. The grille was smashed in from the time the emergency brake had failed when Marge was doing a surveying job up on Tin Can Hill, and Delilah had rolled into a tree. The truck's roof sported a large pit from the time Marge was playing ball at Tommy Forrest Park, and Shorty LaRue hit a foul that arched over the fence and into the parking lot. Delilah's tailpipe, loosely fastened to her chassis with a length of coat hanger, shook and rattled with each belch and roar of the muffler. The wheel wells were filigreed with rust, while the windshield was cracked and the body paint chipped from many trips down the highway that connects Yellowknife to the outside world. It was on one of these jaunts that the fender had caved in when a bison bounced off it just south of Fort Providence.

But Delilah alone was not enough to win the contest. One thing Marge knew from touring the Ugly Truck and Dog entrants year after year was that while all the trucks were fairly ugly, all the dogs were fairly cute. Oh, people tried to uglify their dogs in various ways—sticking bright pink tutus around their bellies, or clown collars around their necks. But none of the dogs were really ugly and Marge herself was willing to wait until a truly gawd-awful-looking beast came along. Until that day, she'd let wannabes continue to think they were winners.

Now, she'd received a sign. Delilah was nicely seasoned, but this collision brought her close to the height of hideousness. All she needed was a final touch. The two of them chugged off to the junkyard, where Marge wandered amongst the decaying vehicles reposing in the snow, looking for ideas. Then she saw it—the corroded shell of a truck that was the same model as Delilah. The salvage yard owner helped Marge remove Delilah's hood and replace it with the mangled one from the deceased vehicle. Few would have been able to detect a transplant, except that the "new" hood was canary yellow. Perfect.

Marge was about to leave when an absolute gargoyle of a dog appeared from behind a pile of flattened vehicles and wandered toward Delilah. He inspected the front tire on the driver's side, lifted a leg, and marked it. The beast had a thick, over-muscled body. A disproportionately small head was graced with a long, pointy snout, giving the animal a rat-like appearance normally reserved for much smaller dogs. Its eyes were an eerie ice blue, although it was hard to see the left one because the eyelid drooped badly. Spiky ears stuck out crookedly from either side of its head. The torso was covered with patchy, grey-white fur.

"Fantastic," murmured Marge. "Can I buy him?"

"Buy him?" said the junkyard owner. "Hell, lady, I've been trying to get rid of him for months. Would've put him down by now, but I keep forgettin' to buy shotgun shells."

The dog, who had been sniffing one of Delilah's bumpers, squinted up at the man and broke into a string of high-pitched barks. The junkyard owner threw a piece of rusty pipe at the animal, who easily dodged it before lunging and latching onto his pant leg. Striking at the dog's head with a monkey wrench, he missed and whacked his own shin. The dog released his grip, then trotted over and sat beside Marge.

"It's your life," the man gasped between grunts of pain. "If you want to share it with an ugly and mean-tempered mongrel, that's your business. Just get it the hell out of here."

Marge named the dog Hubcap in honour of how they first met. Delilah did not, in fact, have any hubcaps, but Marge thought it sounded more poetical than Wheelrim.

Things were falling into place, and the timing couldn't be better. Victoria, one of Marge's cousins, was about to pay a visit—if the perky and polished suburban chatelaine couldn't conceal her repulsion for Delilah and Hubcap, Marge knew she had the winning combination. Victoria was one of a long line of Marge's cousins who lived in southern Canada and had the unfortunate habit of watching educational television. After seeing too many documentaries on the North, they inevitably wanted to experience its glamour first-hand. As children, Marge and her cousins had enjoyed a mutual animosity, since the cousins were unable to appreciate the resounding splat of one of Marge's well-made spit balls as it hit a cheek, or the sinister elegance of her snake collection. But after pricing the cost of a trip north, the cousins remembered Marge with inordinate fondness. Over the years, every now and then, one or two of them would arrive expecting to see the northern lights and herds of caribou undulating across the taiga; instead, Marge showed them a couple of smoggy bingo games at the Elks Hall and a midnight fistfight outside the Gold Range Bar. It was usually enough to send them packing for good—not that they'd confess their disappointment to themselves or anyone else. Most sent a card the following Christmas, enclosing a small studio photo of the family. Their vanilla-pudding good looks gave Marge the heebie-jeebies.

This time she would have the pleasure of introducing the worst of her cousins to the best of Yellowknife. When they were little, Marge had delighted in putting Victoria's daintily dressed dolls out of their misery, sometimes by decapitation, sometimes by drowning. Victoria squawked at the time, but by their teen years, she was trying to reform Marge. She often tried to convince Marge to have her hair permed or to try nail polish at least once before graduation. Her wheedling insistence was no match for Marge's rugged individuality, however. And now, the Ugly Truck Gods were bringing Victoria to Yellowknife. Marge could hardly wait to see her face when she saw Delilah and Hubcap.

*****

Marge spotted her cousin's luggage before she spotted Victoria, since the pristine, shell-pink suitcases were distinctly out of place among the dirty duffle bags and plastic-tubs-sealed-with-duct-tape favoured by seasoned northern travellers. Victoria didn't fit in much better, clad in a pale yellow parka that obviously came from some boutique. Marge endured Victoria's ritual greeting of a vague kiss on each cheek because she had her own special greeting planned for her cousin out in the parking lot.

They left the terminal, Marge lugging two suitcases, Victoria following with her cosmetics case. Marge stopped for moment beside a shiny new truck to let her arms rest. Victoria promptly tried to open the passenger-side door.

"Why'd you lock it, Margie?" She pouted, and tried the handle again.

"We're not there yet."

Marge picked up the suitcases and trudged forward. She soon plunked them down beside her prize vehicle. Victoria kept walking. Marge yelled for her to stop.

"You rest for a bit," Victoria called back. "Just tell me where your truck is."

Marge pointed to Delilah. Victoria froze. Marge heaved the luggage into the box of the truck. She looked up to find that Victoria hadn't budged.

"Come on!"

Victoria reluctantly retraced her steps.

"You'll have to get in the driver's side—had a bit of an accident a few days ago, and the passenger door won't open any more."

Victoria reached toward the door handle. Hubcap, who had been lounging out of sight, suddenly threw himself against the window, barking wildly. Victoria shrieked.

"What is that?"

"My dog."

"Dog?"

"Dog."

"Can't you put it in the back?"

"Can't guarantee he won't pee on your suitcases."

"Well, poor thing, can't help the way it looks, I suppose." Victoria cautiously opened the door and slid in next to Hubcap, who took a break from his frenzy and licked her face.

"See, he likes you."

Victoria tried to smile as she wiped her cheek with a tissue. Marge snickered as they trundled off to her home, a derelict Quonset hut. As they pulled up a few minutes later, Marge spotted Freddy lugging some scrap metal into his garage.

"Hey, Freddy! I want you to meet my cousin." Marge dragged Victoria across the road.

Freddy wiped his hand on his coveralls before extending it toward Victoria. Victoria grasped his fingers lightly.

"Pretty jacket," he said.

Victoria smiled stiffly.

"Nice colour. Nice to see a *lady* in the neighbourhood for a change." He sneered at Marge's checked hunting coat, work boots, and ball cap.

Victoria's smile soured when she realized that Freddy's oily sleeve had brushed against her and left a dark streak on her parka.

"He's right, Margie," she said. "I wish you'd let me do something with your hair while I'm here."

"Ya, Margie," Freddy said. "It's kind of ugly."

"Nothing wrong with my hair." Marge ran a hand over her greying ponytail. "And you wouldn't know ugly if it bit you in the knee, Freddy—as the judges keep pointing out, year after year."

"People, please!" Victoria said. "Where are our manners?"

"Speaking of manners, I'm here to give Freddy a chance to show how neighbourly he is," Marge said. "I have to go out of town for a few days, so I'd appreciate it if you could help Victoria while I'm gone."

Freddy scanned Victoria from top to toe and grinned. "Do what I can."

Victoria shuffled closer to Marge. "Where are you going?"

"Have to do some surveying out of town. Duty calls, you know." Marge marshalled Victoria back across the street.

"Can I come along?"

"Nope. This is business. Besides, I'll be out in the bush. You'd hate it. You can use the time to get to know Hubcap. I'll give you the keys for Delilah, so you can travel around. And you'll have free run of my home." She flung open the door to the tunnel-like hut.

"Oh, Margie, how can you live like this?" Victoria stepped around a snowmobile engine just inside the door. She bent to gather a clump of open magazines from the floor, smoothing them shut and stacking them beside the patched Naugahyde couch. Marge shrugged. There was no point trying to explain—all she could hope for was quick release from her cousin's company. Marge figured a few days with Hubcap, Delilah, and Freddy should be enough to exorcise even someone as demonically decorous as Victoria. By the time she returned for Caribou Carnival and the Ugly Truck and Dog Contest, her cousin would be long gone.

"You could really do something with this place if you tried." Victoria made her way around the area that served as living room, dining room, kitchen, and guest bedroom. "Thank heaven I brought my swatches," she added as she launched into a stream of renovation and decorating ideas, holding up little pieces of coloured cloth to illustrate her points.

Marge turned her mind to preparations for the contest. She'd been scrounging at the city dump for months, stockpiling "decorations." The Ugly Truck Gods had been particularly kind the day she managed to excavate a six-foot-high plastic polar bear from a pile of debris. He stood on his back legs, his front feet pawing the air, his menacing stance matched by the gape of his maw.

Marge planned to create a little tableau on some plywood placed across the box of her truck. She would perch the bear nice and high and arrange some garden gnomes around him, like he was holding court. A wind chime made of enamel cups would be suspended from one paw to provide sound effects. Christmas lawn ornaments—candles and candy canes that stood about waist-high—would lend a festive air. A pair of battle-fatigued snowshoes would grace Delilah's tailgate; a moth-eaten caribou head would be mounted on the grille. The rest of the truck would be hung with old work boots and coffee cans filled with those puffy flowers they put on wedding cars. Marge figured that should suffice—a lot of contestants over-decorated their trucks, which she thought was a mistake. Then, of course, they probably had to, since their trucks were not of the same calibre as Delilah. It would take her only one evening to put everything together.

Marge toured Victoria around Yellowknife's hot spots the next day, before turning her over to Freddy. First, however, Marge insisted that Victoria drive her out to the airport so she could catch her flight into the bush. Marge told her cousin that she wanted to be sure she could handle Delilah, though in reality she just wanted to see Victoria spluttering down Yellowknife's main street in a first-class heap. Victoria tried to hide herself by sliding down on the seat. But driving Delilah was a full-body experience, and Victoria soon had to sit up so she could wrestle with the steering wheel and get enough leverage to stomp on the clutch. Victoria had to be satisfied with hiding behind her designer sunglasses, which she wore even though the day was overcast.

*****

Marge returned to Yellowknife the afternoon before the contest. Neither Victoria nor Delilah was there to pick her up. Congratulating herself on her success in ditching her cousin, she caught a cab home. As the car neared her house, she noticed a strange truck parked outside. She didn't give it much thought, though, because her attention was arrested by Hubcap. In the few days he'd been resident in the front yard, he'd developed a habit of flinging himself toward the road whenever a vehicle passed, his shrill barks breaking off in a dry choke as he hit the end of his chain. He would then stagger to his feet and continue his yipping. But now the cab had pulled all the way up the driveway and there he sat, still as a stick in the middle of the yard, his head turned slightly to the side.

"Oh my God—he's dead." Marge threw a twenty-dollar bill at the cabbie and raced over to her prized pooch. As she reached him, Hubcap slowly turned his head toward her.

A bellow of outrage erupted from Marge. Hubcap wasn't dead—he was posing. Someone had groomed him. Someone had washed and brushed him, then tied a blue bow around his neck, just like he was a damned poodle.

"Stop that, you ingrate," she snapped at the dog, who simply tipped his nose a little higher into the air.

That was when Marge realized that Delilah was nowhere to be seen. She recognized the crisis that was upon her—some scurvy knave, some slimy, snake-in-the-grass competitor had trucknapped Delilah!

Marge collapsed on the hood of the strange truck, beating her fists against the shiny blue enamel. She lifted her head and stared over toward Hubcap, who sat so that his profile was silhouetted against the snow. She turned back and examined the paint beneath her hands. Her head whipped toward Hubcap. Then she realized that the bow tied around his neck was exactly the same colour as the paint on the truck. She gasped. The dents had been smoothed out, the rusty patches filled in, the cracked windshield replaced, and the entire thing repainted, but there could be no doubt—it was Delilah. Marge ran a hand over the hood and along a fender. Whereas baby blue had suited Delilah in her decrepitude, she now looked cute. Insipidly cute.

Marge peered into the cab to find a bundle of silk flowers protruding from the freshly cleaned ashtray. A note lay on the seat. Knees shaking, she threw open the door and climbed in to read it:

> *Thanks for introducing me to Freddy. I've never met anyone who actually did autobody work, but it's a lot like doing house renovations, so we had plenty to talk about. I convinced him to fix your truck in exchange for some home-cooked meals. I couldn't believe he'd do all that work for nothing, really, but he said that the satisfaction of seeing the look on your face would be reward enough. You really do underestimate him, Margie. He's very nice. I must say, I was much happier driving your truck after her little "makeover." (I wish you'd let me do the same for you!) I'm the one who added the flowers in*

the ashtray, of course—just that final touch it needed. Thanks for everything. I'll write at Christmas.

—Victoria

Marge slumped against the steering wheel and howled.

The Prospector's Trail

"Noise! Traffic! Filth! Can't stand the commotion of the city. That's why I come out here," said the grizzled old guy. He leaned back in his lawn chair and contemplated the campfire, then took a long pull of tea from a tin cup. The light from the flames glittered off his creased face and greying beard. The old-timer stared upwards. Norman and Jennifer followed his eyes, examining the dome of the northern night sky, which was still blue at 9:30 p.m. They could hear a loon call from the nearby lake, and the lap of the waves on the shore.

A grumble emanated from the far-off heavens. Thunder? No—the grumble grew into a growl and then into a roar, which gained intensity until it filled the air. Their eyes searched for the source of the clamour. Jennifer covered her ears. Then they saw it. A jetliner, glowing gold with the reflected light of the night sun, made an elegant curve over the city dump and moved in over Long Lake. It lined up with a runway and continued its descent, swooping across Highway 3 for a perfect landing at the Yellowknife airport.

"Flight 592 from Edmonton, right on schedule." The old-timer took another drink of tea. He winced.

"You know, when I invited you over for 'tea,' I actually meant we'd be drinking something stronger—you must be thirsty after your long drive. But all the beer's disappeared.

Elsie must have had one of her damned card parties this afternoon, while I was out in the bush. And now all the peanuts are gone." He shook the empty bag. "Elsie! ELSIE!" he screamed toward an immense camper a few feet away. A tall, skinny woman came to the door. It was hard to see her features because an electric light was burning behind her.

"What?"

"We're out of peanuts."

"So go get some more. And buy some beer while you're at it."

"You know I hate going into that damned city."

"I'm missing my show." She slammed the door.

"Damned TV," he muttered toward the fire. "Supposed to be enjoying the beauties of nature. Get away from all that city stuff . . ."

He continued speaking, but the rest of what he said was drowned out by the whine of a semi-trailer zooming past on the highway a few hundred yards behind them. He finished his diatribe about the same time the noise of the semi faded into the distance. He rooted in his tin cup with a grubby finger, then flicked something onto the ground.

"Skeeter." He turned to Norman. "What kind of work you looking for?"

"Anything," Norman replied. "For now, anyway. I want to start a tourist operation. An interpretive centre—old buildings, dog sled rides in the winter, that sort of thing."

Roy nodded sagely.

"It's the old story. People been comin' to Yellowknife since the '30s, hoping to strike gold. Some did. Giant Mine's that way, Con's over there." He waved vaguely in opposite directions. "Then there's the others. Business tycoons. Government people. All want a piece of it. Some make it, some don't."

"Can't be any worse than southern Canada," Norman said.

Roy snorted.

"Bet you think differently when you're still living in a tent at forty below," he said.

Jennifer shuddered.

"Well, Yellowknife is the end of the road for me—and I don't mean just because the highway ends here." Norman's voice had a touch of bravado. "If I can't make it here, I can't make it anywhere."

"It's the end of the road for all true Yellowknifers. Place pulls a lot of people to it. The right ones stay."

"Any chance you could dig up something for us, Roy?" Jennifer asked.

"What do you mean?" the old-timer said. "What have you heard?"

"Nothing!" Norman jumped to his feet. His half-finished cup of tea, which had been balanced on his thigh, catapulted across the fire and hit Roy in the chest. The old man leaned forward and pulled the wet plaid flannel away from his skin.

"Good thing that wasn't hot," he said.

Jennifer stood and stomped off.

"Little missus gets a bit testy at times, eh? Know what that's like." Roy winked and nodded toward the camper. "I'd better pack it in—gotta rise and shine tomorrow."

As Roy collected the tin cups, Norman said goodnight and started off. Moments later, the old man heard a thud and turned to find Norman splayed on the ground.

"Tree root." Norman hoisted himself upright and limped away.

Roy shook his head. "Watch your step, son."

Norman found Jennifer standing next to their tent, an artefact he'd bought at a garage sale in Winnipeg a couple of weeks earlier. It consisted of mildew and, to a lesser extent, beige canvas.

"Get in," she said.

The tent came with an odd assortment of poles and guys that more or less kept everything in place. One of the poles was a bit too short, however, and if someone brushed against it, the tent collapsed. Since it was currently in its flattened state, Norman had to dive amongst the loose canvas and restore the poles. Jennifer then went around the outside, refastening guys. She gingerly crawled in. Norman was lying on top of his sleeping bag. Jennifer sat down on top of hers and shook her finger at him.

"Don't move for the rest of the night. Got it?"

"Got it."

Jennifer began to change into her pyjamas. The top was part-way over her head when she was seized by convulsions. She gasped. She panted. Her shoulders jerked.

"Achoo!"

The tent rocked ominously. Jennifer froze. When she was certain the tent would remain upright, she popped her head through her pyjama top. She glared at Norman through the dim light.

"You realize I'm allergic to this damned thing."

"It's all we can afford."

"No kidding," she said.

"You shouldn't be so hard on people."

"It's not my fault I'm allergic." She blew her nose.

"I meant Roy. I think he can help us."

"I know he can—that camper's brand new."

"Don't push too hard, or you'll scare him away."

Jennifer pulled on her pyjama bottoms, then carefully tossed her clothes toward the few inches of floor at the foot of her sleeping bag.

"You'll never get ahead by pussyfooting around," she said.

"We'll just have to give it some time."

Jennifer sneezed again. She wiped her nose. She turned to her husband.

"I'll give it six weeks," she said. "Until Labour Day."

"That's not much time to start a new life."

"Norman. We're living in a tent. This is not a life."

"We've only been here a few hours and we're already accumulating authentic northern experience."

"That's what you call drinking tea with that old guy? Authentic northern experience?"

"He's a character. Local colour. It'll be important when I set up the interpretive centre. Maybe I can get him to work there."

"If you can get something useful out of him, fine. But keep your distance while you're doing it. I don't want you playing the role of hillbilly—trying to out-northern the northerners for the sake of your 'interpretive centre.' You're going to be the owner, so you'll have show some decorum. Besides, you're lucky you didn't scald him. Like before."

"That was an accident."

"It's always an accident."

Norman sighed.

"Six weeks!" Jennifer said. "Unless I catch you wearing a plaid flannel shirt, in which case I'll leave you on the spot."

She climbed into her sleeping bag and turned her back on her husband. Norman heard her sniffling well into the night. He wasn't sure if she was crying, or just needed an antihistamine. It could be hard to tell with Jennifer.

Norman and Jennifer had arrived at Fred Henne Territorial Park, on the outskirts of Yellowknife, about suppertime that day. It was, indeed, the end of a long road for them. A year earlier, they had received their tourism studies certificates at a college in Winnipeg, then promptly got married. Norman still couldn't believe it—Jennifer had been a star student throughout the program, and he'd been flattered when she consented to date him because she liked his sense of whimsy.

With a sharp mind and an eye for the big picture, Jennifer was a whiz at developing tourism marketing programs. Norman's first love was "interpretation"—dressing up and acting like historical personages for the entertainment and edification of tourists. Jennifer's appreciation of his sense of whimsy had soon evaporated, however. She'd decided interpretation was undignified and convinced him to get into the corporate side of the industry. Norman found a decent job shortly after graduation, but was unnerved by the formality and high expectations of the office. Plagued by insomnia, he'd become clumsy. His boss had laughed when Norman tripped on the carpet in the waiting room and landed face-first in the fish tank. He had been less amused when Norman spilled a glass of Beaujolais on a client's silk dress. He was livid when Norman gave another client second degree burns by dumping a pot of coffee on him. Norman's reputation spread and he could no longer get work. Jennifer became the sole breadwinner, but as a recent graduate, she couldn't earn enough to support them both. When Norman begged her to let him pursue his dream of opening an interpretive centre, Jennifer agreed, on the condition that he did it far away from anyone they knew. They scraped together a few hundred dollars, loaded their sparse belongings into Norman's battered Chevy van, and headed north.

The morning after their arrival, Norman walked by Roy's camping spot, where he found the old man seated at a concrete picnic table. He was wearing tattered work pants and a murky T-shirt, his omnipresent red plaid flannel shirt draped over the ensemble. The tea stain from the previous night was lost in a patchwork of grease and dirt. Norman smoothed his own spotless rugby shirt, and adjusted his collar.

"Come have breakfast," Roy said. "Can't get Elsie out here. We're supposed to be enjoying nature and all she does is complain about the bugs. The simple life! That's what it's all about! Wanna Pop Tart?"

"It's okay—I have some granola back at the tent." Norman sat down anyway.

"Suit yourself." Roy ripped open a package and took a big bite out of one of the pastries. "You're supposed to toast them, but we're roughing it, after all," he mumbled around the glob in his mouth. "Where's the little lady?"

"Gone into town to look for work."

"Why ain't you with her?"

"She said she wasn't ready to unleash me upon an unsuspecting population."

"Ah. I see her point."

Norman noticed a dark rock with flecks of gold in it lying in the dirt. He kicked at it, but missed and jammed his toe into one of the table's concrete supports. He gasped. Roy leaned over and scooped up the rock. He examined it, then tossed it away.

"Fool's gold," he said.

"Are you a miner, Roy?"

"You bet. A little prospecting. A little mining."

"Mining pays well, doesn't it?"

"Well enough." Roy cast a self-conscious look toward the shiny new camper. "Thought you were a big tourism entrepreneur."

Norman straightened his shoulders. "True. But I need to build up a nest egg. I also need to get to know the place. Develop some authentic northern experience. I was hoping you could help me. I'd like to follow you around. To observe."

Roy looked grim. He picked at the dirt under his fingernails.

"What are you going to do today?" Norman coaxed.

Roy remained silent as he continued working at his nails. "Prospector's Trail, I suppose," he finally said.

"Prospecting? Excellent! Can I come?"

"Son! You don't ask a lady her age, and you don't ask a prospector to show you where he's working."

Norman's shoulders drooped as he studied the stubborn set of Roy's jaw. Then he smiled. "It's just that I wanted to use you as the role model for the interpretive centre."

"Oh?"

"If you don't mind being famous, that is."

Roy abandoned his impromptu manicure. "Well, maybe I could help a bit. You can come with me this morning. But this morning only, hear? Better take some provisions with you." He tossed a foil pack of Pop Tarts at Norman. "Just don't try to chew and walk at the same time."

Roy strode across the campground, Norman close behind. They reached the road that wound through the park and followed it for a few minutes before Roy veered into the bush. Norman was able to keep pace as they trekked across the huge lumps of Precambrian rock. The strips of dirt that snaked between them were the real challenge. They were littered with spindly jack pines and poplars that slapped at the face, and mined with traps for the feet: lumps of rock sticking through the soil, loose stones, tree roots. They didn't slow Roy. Norman teetered after him, but managed to stay upright.

"What are those little footprints painted on the rock?" he asked when he finally caught up with the sure-footed Roy.

"Directions."

"This is a walking trail?"

"Of course. Didn't think I'd really show you where I prospect, do you?"

Norman looked as deflated as his mildewed tent.

"I'm willing to share general knowledge, though. See that pillow of grey rock over there?"

Norman walked to the spot.

"Run your fingers over the surface. Feel the bumps?"

Norman nodded.

"What do you see?"

"Brownish-red granules."

"Good. They're garnets."

"Wow." Norman bent closer to the rock to examine them.

They continued on in silence for some time, until they reached the tumble-down remains of a cabin. The skeleton of a bedframe, a rusted-out wood stove, and a few pieces of decaying cutlery were scattered around.

"Reminds me of the shack I lived in when I moved up in the '40s. Made of plywood and packing crates." Roy sighed.

"Elsie didn't mind?"

"Living in a shack? Of course she did—but she saw the potential of the place." Roy smiled. "And of me."

"You're lucky. I don't think Jennifer is that optimistic."

"Chin up, son." Roy watched Norman wander toward the trail. Half a dozen steps, and he stumbled on some loose rock. "On second thought, better keep your eyes on the ground."

They later found a vein of white quartz that prospectors had blasted.

"Quartz is the key," Roy said. "Find it, and you just might find gold. Time for a rest."

The old man sat cross-legged beside the mutilated rock and closed his eyes. The sky clouded over, and a breeze came up. Roy's red plaid shirt fluttered around him. He swayed with the wind. His breathing became slower and deeper. Norman cautiously ripped open his pouch of Pop Tarts and nibbled a corner. Finding that it hit the spot, he gobbled both pastries in the packet. Then, exhausted after another sleepless night, Norman closed his eyes. He, too, swayed with the wind. He drifted off, but jerked himself awake just as his head started to topple toward the ancient and very hard rock. He started to worry about the old man.

"Roy," he whispered. There was no reaction, so he hissed louder. "Roy!"

"What?"

"I thought you'd fallen asleep."

"Asleep! Ain't you ever seen anyone meditating, son?"

"Meditating?"

"I thought you were educated. You know—meditating. Getting into the zone. Becoming one with the earth. The earth don't give up her secrets too easily. You gotta get to know her on a personal level."

"Oh."

"Time to go." Roy jumped to his feet. He completed the circuit of the trail, which led them back to the campground. "Nice spending the morning with you. Now I have get on with business."

Norman wiped a couple of drops of moisture from his arm. Roy had been generous toward him, but Norman would prefer if he didn't spit while he talked. Roy turned away. A large drop hit Norman's face. Rain.

Norman sprinted toward his tent as the deluge began. Moments later, Roy heard a stomach-turning shriek. The old-timer found Norman staring at the sodden puddle of his so-called shelter.

"You can stay in your van," he suggested.

"It's full of boxes and furniture." Norman began to pace. "What was I thinking? This is never going to work. Jen's going to leave me. I have no money. I can't earn any. It's over." He stopped moving and stared at Roy. "It's all over," he repeated in disbelief.

"You're packing it in? Just like that?" Roy said. "No interpretive centre?"

"I'm sorry, Roy. No interpretive centre."

Roy chewed his bottom lip. He assessed the state of the tent. Then he nodded at Norman. "Don't panic. I'll help you. Get in your van. We're going prospecting."

They stopped by the camper to pick up some gumboots. Roy instructed Norman to drive away from Yellowknife, but they hadn't travelled for more than a minute before the old man told him to turn down a wide, well-maintained road that led past an industrial building. They were heading for the city dump.

"Now what?" Norman muttered.

"Right over there," Roy said.

The rain eased as Norman pulled up next to a row of a half-dozen vehicles. Roy climbed out of the van and rambled amongst the hills of debris, his gaze locked on the ground. Every now and then he would stop and bounce on an abandoned couch to test the springs, or lift a piece of plywood to see what was underneath. Other people were wandering in a similar fashion, but Roy ignored them. He motioned to Norman to join him, but Norman couldn't bring himself to leave the van, where he stared vacantly through the windshield. A scuffling from the back of the vehicle caught his attention, and he realized someone was peering through the rear window. Norman got out.

"You going to dump that stuff, or what? I don't have all day," said a young man in ragged jeans and a grimy windbreaker.

"I am not dumping anything. That's my furniture. Back off."

"Settle down. I can find better out here anyway." As he stalked off, Norman locked the van, put on Roy's extra pair of gumboots and set out after his mentor, stepping cautiously so as not to do a face-plant in the mud. He found Roy digging in a pile of garbage, a battered television and some lengths of two-by-four stacked beside him.

"I thought you hated the noise and traffic and filth of the city," Norman said.

"This ain't the city," the old man replied, surprised Norman hadn't noticed. He paused to wipe the drizzle from his forehead with a grimy hanky, then continued to root in the mud. "Eureka!" He extracted a dirty orange tarpaulin with a long rip in it. "Can I read 'em, or what?"

"What's it for?"

"It's for you. A fly for your tent. We'll wash it in the lake. Patch it with a little duct tape. Good as new!" He examined Norman's face. "What's with you, boy? I thought you wanted to accumulate authentic northern experiences, and here you've been missin' one of the most authentic of them all."

Norman mustered as much patience as he could. "Can we go prospecting now?"

Roy beamed at him.

"Oh, no! This is how you made your money?" Norman said. "Prospecting and mining. At the dump?"

"After the first few years there was so much competition in the bush that I decided to use my skills here. You'd be amazed at what I find. Take it home, clean it up, sell it. Got so much now, I'm having trouble shifting it."

Norman eyes misted over and his throat constricted, but the cause was neither the rain in his eyes nor the stench in his nose. The rubble he saw before him was more than just the detritus of the Yellowknife dump—it was the wreckage of his future. Wifeless. Homeless. Hopeless. Suddenly, he bent over. He wasn't sure why, since he could see little through the blur of tears. He ran his fingers over a pile of mud. He felt a bump. He wiped his eyes on the back of his sleeve and examined the mound more closely. A point of brownish-red was poking through. He flicked at it with his finger. A little more red showed. He dug deeper. It was cloth. He grabbed it and pulled out a red plaid flannel shirt, much like Roy's. The old-timer whistled as he took it from his protégé.

"Impressive. One little rip, but otherwise, good as new." He held it close to Norman's chest. Norman tried to push away the old man's hand, but Roy insisted on checking the size. "It'll fit you perfectly. Let's see what else you can do. Try over there."

Roy pointed him toward the back of the dump and gave him a little push. Norman meandered through the piles. He saw a strip of white gleaming through the mud. He wiped at it with the shirt he had unearthed. Not quartz this time, but porcelain. It was an old bathtub, the kind with feet.

"Excellent," Roy said. "That'll get you a couple hundred dollars. If you refinish it, you can get more. I'll find some packing crates—we can use them as skids to drag it out of here. Good thing I took you on that walk. Sure got you into the zone."

Norman sagged onto the side of the bathtub.

"Don't knock it, son. You have a gift. You're in your element. Do you realize you haven't fallen once since you been out here?"

It was true. Norman felt himself relaxing. He took a deep breath and promptly choked.

"You'll get used to it," Roy said.

Norman surveyed the terrain through the mist. He instinctively headed toward the edge of the landfill. He came around a hill of debris and found some freshly dumped computers.

"You've hit the motherlode!" Roy said.

Norman inspected them. He shook his head. "Fool's gold."

"I thought computers were worth a fortune."

"These are too old. Got a screwdriver?"

Roy searched the pockets of his work pants and produced a rather nice multi-tool.

"Found it here last week," he said.

Norman used his sleeve to wipe the rain from one of the computers, then removed the case and looked inside.

"You know about these things?" Roy asked.

"A bit. I think this one's a 486. Might work if it hasn't taken on too much dirt and rain. Not high-powered, but we can use them for parts, if nothing else."

"You know how to set up one of those website things?"

"Ya. It's not so hard."

"A little e-commerce might move my inventory."

"Who's your market?" Norman asked.

"People who can't come to visit, but want authentic northern artefacts just the same. You can make a planter out of anything," he said with a wink. "I'll cut you in for a percentage. Best way to build up your nest egg."

Norman grinned. "We'll need a catchy name. And a logo."

"Ain't you the marketing genius?"

"Maybe I am, after all." He handed back Roy's multi-tool.

"Your little lady's not going to like it. She's more upscale than my Elsie."

Norman's smiled drooped. He made his way to a shabby rocking chair that teetered nearby and eased himself onto it. He picked at its chipped wooden arms. He surveyed the surrounding hills of debris. He inhaled deeply, and gagged only slightly this time. Jennifer, he knew, could never belong to this world of plaid flannel shirts, odd characters and strange business opportunities. And previous experience had shown that he couldn't belong to her world of dark suits, high-powered meetings and constant pressure.

"You're right. She won't see the potential. But like I said—this is the end of the road for me." Norman stood. "Let's take this chair for the interpretive centre."

The sun was shining again when Jennifer returned to the campground with news that she'd landed a job. She found Norman outside Roy's camper. He was seated at the concrete picnic table, which was strewn with computer parts. Roy was peering over Norman's shoulder, which was clad in a red plaid flannel shirt. Jennifer gasped.

"I found it at the dump. Elsie washed it for me." Norman was monkeying with a partially assembled computer.

"Me and your boy are going into business together," Roy said. "First e-commerce, then the interpretive centre."

"I think I've got it." Norman connected the computer to an extension cord that stretched from the camper. A puff of smoke rose into the air. The two men looked at each other.

"Planter," they sang in unison.

"Grab me another," Norman told Roy. Jennifer's glance shifted to the computers stacked beside the table.

"Found them at the dump," Norman repeated, but this time he looked her straight in the eye. "You wouldn't believe the business potential out there."

It was midnight when Norman wandered over to the tent, now protected by the freshly patched orange tarp. His van was gone, and several boxes of his possessions were sitting on the ground. She hadn't left a note. Norman sighed and crawled into the rickety tent. It swayed slightly but remained upright. He slept soundly for the first time in months.

The Yellowknife Yeti

"Leonard—this question's for you. You have thirty seconds. What is another name for the yeti? Y-e-t-i. The yeti. Go."

All eyes swivelled toward the reigning champion of the Great Northern Trivia Tournament. Every few seconds Quiz Master Bob pulled his gaze from Leonard's face to check the time as it whirled past on his stop-watch. Ed, Leonard's opponent, had started to twitch in his chair and was making little hiccuping noises, a sure sign he knew the correct answer. Leonard, on the other hand, didn't have the least clue as to what a yeti might be, or what an alternative appellation for it was, but he was enjoying the suspense of the audience and the near-panic of his rival. A man with few pleasures in life, he was damned if he was going to cut this one short. The stop-watch beeped.

"Ed—over to you. Can you tell me another name for the yeti?"

"The Abominable Snowman!" Ed sprang from his chair and did a little victory dance.

"Correct!" said Quiz Master Bob. "Ed wins another round and moves on to the A side of the tournament. Leonard—buy the man a drink."

Leonard stepped onto the deck of the cabin at Cassidy Point and pulled a bottle of premium beer from a snowbank.

During the few seconds of his absence, Ed's solo jig had grown into a conga line. Leonard handed the beer to the victor as he cavorted past the door, leading the other contestants around the room. Despite the sub-zero temperature, Leonard decided that he preferred the ambience of the deck to that of the cabin. He slowly inhaled the crisp air, then released a cloud of breath that faded into the uncertain light cast by the full moon and the snaking green shimmer of the northern lights. He leaned his elbows on the deck railing and peered into the yard, where bright patches of snow quickly gave way to deep shadows created by a jagged wall of jack pines and willow bushes. He thought he saw something move.

Something creeping around in the shadows. It's getting to be a regular thing.

A burst of laughter came from inside the cabin. Through a window, Leonard saw Ed—the newest member of the Yellowknife Raven Lodge and its self-appointed court jester—standing on a chair telling jokes. He was underneath a propane lantern, its harsh light falling upon a ring of admiring faces. It had been a long time since Leonard had seen his brother Ravens gaze upon anyone with that rather stupid look of awe. He'd first seen it when *he* was the lodge's newest member, and had managed to make order out of the morass of its so-called accounting system. He'd seen it when he introduced the Saturday Night Super Bingo, which now constituted a major source of revenue. He'd seen it when the head of the local hospital committee dedicated a plaque recognizing the lodge as the number one donor of specialized screening equipment. Over the years, many of the actual faces had changed as lodge members died or moved away and new people joined, but that idiotic look of reverence remained the same. It had, however, been a long while since Leonard had been on the receiving end.

As Grand Master of the lodge, Leonard carried out his duties with diligence, and his exacting standards extended to the rest of the membership. But there had recently been growing resentment of the rigour with which he ruled the roost. He had a seemingly supernatural knowledge of everyone's activities, or lack thereof: when the lodge held a raffle, Leonard didn't have to check the records to know who was not selling tickets with adequate vigour; on bingo nights he didn't have to emerge from his office to know which members had tried to skip their shifts in the canteen. The Ravens muttered that he must be in league with the devil—and some actually believed it.

Leonard was aware that a vague belief in his supernatural abilities had become part of lodge legend, and he'd found it increasing useful in controlling the membership. One of his favourite techniques was rolling his eyes and muttering a few choice phrases in Latin whenever a Raven was being particularly irksome. It scared the bejabbers out of the more impressionable members, and even the sceptics had to admit that his chanting had a certain hypnotic effect. No one dared tell him to lighten up, though, since he could condemn you to an eternity of scrambling around, doing the garbage jobs.

A few days before the Great Northern Trivia Tournament, Leonard had been gliding down the hall toward his office when he saw something moving in the gloom within. Sliding closer, he discovered Ed stroking the artificial feathers of the Grand Master's ceremonial head-dress. Ed had slipped a hand underneath and lifted it to see how heavy it was. Leonard cleared his throat.

"Hey, Leonard!" Ed put down the head-dress, unabashed.

"Can I help you?"

"Just came by for a little chat. Cool tunes, by the way," he said as the chords of a fugue emanating from an ancient tape player faded away.

"Bach," Leonard replied as he sat, stiff-backed, behind his well-scarred wooden desk.

"Bach, bach, bach," Ed chirped, sticking his thumbs in his armpits and flapping his elbows in imitation of a chicken. "BACH-A!" he crowed as a finale before dropping into a chair in front of the desk. He squinted at the dim gallery of photos hung on the cheap wood panelling, each one showing Leonard front and centre at an important lodge function.

"You've been Grand Master for a long time," he said.

"Yes."

"Most of the lodge members can't even remember when you weren't the Grand Master."

"I dare say."

"Ever get tired of it?"

"No."

"Wife doesn't mind?"

"No."

"Do you have a wife?"

"Not any more."

"Ah. How come you don't have any of your university stuff on the walls?" Bob leaned into the light from a small lamp and blinked with mock innocence.

"Like?"

"Grad photos. Diplomas. Most of the guys I work with have all that stuff in their offices."

"Irrelevant."

"Where did you graduate? Smart guy like you must have gone to university somewhere."

"What do you want?"

Ed returned to the shadows, lolling in his chair.

"Just to chat."

"I'm too busy to chat."

"Where do you live?"

"*What?*"

"Look—no one in this club seems to know much about you."

"They don't need to."

"Didn't you know that the ability to communicate is now considered the most important leadership skill?"

Leonard remained silent.

"Got to have the right image if you want people to follow you," Ed continued. "Image is everything."

"True."

"So astound me with your communication skills. Where do you live?"

"Downtown."

"Basement suite?"

Leonard nodded.

"In one of those little houses built in the '40s, insulated with sawdust, no doubt?" Ed said.

"I'm not at home much. No need for anything swanky."

"And I'll bet your living room looks like this." A wave of Ed's hand encompassed the dusty and rather tatty office. Not a muscle twitched in Leonard's face as he tried to decide if Ed had been spying on him. He came to the conclusion that Ed had just guessed correctly.

"Well, it's good you're dedicated to the job. I understand the lodge pays you."

"It's on the books."

"Nice gig after you lost your other job."

Leonard winced. Ed had obviously heard the rumours that Leonard didn't have a Grade 12 diploma—

rumours that happened to be true. He'd been close to fifty when he'd been laid off from the government warehouse. All the reading he'd done over the space of thirty years didn't matter. He was erudite, he was self-taught, he was unemployable. With no Grade 12 diploma, it had been impossible for him to find a decent job. Some of the lodge members had tried to help him get hired on at different places, to no avail. Paying him for his work as Grand Master was the best they could do, and the solution suited Leonard perfectly. He just wished that his layoff had happened so long ago that no one remembered why he was on the lodge payroll.

Ed pursed his lips and began to re-examine the photos.

"You know, the lodge could make way more money."

"We make plenty."

"I have some ideas."

"We make enough money."

Ed leaned into the light and looked Leonard in the eye.

"Did I tell you I have a Master of Business Administration?"

"So?"

"Just thought it would be an interesting little project to see if I couldn't improve cash flow."

"Not while I'm Grand Master."

Ed smiled. He lounged back in his chair and planted one foot and then the other on Leonard's desk. Leonard began to mumble furiously.

"Whaddja say?" Ed was unfazed.

Leonard cleared his throat.

"If you have an MBA, why would you want to be Grand Master? It doesn't pay anything close to what you can earn elsewhere."

"I just said—it would be an interesting little project.

I can easily do all this in addition to my real job. It would be a hobby, really."

Ed stood up.

"I'll put a few ideas on paper for the membership's consideration," he added. Then he winked at Leonard and strolled out of the room.

Leonard stared at his ceremonial head-dress perched on a low cupboard across the room. He slammed his hands on the desktop.

Ravens!

They called themselves Ravens, but they acted like ptarmigan: birds too stupid or too lazy to use their wings and actually fly, preferring to remain earthbound and waddle around town. His brother Ravens had been too stupid and lazy to make a success of the lodge before Leonard came along, and now they were too stupid and lazy to get rid of him on their own. They were hiding behind Ed, and probably figured Leonard couldn't see what they were up to. The problem with ptarmigan, however, was that their camouflage often proved to be their undoing: the white winter coat that was supposed to protect them from predators also meant they were frequently hit by vehicles as they wandered down the middle of a Yellowknife street, oblivious to danger. Even ptarmigan had their purpose, Leonard told himself—if nothing else, the roadkill kept the scavengers well fed.

Now, staring into the darkness outside Quiz Master Bob's cabin, Leonard wondered just how many of the lodge members had sided with Ed, and who they were. Leonard had been the perennial Quiz Wizard of the Great Northern Trivia Tournament ever since the mid-winter ritual had been established some years earlier. A quick count of his beer supply revealed that, at the rate he was being forced to hand over bottles to Ed, his cache would be depleted long before the weekend was over—a sure sign of defeat and the first step on the slippery slope to ignominy and unemployment. Well, he still had a few tricks up his sleeve.

The cabin door swung open and Quiz Master Bob wandered over to the snowbank that was serving as a beer cooler. He started rooting through the bottles.

"Hello, Bob," Leonard intoned.

Bob squealed. A beer bottle hit the deck and rolled toward Leonard. He picked it up.

"Jeepers, Grand Master, you scared the daylights out of me. I d-didn't see you there."

Leonard emerged from the shadows. With his perpetually black clothing, black hair, and hooked nose, Leonard actually looked liked a raven. The effect was somewhat disrupted, though, by the sheen of his greyish-white skin. The moonlight bounced off Leonard's forehead, nose, and cheekbones, sinking the rest of his face into shadow and giving it a cadaverous look. Bob shivered as Leonard handed him the bottle.

"Ed's doing well," Leonard said.

"Maybe." Bob returned the shaken bottle of beer to the snowbank and selected a new one.

"He could win."

Bob shrugged.

Leonard studied the sky. He started whispering. The words were barely audible, but Bob realized they were Latin. He picked at the label on his beer bottle but had to stop because his hands were shaking, a clear sign of where he stood on the question of Leonard's leadership. He following Leonard's gaze.

"So, you w-wishing on a star, or what?"

"In a way."

"What's that bright one?"

"The Evening Star. Actually, it's Venus, which is a planet, as I'm sure you know."

Bob nodded vaguely.

"Interesting fact: Venus is known as the Morning Star, as well as the Evening Star."

"Is it?"

"Did you know that both the Morning Star and the Evening Star are associated with Lucifer?"

Bob twitched. "Are they?"

Leonard treated Bob to one of his best sinister smirks.

"Oh, yes. 'How are you fallen from heaven, Bright One, Son of the Dawn!' says the prophet Isaiah. I notice there are no astronomy questions in this year's tournament," Leonard said.

Bob studied the outline of his boot in the moonlight.

"Or history. Or English literature. Lots of questions about science fiction, though. Yetis and such."

Bob shrugged again. Employing another favourite technique for subduing recalcitrant lodge members, Leonard fixed his gaze on Bob, who thought for a moment that he could see a red glow coming from the darkness of the Grand Master's eye sockets.

"'From morn to noon he fell, from noon to dewy eve,'" Leonard thundered, striding into the Quiz Master's personal space, his beak-like nose only a couple of inches from Bob's. "'A summer's day and with the setting sun, dropped from the zenith like a falling star.'"

Immobilized, Bob gaped at Leonard.

"That's Milton." Leonard took a baby step backwards.

Bob remained frozen.

"John Milton. The poet," Leonard said. "Not Milton Biddle, the plumber."

A look of panic crossed Bob's face. He was clearly wondering if Leonard could read all his thoughts.

"Didn't think it sounded like anything Milt would say," Bob murmured. Released from his paralysis, he scurried toward the door and entered the cabin.

The music started again. Through the window Leonard watched his lodge brothers hopping and bobbing around the cabin. He imagined them as just so many ptarmigan in the road. He imagined himself behind the wheel of his big old Buick bearing down on them—heaven knows, he could flatten them and pretend he'd never even seen the stupid creatures. Or maybe it didn't matter. Maybe it was truly over after all these years, and he was the one who was going to end up as roadkill.

Leonard resumed his meditation under the stars. *Over a question about a yeti. Yeti, yeti, yeti . . .* The cabin door swung open and Ed strolled onto the deck.

"Len! Buddy! No hard feelings, eh?" He slapped Leonard on the back.

"Not at all. Let the better man win, and all that."

"Adda boy." Ed whacked Leonard again. Leonard, unfortunately, had just taken a sip of beer, which promptly exited through his nose.

"Priddy," Ed said.

"What?"

"Sky." Ed motioned toward the swirling green lights with his beer bottle.

"Aurora Borealis," Leonard spluttered. "Caused by the interplay of solar winds and the earth's magnetic field."

"I know." Ed gave Leonard a lopsided wink.

"Of course you do."

Ed swung his beer bottle toward his mouth and banged it against his front teeth. He squinted at the bottle, and then gingerly tried another sip.

"They're almost hypnotic, aren't they?" Leonard said.

"Oh, ya. Jus' like those guys in Vegas. You are getting sleeeeeepy . . ."

"How long have you been up here, Ed?"

Propping his back against the deck railing, Ed stared through the darkness at Leonard. "Why so chid-chaddy tonight?"

"I don't think I gave you your due the other day. How long have you been up here?"

Ed shrugged. "Coupl'a months."

"So you're just starting to experience the enchantment of the North."

"If that's what ya wanna call it."

Leonard uttered a low-pitched chuckle.

"Look, Leonard." Ed leaned toward him as if he was about to share a confidence. "Cut the crap, okay? You might be able to scare those bird-brains in the cabin with all that spooky stuff, but don' bother with me."

Ed tried to stare him down, but the moon-lit mask of Leonard's face made him shudder.

"Ed, my good man, you misunderstand. I was merely observing that the aurora imparts a sense of peace. Look over there." He traced the flow of the lights with his finger. "They look like waves. Just like the ocean. Rocking like the ocean."

Ed yawned. Leonard slid over and leaned toward his ear, the grey vapour emanating from his lips enveloping Ed's face.

"Rocking waves. Waves rocking. Rocking."

Ed shook his head.

"Keep it up, buddy, and I'll get sea-sick." He stumbled sideways. "Don' want me barfing up all your high-priced beer, do ya?" He swallowed hard.

"Certainly not," Leonard said. "But people get seasick only when they try to resist the waves. It's best to relax

. . . let yourself go . . . abandon yourself to the waves. The back-and-forth, the gentle toss of the waves. The rocking of the waves."

Ed's eyes became bleary, but they remained fixed on the undulating lights.

"Ed?" Leonard moved in close once again.

"Hmm?"

"Have you heard of the Yellowknife's Abominable Snowman?"

"Nope," he mumbled.

"Or maybe I should say 'yeti'?"

Ed continued to stare at the lights.

"Yedi," he said.

"The Yellowknife Yeti is a ferocious snow monster, who only lives in the winter. When the time is right, he starts to form from little lumps of snow. They say you can see bits and pieces of him scurrying across the ground as they come together. It starts at the top. A couple of lumps will run in from opposite directions to form his head; an arm will rear up out of a snowbank and drag itself toward him; a foot will appear from under a bush and lurch over. Once he's pulled himself together, he rises and goes looking for breakfast."

"Breakfast," Ed muttered.

"You see, he's been hibernating all summer. He's not particular about what he eats—usually just the first thing he comes across. Lost two snowshoers that way last year. Third one got away."

A drowsy snort erupted from Ed's nose. Leonard paused.

"Look at those pink lights over there." He pointed at a new quadrant of the sky. Ed's gaze drifted across to the spot. "Look at the lights waving. Waving. Waves rocking . . ."

"Rocking waves. Rocking," Ed said.

"That's better. As I was saying, the Yellowknife Yeti is voracious. Could easily clean out this crowd." Leonard gestured toward the cabin.

"Mmmmm."

"So we must beware of the yeti."

"Beware . . . ," Ed murmured.

"Beware of the yeti."

"Beware . . ."

Leonard observed his adversary for a moment. Then he snapped his fingers and moved away.

"Wha?" Ed shook his head.

"I think you fell asleep."

"No way. I heard ya. Yanking my chain. Telling me about some Yellowknife Yeti. Too bad I beat ya Leonard, but ya better get used to it. I'm going to take a whiz."

Ed thumped down the steps and went around the side of the cabin. He returned a few moments later and was about to climb the stairs, when Leonard gasped.

"Look!" He pointed at a clump of willows.

Ed stumbled toward the bushes, squinting through the mottled light. Then he saw it. A lump of snow appeared from behind a stand of jack pine and lumbered toward the willows. Ed rubbed his eyes. As he watched, another blob of snow fell—or perhaps flew—from the top of the willow bushes to join with the other. Another soon materialized and ran toward the ever-growing, writhing mass of snow. Almost paralyzed, Ed managed to turn his head toward Leonard, who had a better vantage point up on the deck. Leonard gaped at him.

"Run!" he breathed.

Ed bolted for his truck. He leapt in, threw it into reverse, hit a pocket of snow and spun his tires. For a moment Leonard thought he'd have to give him a push. Then the tires caught, and Ed swerved out of the driveway, side-swiping

Quiz Master Bob's car as he went. He popped the truck into gear and roared away. Leonard smiled.

"Roadkill!" he whispered, savouring the thought of what this abandonment would do to Ed's image.

The cabin door opened. The beam of a flashlight cut across the moonlit snow, then came to rest on Leonard. He squinted into the glare.

"Someone leave?" asked Quiz Master Bob.

"Ed."

Bob's eyes popped wide open, two white orbs in the gloom. "Why'd he do that?"

"I don't know. He saw the ptarmigan over under the willows, then took off."

The Quiz Master aimed his flashlight toward the willows, where a flock of fat white birds—each looking like a good-sized lump of snow—were ambling in search of buds to nibble.

"Too bad," Bob said.

"Too much beer, maybe. I don't think he's used to the good stuff."

"Jeepers. That means he forfeits the lead. Well, I g-guess you take his place on the A side. Better come in—we're ready for the final round."

Leonard stood gazing toward the Evening Star. He gave it a quick salute, then turned toward the cabin door.

Bug Bites

It was the whack upside the head that finally awoke Ariel. She'd been semi-conscious for some time, thrashing in the sheets as she tried to fend off her tormentor. Just as the slap from her own hand summoned her to consciousness, her adversary—showing a predictable perversity—went silent. Muscles tensed, she waited for the attack to resume.

Zzzzzzzzzzzzzzzzzzzz.

Her arms flailed, with no effect. Then she realized the buzzing was coming from outside. Pushing herself upright and squinting through the dusty little window, she rubbed her still-stinging temple. Through the gaps between the houses, she caught a glimpse of an all-too-familiar bush plane taxiing back to the floatbase. Herb had probably made three or four attempts at a takeoff before conceding he was carrying too much cargo. Again.

Now fully awake, Ariel lay back and closed her eyes. She slowed her breathing. She relaxed her muscles. She pictured herself beside a gentle waterfall.

"I go calmly amid life's turmoil," she said.

Zzzzzzzzzzzzzzzzzzzz.

Her muscles contracted. It was inside this time.

"I accept and value my fellow beings," she said more loudly.

Zzzzzzzzzzzzzzzzzzzz.

"I am at one with myself and the world," she shrieked.

Zzzzzzzzzzzzzzzzzzzz.

Smack!

Ariel pulled her hand from her temple and examined the palm. It contained one dead mosquito and a lot of blood.

"Oh, oh, oh!"

Eight steps took her from the alcove in which her bed rested, through the living room, and into the kitchen at the opposite end of her shack. Jamming her hand under the spout of an orange plastic jug next to the sink, she pushed the release button and scrubbed away the blood. A relaxing mug of chamomile tea would help; Ariel filled the kettle and lit her propane stove.

She pushed back the tea towel nailed over the kitchen window and sighed. Her gaze travelled along the side of her landlords' little green house, then proceeded across the road, where it collided with a large maroon building. Ariel thought wistfully of the waters of Yellowknife Bay that twinkled beyond her view, behind the monstrosity. For years she'd stood at this window and watched the float planes taxi to and from the stretch of water they used for takeoff and landing. That pleasure ended a year earlier, when Herb built his mammoth house.

Ariel closed her eyes and pictured them. Twin Otters. Turbo Beavers. Caravans. As they wound up for takeoff, the roar of their motors resonated in her chest; as they freed themselves from the constraints of the water, Ariel's heart lifted with them as if it would float right out of her body. The whine of Herb's nasty little puddle jumper, on the other hand, resonated in her nasal passages and left her with a sinus headache.

The kettle whistled and Ariel sat down, inhaling the tea's soothing vapours. The bite on her temple started to itch. She tried, unsuccessfully, to keep her fingernails away. One hand was scratching, the other lifting her tea to her mouth, when something bit her ankle. As she jerked to swat the mosquito, her mug flew across the table. Now suffering from a full-scale attack of the heebie-jeebies, she danced around the shack clawing her head, her neck, her legs.

The door banged. Loretta, her landlady, marched to the kitchen table and set down a terra cotta dish holding a mosquito coil. Ariel's twitching slowed.

"That's cruel," she said. "It paralyzes them."

"Sacrifice your principles just this once."

The coil smelled like incense. Ariel started to relax.

Loretta mopped up the spilled tea, pulled a chair from the kitchen table, and sat down.

"Don't move the chair so far away—you'll disrupt the harmony of the room."

"This shack is no hotbed of harmony these days, feng shui and mantras not withstanding. I was watering the flowers when you started screaming."

"There are just so many bugs this year." Ariel scratched her ankle. The motor of Herb's plane started up.

"And he's the biggest bug of them all. Right?"

Ariel shook her head, her fluffy blonde hair swaying all the way down to her waist.

"He has the right to live as he feels best. I accept and value my fellow beings."

"Whatever."

Ariel contemplated the stream of smoke rising from the bug coil. Her thin face and pale colouring gave the impression of a white rabbit, an image reinforced this morning by reddened eyes. Loretta glanced into the living room, where a dusty sunbeam lit up a pile of cloth sitting on an ancient treadle sewing machine. Ariel, who described herself as a "textile artisan," had been working late, preparing for a big craft sale.

"When did you last eat?" Loretta asked. "Want some scrambled tofu?"

Ariel nodded. Loretta searched the rough wooden shelves under the kitchen counter as Ariel returned to the bedroom alcove, pulling a tie-dyed curtain across the entrance. She was slipping out of her cotton nightgown when Herb attempted another takeoff. As the scream of the motor faded, it was replaced by Loretta's competent banging as she found the frying pan, spice mix, and tofu. Ariel put on a calico skirt and a sweatshirt and returned to the table. Loretta soon placed the tofu, toast, and a glass of orange juice in front of her.

"Aren't you eating?" Ariel asked.

Loretta removed the kerchief covering her short grey hair and shook her head.

"I'm stuffed. Floyd and I had breakfast with Herb. Steak and eggs."

Ariel almost gagged. That's what they'd served the first time she met Herb. Not eggs, because it was suppertime, but steak. T-bones. Herb had just moved into his house, and friendly Old Towners that they were, Floyd and Loretta had invited him over. The pudgy, balding newcomer had a chunk of rare meat impaled on his fork, blood dripping, when he discovered that Ariel sold the clothes she made at craft fairs and at the Yellowknife City Market on Saturday mornings.

"I'd better take a boo at your marketing plan."

Ariel frowned as she nibbled the lima bean casserole that served as her main course.

"You must have a marketing plan." Herb hadn't swallowed his previous forkful, and Ariel could see the glob of half-chewed meat as he spoke. "What's your production schedule? Are you achieving economies of scale?" He waved his fork. Blood splattered onto Ariel's white peasant blouse.

"Did you make that thing you're wearing?" Herb fondled Ariel's patchwork skirt. "How long is the fad for '60s revival clothing supposed to last?"

Ariel launched a series of little slaps at his hand. He released her skirt.

"The clothing I make reflects my lifestyle and world view, neither of which is 'a fad.' I gather the raw materials at garage sales and thrift stores. Every piece is unique, created without damage to the planet, and without promoting rampant consumerism."

Floyd and Loretta raised their eyebrows. Neither had ever heard Ariel speak so loudly.

It had been Herb's turn to frown.

"Okay, lady. But you could make serious money if you do things right. At least you could move out of that garden shed."

Chewing her scrambled tofu, Ariel gazed around her "garden shed," the sparse furniture aligned to maximize the flow of positive energy. The low rent saved her from the hubbub of a regular job. Sometimes she had to put in long hours at her sewing machine, but her work was blessedly solitary. Or it had been, until Herb arrived. Despite his entrepreneurial endeavours across the street—an air charter company, a bicycle repair shop and an ice cream parlour, each of which had failed within months—he still found time to pester Ariel with promotional schemes for her clothing. Visiting one evening, he'd found the flat wooden box that held Ariel's oil paints. He was playing with a twisted, half-used tube of crimson when Ariel returned from the kitchen. She grabbed the tube and replaced it in the box, which she snapped shut and restored to its spot under her bed.

"Floyd and Loretta told me you used to paint." Herb leaned back and draped his arm across the back of the couch. "They said some of your pictures are hanging in swanky lobbies all over Yellowknife."

"That's right."

"I saw a couple. Not bad at all."

"And you'd know?"

"Betcha got good money for them."

"Maybe."

He'd borrowed her book on Tom Thomson and subsequently decided to become a world-famous northern landscape artist. Market research had revealed that the Germans are wild for the Northwest Territories.

"Japanese, too," he said. "If I can get a foothold in those markets, I can make serious money. I'll open my own gallery—cut out the middleman. I'd sell your stuff, too."

Ariel took another mouthful of scrambled tofu. Herb still hadn't returned her book. Her scalp started to itch again.

"Ariel!"

"Sorry—"

"For the third time: when do you want to go to Herb's grand opening tonight?"

"I can't. He'll be a laughing stock."

"He invited you specially. And you haven't even seen his paintings."

"No one has."

"Part of his marketing strategy—keep them in suspense while you stir up the media hype," Loretta said. "Floyd told me. He's learning a ton managing the gallery for Herb. They've invited all the big names: CBC, *Globe and Mail*, *Edmonton Journal*, the *Yellowknifer*."

"Was it wise for Floyd to quit his job and take a chance on one of Herb's schemes?"

"He's got plumber's thumb. Can't torque a wrench any more. Herb's giving him a steady salary and a percentage of every painting sold. This new job's saved our bacon."

Ariel trailed her fork through the mashed tofu.

"Loretta—all the media hype in the world can't hide the fact that Herb has been painting for only three months."

Loretta's back stiffened and she crossed her arms.

"He's a high flyer."

"Not in that little plane."

"You know what I mean. And don't make fun of his plane. You can't even look at one without getting airsick."

"That's not true—I don't get sick unless I'm actually in one and it actually lifts off."

"Which is what happened to your painting career, if I remember correctly. Never achieved lift-off because you puked during the opening of your one and only show."

"They wanted me to make a speech. At least I didn't hit any of the canvases—just a pair of expensive shoes." Ariel shuddered. "Herb can keep his hype."

"He's onto something this time. He spent the entire summer sketching in the bush and painting in the studio. That's dedication. He's even sketching on the day of his gala."

Ariel set down her fork. "What weighs him down so much? The noise is horrible when he tries to take off."

"He docks his plane ten feet from his front door—we can't see what he's doing. Maybe he's still re-supplying canoeists. He doesn't tell us everything."

Ariel took a big bite of her toast.

*****

When Loretta shouted from her back door that evening, Ariel was dressed in an emerald three-tiered skirt, topped with a jacket she'd fashioned from an old quilt. In the seconds it took to reach Loretta's house, a swarm of mosquitoes formed around her. The two women headed across the street, Ariel scurrying in front, beating away the bugs. She was so preoccupied that she barely noticed the line of parked cars.

Ariel pushed through the door into the main level of Herb's house. Except for a glassed-in office in one corner, it was a large, open space facing Great Slave Lake that had been home to his various enterprises. Ariel backed out, tripping over Loretta.

"There's a million people."

"Herb's a popular guy," Loretta said, propelling Ariel back inside. "Most don't mind the rough edges."

Practically everyone was dressed in black, and all were sipping wine. Within moments, the crowd carried Loretta away and Ariel was left alone.

"I am calm amid life's turmoil," she whispered as she edged through the throng. Peace was hard to maintain, however—people were standing in clumps around Herb's paintings, disrupting the flow of energy. It also made it impossible to see the artwork. Ariel passed Herb and a man scribbling in a tiny notebook.

"I see myself as a latter-day Tom Thomson," Herb said. Breaking into a coughing fit, he turned from the reporter and slipped a white index card from his jacket pocket. Snorting and hacking, he ran his eyes over it and tucked it away. He turned back. "Excuse me. Like Mr. Thomson, I'm not interested in producing a literal depiction of the northern landscape, but in conveying its soul, its spirituality. Unlike Mr. Thomson, however, I have no intention of disappearing into the wilderness."

They both laughed.

"Wanna picture of me and my plane?"

The reporter accompanied Herb outside.

A quiver passed through Ariel's body and she scratched her arms as she made her way to the far corner. Floyd was mopping his brow as he watched two men and a woman, who were wearing expensive-looking suits and conferring intensely in German. Sales were probably not good. Ariel realized that, given Herb's track record, he must be in serious financial trouble. If the gallery failed, Herb's monster house would remain, but Herb would be gone and there would be peace in the floatbase again. Floyd could find other work. Ariel smiled. She was at one with herself and the world.

The glow was extinguished when Herb swooped down and pulled her toward a table loaded with kebabs of muskox teriyaki and buffalo satay, sides of smoked Arctic char, and caribou pepperoni. Ariel recoiled. Garlic, ginger, and peanut sauce could not mask the stench of blood that rose to her vegetarian nostrils. A low buzzing started in her ears, a warning sign that she was going to be sick. She backed away.

"I forgot about that vegetarian thing," Herb said. "Look around—we've got celery sticks somewhere."

Loretta emerged from the crowd. "This is great." She popped a caribou canapé into her mouth. "But why only fifteen paintings? Thought you'd be going for economies of scale."

"Only the best for this crowd," Herb said. "I have others, of course. My early works."

"From last week, you mean?" Ariel said.

"This might be a good time for a mantra," Loretta replied drily.

Ariel closed her eyes and whispered. Herb put an arm around her shoulder. Ariel's eyes sprang open.

"There'd be more stuff on the walls if Ariel would start painting again. I've got some other artists lined up, but no one of her calibre. Whadda ya say? Serious money. I'd only take forty per cent."

The heebie-jeebies struck Ariel once again. Herb withdrew his arm.

"I've told you. I am not of this world." Her hand fluttered toward the crowd as she tried to stop twitching.

Herb bent close to her. His self-confident grin twisted into something menacing and his garlic breath was stifling. The buzzing in Ariel's ears became louder.

"It's time you joined the real world."

"I will live as I see fit."

"I think not. Remember all that marketing advice? You owe me."

"As if."

Ariel tried to move away, but Herb grabbed her wrist.

"No, Herb. Better go to Plan B. If you have one." Ariel shook herself free.

"That's the last thing you want." Herb straightened up. "Give me a testimonial, at least. People from the German trade commission are here."

"How can I? I haven't actually seen your so-called art."

Herb let out a whoop.

"Listen up, folks. This is Ariel Sommers, the renowned Yellowknife *artiste*. Move away from the paintings, please, so she can give us her esteemed opinion."

"Herb!"

The crowd shifted to the edges of the room. All eyes were on Ariel. The German trio watched her intensely.

"Make it good," Herb hissed, pushing her toward a row of paintings. The buzzing in her ears became insistent, and she swallowed hard. Vivid greens and blues, punctuated with grey, swam before her eyes. A flash went off in Ariel's face.

She fainted.

*****

Ariel spent the night on Loretta and Floyd's couch. Loretta was handing her a glass of water and some painkillers the next morning, when Herb's plane whined toward takeoff. Placing her hands over her ears and quelling the urge to scream, Ariel waited for Herb to cut the motor. He persevered, however, and even when he made it off the ground the clamour did not dissipate. Ariel stumbled outside to find Herb making a circuit over the floatbase. Loretta and Floyd joined her, hands shading their eyes, as Herb flew over them.

"Gone for a week," Floyd yelled. "Sketching trip."

Herb turned west. The sound melted away.

The media hype amounted to a few column inches in the *Yellowknifer*, accompanied by a picture of Herb silhouetted against the setting sun of late summer, arms crossed and a foot braced against one of his plane's floats. A handful of paintings were purchased at the gala, but then sales had come to a halt.

"We're finished because of you," Floyd told Ariel.

"Because I won't paint?"

"Partly. But also because of your marketing strategy. Herb liked it once he thought about it. Low supply equals high demand and high prices. 'Keep 'em drooling for more, and you can make serious money without a whole lot of work,' he said. But no one wants to pay those prices. I'm ruined. I've got plumber's thumb, you know."

Despite Floyd's predicament, a surge of positive energy buoyed Ariel through the next few days. She slept late.

She made the rounds of the thrift stores. When the breeze was strong enough to keep away the bugs, she'd climb to Bush Pilot's Monument, atop the hump of grey rock that dominated Yellowknife's Old Town, and watch the planes come and go. She looked forward to the day when Herb was gone for good.

Eight days later, Floyd was worried.

"Herb should be back by now."

"Maybe he got side-tracked," Ariel said.

Floyd called the RCMP.

The search and rescue started the next day, with a number of local pilots joining the official search. Loretta spent hours in the air as a "spotter," her eyes red and weepy from the strain of scanning the ground, and from fear of Herb's fate. Floyd wanted to help, but once word got out about Herb's disappearance, the gallery did brisk business.

The media coverage was heightened by the propaganda of Herb's press kit, which paralleled his "artistic vision" with that of Tom Thomson. If the similarity of their skills was a stretch, the similarity of their fates stirred the popular imagination. An old television documentary was hastily re-aired, describing the fate of the forerunner of the Group of Seven, who disappeared in Algonquin Park in 1917. A local folk group wrote a song about the two men, which played incessantly on the radio.

"Those people from the German trade commission bought the rest of the paintings from the show, even at the higher, post-disappearance prices," Floyd told Loretta and Ariel at supper on the fourth day of the search. "I'm reduced to selling his paint-on-canvas-board roughs, and they're going at a good clip."

Surprised by the reversal of Herb's fortunes, Ariel followed Floyd across the road after supper. She'd avoided the gallery since opening night, so she'd still not seen Herb's work. Floyd flipped on the lights, and Ariel moved toward the paintings. Pillows of grey rock rose from rippling blue lakes; green-leafed birch and scraggy tamaracks bent with the breeze. Herb had natural talent, it seemed—his style was naive, but the paintings had charm. Ariel felt a twinge of irritation that she knew was unworthy of her.

From early in the morning until late at night, Yellowknife Bay was a-buzz with the comings and goings of float planes searching for Herb, but they no longer filled Ariel with delight. A stream of people found their way to Ariel's front door: a police officer wanting to know if Herb was depressed before he disappeared; a woman wanting to borrow some tea for the volunteer pilots resting at Herb's house; a tourist who couldn't find the gallery, despite the large sign posted outside. The crunch of tires and slamming of car doors from the gallery parking lot became unbearable.

Then Herb's plane was spotted, exposed by the defoliated trees of late autumn. It was tied up and undamaged on a lake about a hundred miles from Yellowknife. The fuel tank was drained, as if Herb had run out of gas and glided in for a landing. There was no sign of him; it seemed he had gone into the bush looking for food and got lost. The tragedy was greater because there was a brand-new squatter's cabin, built from two-by-fours and plywood, about a mile away. Not only would Herb have had shelter, he would have been well fed: cases of baked beans, Spam, and cling peaches were stacked on the floor. It was obvious Herb had never found the cabin, though—if he had, he'd have stayed put until help arrived.

*****

Floyd was occupied with running the gallery, so Loretta and Ariel were enlisted to inventory Herb's "early works." Floyd had been instructed to prepare them for auction.

"Instructed by whom?" Ariel asked as she wandered around the gallery storage room.

"Herb's brother." Loretta was standing before a painting, making notes in a coil-bound book.

"Since when does Herb have a brother?"

Loretta shrugged.

"Herb said if anything happened to him, his brother would send instructions. He got in touch with Floyd the day after the search started. I think he lives in the States."

"He's spoken to the guy?"

"Nope. E-mail."

The storage room was filled with negative energy, so Ariel tried to rearrange things to help it flow out the door. She was edging a sheet of plywood across the floor when she tripped over a wooden palette. Her foot flipped back a tarp, revealing cases of baked beans, Spam, and cling peaches.

"What's this for?"

"I told you. Re-supplying canoeists."

Ariel cleared a space along one wall and set out a half-dozen paintings that had been stacked in a corner. They all had Herb's signature, the style was consistent with his work, but something bothered her.

"The leaves are yellow."

"So?" Loretta continued to make notes.

"The leaves hadn't turned when Herb disappeared. Where'd these come from?"

Loretta pulled her gaze from her notebook and stared at the row of paintings.

"The storage locker in the industrial area."

"At the other end of town."

"Yup. Herb's brother told Floyd to check out there. Good thing, or we'd have missed them."

Ariel's body shuddered with another case of the hee-bie-jeebies.

"Herb's not dead," she said.

Loretta's head snapped toward her.

"Of course he's dead. He imagined what the trees were like in the fall."

"His 'brother' has access to the corporate account, doesn't he?"

Loretta moved close to Ariel.

"Herb's a legend."

"Herb's alive!"

"Who's going to prove it?" Loretta placed her face within inches of Ariel's. "A scared little rabbit like you?"

"Loretta!"

"Do you understand the amount of money Frank can make off these paintings? Need I remind you that his plumbing career is over?"

"I know, I know. He can't torque a wrench." Ariel took a step backward.

"For years we've helped you out with cheap rent. So now you can help us out by keeping your lip buttoned."

It felt as if a thousand mosquitoes were crawling through Ariel's hair and along her neck. With a shudder and a shriek, she bolted out the door and toward her shack. Throwing herself on her bed, Ariel tried to slow her breathing to match the chugging of a Twin Otter out on the water. The slam of a car door broke her concentration. She realized that Herb's "estate" would retain marketing rights to his work. There'd be posters, art cards, books. "Early works" would occasionally surface for auction. The gallery would become a tourist trap. Unless, of course, Herb's legend died.

Rooting under her bed, Ariel found her paint box. She opened it and ran her fingers over the contorted tubes.

Because of Herb, she really did have to join the real world. Tourists would swarm to the gallery as long as his disappearance remained a mystery. There'd be no peace in the neighbourhood until she exposed him; there'd be no peace with Loretta and Floyd if she did. Either way, she'd need serious money—to find him or to find another place to live. From out on Yellowknife Bay, the Twin Otter roared. Ariel closed her eyes. It sounded different today. Instead of soaring toward parts unknown, it seemed to climb slowly, steadily. Not thrilling, perhaps, but heartening. Ariel opened her eyes to find a mosquito drilling into her arm. Muscled tensed, she watched it fill with blood. Then she killed it with a slow, deliberate slap.

Diamond Girl

"Quick, Claire! Here he comes!"

A salesclerk strolled out to join her co-worker bundling daisies at the counter of the florist shop in Yellowknife's downtown mall. The women watched a scrawny young man in jeans, a black bomber jacket, and white sneakers wander past. He headed into the public washroom, a large backpack slung over his shoulder.

Work on the daisies slowed. A few minutes later, a businessman wearing a rumpled suit—and white sneakers—emerged from the men's room, one hand carrying a briefcase, the other smoothing his moustache. He strutted to the florist shop and attempted to lean on the counter. Peering through a low-hanging grey wig, he misjudged the distance. His elbow slipped and he pitched forward, almost smacking his chin on the counter top. A second attempt to strike a pose succeeded.

"Cheerio, love," he said in a well-practised English accent. "A perfect red rose—there's a good girl."

Claire smirked at her co-worker, who hurried into the cooler. Claire's fingers arranged and re-arranged pieces of ribbon, while she stared at the man. He smiled and winked in her general direction, but the gesture went wide of the mark; he appeared to be flirting with a large bouquet of yellow chrysanthemums sitting against the back wall. He shook his head and tried again to make eye contact, but the over-powered glasses perched on his beaked nose caused Claire's face to swim in the middle distance.

"Your 'stache is slipping, Gerald," she said.

Gerald hiked the drooping corner of his false moustache into place. He glanced around.

"I don't think the enemy agents noticed," Claire said.

The other clerk returned and was about to wrap the rose. Gerald took it from her.

"I prefer it *au natural*." He trailed the blossom under the clerk's chin.

"What would Krystal say?" she asked.

"It's okay, babe. Everyone knows I'm out playing the field."

"Ya. Left field," Claire said. "And I think Krystal'd be happy to hear you'd transferred your affections elsewhere."

Gerald tossed his head in scorn. The wig flew off, arched across the corridor, and, like a misguided sparrow, hit the display window of the facing store. Gerald scuttled over, retrieved his wig from the floor, and scuttled back. The clerk gave him his change, and he slunk from the mall.

As he reconnoitred amongst the stumpy office towers and squat, middle-aged buildings of downtown Yellowknife, Gerald pulled at his wig and squinted through his glasses. He stopped to peer at the passing faces, lit by the sunshine of a fall morning. The denizens of Yellowknife seemed oblivious to his existence. Yeah, right. Despite his efforts, the eyes of any number of enemy forces could be trained on him. He removed a pen from his suit jacket, clicked a button, and lifted it to his lips.

"Monday. Ten-hundred hours. Corner of 50 and 50. Code orange."

As Gerald replaced the pen, his fingers brushed a warm piece of metal. He smiled and pulled it out. Scratched and worn, it was his father's "James Bond" knife. Years earlier, eight-year-old Gerald had awoken to find it under his pillow, the very day his father had disappeared on his secret government mission. Gerald's father had often shown his son the wonders of the multi-blade knife: a saw for severing bonds; razor-sharp edges for dispatching your enemy to the next world; and, most importantly, a corkscrew for wining and dining the babes. If only his dad could see him now.

A pedestrian crashed into Gerald. He dropped the knife.

"Sorry, buddy," the pedestrian said. "Didn't see you."

Gerald retrieved his keepsake, then watched the man disappear down the street. It was time to conclude his day's mission.

Moments later, Gerald arrived at the offices of the Borealis Diamond Mining Company, not far from where he'd started his trek almost an hour earlier. His impaired vision was no hindrance to finding his way into the main reception area—he was guided by the gleam of platinum hair and a pink V-neck sweater emanating from the far end of the lobby.

Krystal.

Her radiance was not the glow of the midnight sun on a summer's eve; it was the winter glare of afternoon snow, a brilliance so sharp it could blind. Sitting behind the large reception desk, she was using a nail file to attack one of her talons, and her molars to assault a wad of chewing gum. Gerald smoothed his creased suit, approached, and laid the rose in front of her.

"Cheerio, love," he said.

Krystal stopped sawing and looked up.

"You're late. I missed coffee because of you."

"You're beautiful when you're angry, babe."

"The security company called forty-five minutes ago to say you'd left their office. Barry's been tearing his hair out."

Gerald patted his bulging briefcase. "Had to make sure no one was following. Special dispatches today."

"As if you'd know. Has it occurred to you that we don't need a courier, considering Wolverine Security is a block away, and one of their staff could run stuff over in two minutes? Barry only hired you because Borealis promised to support local business in return for the privilege of opening a diamond mine in the Northwest Territories. You are pushing your luck, big time, mister." She jabbed the nail file at him for emphasis.

Gerald almost tossed his head again, but thought better of it. Hefting his briefcase onto the counter, he opened it and unloaded the black bomber jacket from his earlier disguise, a hunk of mountain-climbing rope, and a snorkel. He squinted into the bag before removing his spectacles. "These reading glasses are way too strong. All I could find in the bargain bin at the grocery store, though." He located an envelope and presented it to Krystal. "Security arrangements for the Diamond Gala—charity event of the year."

"What do you know about that?" Barry, director of Borealis's Northwest Territories operations, appeared behind Krystal and snatched the envelope from her hand. Barry's thin hair was sticking out at frightening angles as if he had, indeed, been pulling at it. "Speak up, Gerald. How'd you know what's in here?"

"Elementary, my dear Barry."

Barry's face turned a nasty shade of purple. He moved around the desk. "Have you been reading this? Is that what took so long?" Barry shook the envelope in the courier's face.

"Of course not."

Krystal's lips twisted into a mischievous smirk. "Nothing's a secret to an international man of mystery . . . and freelance waiter."

"Sit down while I call the RCMP."

Gerald's shoulders drooped. "I guessed. That's all. Everyone knows the Diamond Gala's coming up. The guys from your security company were at the hotel banquet rooms a couple of days ago deciding where to put the surveillance cameras. They were so paranoid this morning, I assumed the plans were in the envelope."

"You were snooping around the hotel?" The veins in Barry's temples were popping out.

"That's where I currently 'freelance' as a waiter, as Krystal puts it."

"Waiter? You're such a lousy courier you have to moonlight as a waiter? To hell with my northern hiring quotas—you're fired."

"But I've kept your documents safe for months!"

"Your job is to walk them from Point A to Point B in the quickest time possible. That's it. Borealis's security is handled by actual trained professionals, who don't monkey around with this." Barry flipped Gerald's wig into the air and onto the floor. "Now get out!" Barry stormed into the sea of offices behind the reception desk.

Krystal snapped her gum. "Bummer," she said.

Gerald sank into a chair. Krystal leaned over the reception desk to examine him.

"Get your suit at a flea sale?"

Gerald smoothed a sleeve. "Ya. Eight bucks at St. Pat's." He glanced up, his eyes catching on Krystal's cleavage. He fumbled around his left wrist. Krystal noticed her exposed chest and jerked herself upright.

"Hand it over," she said.

"Hmm?"

"Now!"

Gerald sighed, then unclasped what appeared to be a wrist watch and passed it to Krystal.

"I never should have told you I had a wrist camera," he said.

She pushed buttons until she found the digital photo of her cleavage, then erased it.

"Men. You're all the same." She tossed the camera back to him. "How can you afford this stuff, anyway? I'll call Radio Shack and say you're shoplifting. They'll ban you. That'll fix you."

"Hey, I pay my way." Gerald pouted. "And no one complains when James Bond gets friendly with the babes."

"News flash: you're not James Bond. Now get out."

"I just wanted something to remember you by." A tear fell onto his suit as Gerald re-attached his wrist camera. "This was the best job I ever had."

"Oh man, don't cry." Krystal looked away.

"I'm not." Gerald sniffled as he stuffed his jacket and spy accoutrements into his briefcase, then shuffled toward the door. Halfway down the lobby, he stopped beside a high-security display case and peered inside. There floated the showpiece of the Borealis jewellery collection, a necklace called the "North Wind," featuring the splashiest gems from the company's new mine up on the Northwest Territories Barren Lands. The bottom of the L-shaped necklace was white gold, encrusted with tiny diamonds undulating like snowdrifts across a frozen lake. The diamonds arched into a stand of trees made of yellow gold, forming the arm of the L. From the treetops rose a shaman's face, cheeks puffed and mouth forming an "O" as he blew across the snow. Six large stones flew from his mouth like shooting stars.

“Worth half a million.” Gerald wiped his nose on his sleeve.

Krystal fidgeted behind the counter. She came forward. “I’ll tell you a secret about the gala—I’m going to be the Diamond Girl!”

“Cool.”

“Barry’s freaked about taking the necklace out in the open. A public relations firm convinced the board of directors to use the North Wind as the drawing card for the Diamond Gala. Barry tried to talk them out of it, but no go. Just think—I’ll be the first person to wear it.” Krystal’s nose hovered near the glass.

“You going to have a bodyguard?” Gerald asked.

“No. The organizers don’t want to cramp the style of the Yellowknife ruling class. But you saw the cameras they’re putting in. And there’ll be security at the door. Besides, all the diamonds in the North Wind are laser-tattooed with a little moose. The necklace would be impossible to sell on the open market, either in one piece or broken up.”

“There are such things as private collections.”

Krystal straightened and scanned the reception area. “Don’t be melodramatic.”

On her way back to her desk, Krystal picked up Gerald’s wig, lying forgotten on the floor. She twirled it in her fingers.

“Wanna have a drink tonight?”

“Who, me?” Gerald glanced around the empty lobby. “I thought you had a boyfriend.”

“You mean Frank? Long gone.”

Gerald sniffled. “And you want to have a drink with me?”

"IS THAT TWERP STILL HANGING AROUND?" Barry reappeared. His colour hadn't improved.

"He just won't leave," Krystal said loudly.

"Stop drooling on the display case and get away from the North Wind," Barry said.

Krystal marched over to Gerald. "Black Knight Pub. Eight o'clock," she whispered, slipping the wig into his pocket so gently he barely felt it. Then she thumped him on the chest. "For the last time—get out!"

Gerald looked back as he scooted through the door. Krystal and Barry were both watching him, arms crossed and frowning.

*****

Gerald wandered the streets, spontaneously trailing people to keep up his skills. Not that it mattered any more. Borealis Diamonds had been the first—and only—client of his courier business, his unique approach designed for the high-security needs of Canada's new diamond industry. He'd hoped his contract with Borealis would catapult him into a new life: safeguarding secret documents, changing disguises on the fly, canoodling with beautiful women. But now Barry had doomed him to the same old routine: serving rubber chicken at banquets, hanging around Radio Shack, enduring the contempt of the women at the flower shop.

He touched the knife in his pocket. He'd let down his father, wherever he was and whatever he was doing. Gerald's mom had explained that his dad disappeared because of his job with the government, and instructed Gerald never to discuss the matter, with her or with anyone else. The seriousness of his father's mission was underscored when Gerald's mom burned all her husband's possessions, changed their last name, and moved to Yellowknife.

Gerald went home, put on a James Bond movie, and cried himself to sleep.

*****

Shortly after eight o'clock, Gerald stepped into the murk of the Black Knight Pub. Unable to locate Krystal in the crowded, English-style bar, his fingers itched toward the night scope in his jacket pocket. A summer's worth of midnight sun had robbed him of the opportunity to use it.

The throng shifted as Gerald put the scope to his eye, revealing Krystal in a corner. He almost dropped the scope—a monstrous necklace gleaming above her neckline boosted her usual dazzle. A half-moon of yellow metal, sprinkled with rhinestones, was suspended from a thick chain. Up one side rose a pastiche created from old jewellery—a clump of pine trees and some stars, topped by a gold Santa Claus face.

After tucking away the night scope, Gerald approached her table. He nodded at the necklace. "Looks like the North Wind on acid."

Krystal's hand rose to caress the necklace. "I made it myself. Found the bottom part at the drugstore, and the other bits and pieces in my drawer."

"It's quite . . . something."

Krystal smiled. "Thanks."

They ordered drinks—a martini for Gerald and a white wine for Krystal—then Gerald became aware of a set of eyes locked onto the back of his head. A thin, middle-aged man with a hawk-like nose was sitting at the next table, staring at him. Gerald flicked his scraggy hair out of his eyes and stared back. The guy likewise flicked his hair. Then he cracked his knuckles. Gerald dropped his gaze.

Their drinks appeared. One sip of his martini, and

Gerald choked. “They bruised the gin,” he spluttered. “You did hear me say ‘stirred, not shaken,’ didn’t you?”

Krystal rolled her eyes. “Listen, Gerald. I’ve decided I need extra security when I’m the Diamond Girl. You working as a waiter at the gala?”

“Of course. They’ve had to hire extra staff.”

“Good. I want you to double as my bodyguard.”

“Really?” Gerald squirmed in his seat.

“As soon as I enter the banquet room, I want you to stick like glue. I can’t pay you, but if you do this right, your fate as a courier will be sealed.”

“Always ready to help a damsel in distress.” Gerald reached over and touched Krystal’s hand. She withdrew it.

“What’s your disguise?” she asked.

“Have to think about it.”

“I need to know ahead of time. And Barry can’t find out. He’s particular about who I associate with.”

“Why do you put up with him?”

Rifling through her shoulder bag, Krystal found a pack of cigarettes. She pressed the inner sleeve of the pack upward with her thumb, extracted a cigarette and lit up, exhaling her first drag in a long, slow stream of smoke. “I needed a job, he liked my look, so he said he’d give me a chance.”

“Liked your look? Barry notices things like that?”

“Oh, he has an eye for the ladies, all right. And the hands to go with.”

Gerald shivered. “Gross.”

Krystal shrugged. “Small price to pay. I’m just a receptionist now, but I want to be a jewellery designer.” She touched her necklace again. “An Armenian guy who’s up here teaching diamond cutting said I’d be a natural, so that’s my next step.”

"Would Barry let you go? You'd need his recommendation."

"We play the Diamond Gala right, Barry will do whatever I want. Give me a pen, and I'll draw the banquet room." Krystal smoothed a napkin. Groping in his shirt, Gerald pulled out the first thing that came to hand—his new pen that could record a couple of short messages. Krystal was describing her grand entrance when someone appeared beside them. There stood Claire from the florist shop, hand on hip and eyebrows raised. She ignored Gerald.

"Can I see you?" Claire hauled Krystal to her feet and steered her toward a distant table. Claire launched into some sort of a lecture, waving her hands and frowning at Gerald. Krystal stared at the floor, nervously clicking the buttons on Gerald's pen. When Claire had finished her diatribe, she tossed one last sneer Gerald's way, then marched over to a table where her co-worker from the florist shop waited. Krystal started back to where Gerald sat, but the skinny man from the next table stood and intercepted her. After a quick, choppy conversation, Krystal returned to Gerald, throwing the pen on the table so hard it bounced. Gerald shrieked as he grabbed for it.

"Gotta go." She reached for her cigarettes, knocking them to the floor. She scooped them into her purse, bumping Gerald's chair as she stood up.

"Take it easy, babe." Gerald was rubbing at a dent on his spy pen.

"Call me when you know what you're wearing." Krystal headed for the door, the skinny man on her heels. Gerald rose to follow, but Claire had magically reappeared and clamped onto his arm.

"Don't. Barry finds out you've been speaking, she'll be toast in the diamond biz."

"He has no right."

"Doesn't matter. That's why she and Frank broke up. Barry found out about Frank's record. Made him nervous."

"Frank cut a record?"

Claire stared at Gerald.

"Oh! You mean he's a criminal?" Gerald leaned closer. "A real one?"

"They do exist."

Gerald licked his lips. "What was he in for?"

"Embezzlement, if you must know. Skipped the country with his secretary. Got caught anyway." Claire released Gerald's arm. "Stay away from Krystal." She swished out of the pub.

Gerald sat down and inspected his pen. He clicked a button, and Claire's voice was back.

". . . hell are you doing? He'll ruin you," she said.

". . . my chance to get rid of him . . . I'm sick of that loser," Krystal said before the recording chip cut out.

Wow, Gerald thought. *I didn't think she hated Barry that much.*

The other button was stuck. Gerald finished his martini, trudged home, and put the pen in his dresser drawer.

*****

The hope of regaining the Borealis contract buoyed Gerald through the next few days. He spent a lot of time searching for his night scope, which had gone missing, and visiting and revisiting Yellowknife's department stores and thrift shops to develop his new disguise. Two days before the Diamond Gala he spent an hour in the bathroom, strapped on some padding, squeezed into his costume, and examined himself in the mirror.

Perfect.

Gerald reached the mall by ten o'clock. Despite his inexperience with high heels, he looked halfway to sultry as he passed the flower store—neither Claire nor her co-worker batted an eye at the thin woman in the purple dress, black hair cut Cleopatra-style.

He found Krystal chatting with a friend in the coffee shop she frequented. Choosing a nearby table, Gerald stared over the top of his black-rimmed, purple-tinted glasses until Krystal glanced his way. She returned to her conversation, then snapped back toward Gerald. He winked.

Krystal drummed her fingers on the table as her friend sipped her coffee. When the woman finally left, Krystal scanned the restaurant before sliding into the chair across from Gerald.

"What are you doing?" she hissed.

"You wanted to know about the disguise."

"There are more discreet ways. A phone call. A Polaroid in a sealed envelope. You're the frigging spy—you figure it out."

Gerald grinned.

"Okay—stand up, but make it snappy." Gerald was in mid-twirl when a half snort, half scream erupted a couple of tables away. There sat the man from the bar, mopping up coffee he'd sprayed onto the table.

"What's his problem?" Gerald asked.

"Your skirt flipped up. I think he noticed your underwear."

"What's wrong with jockeys? I thought boxers would show with this hemline."

"They just bulge oddly for a female person. Are you going to serve drinks in that outfit?"

"Nope—black skirt, white shirt. Frumpy, but it's what all the waitresses are wearing this season." He smiled down at Krystal and batted his false eyelashes. "I couldn't resist the dress, though. Two dollars at the Sally Ann." Gerald became sombre. "Do I look like a floozie?"

Krystal reconsidered his outfit. "You're okay with pumps. Strappy shoes will make you look cheap."

"Mom's always ranting about floozies. Probably because of dad. But he *has* to cavort with beautiful women. It's part of his job."

"What does your dad do?"

Gerald reddened. "Never mind."

Krystal grabbed Gerald's arm and hoisted herself to her feet. "Give me a head start, then scram before anyone recognizes you." Krystal hurried away, the man from the bar stomping after her. Gerald would have followed, but his wrist camera was missing and he had to retrace his steps.

*****

The hotel catering manager, familiar with Gerald's various personas, rolled her eyes at his latest disguise as she handed him a tray of cutlery and sent him off to set tables for the gala. Dim lighting, the northern lights shimmering in pink and green foil on the walls, and star-like fairy lights sparkling from the ceiling gave the banquet room the ambience of a winter's eve. The room's layout was as Krystal had described. Across the front stretched a platform. From its centre, a catwalk extended into a wooden dance floor, which was rimmed by the round tables Gerald was now setting.

The tables were no sooner finished than the room started to fill with Yellowknife's social elite. Gerald found himself carrying tray after tray of champagne through the growing number of tuxedos and evening gowns. Krystal, he knew, would be in the hotel's executive suite with the Borealis bigwigs, waiting to make her grand entrance. Barry was probably with them. Gerald was relieved he wouldn't have to see him until later in the evening.

"I see you saved one for me," a familiar voice whispered. Turning, he came face to face with Barry.

Grateful for the twilight of the room, Gerald pushed his tinted glasses well up on his arched nose and held out the tray. As Barry helped himself to the last remaining glass of wine, he slid a hand around Gerald's waist. Gerald managed to choke off a scream just in time, so that it came out as little more than a surprised squeak. Barry trailed the champagne glass under Gerald's chin and winked. Stomach heaving, Gerald fixed a stunned smile on his face. Barry had just given Gerald a light slap on the rump and vacated his personal space by a baby step when a robust woman in a black gown appeared.

"Thanks, dear." She was lifting the champagne from Barry's hand when she caught sight of Gerald. She frowned, grabbed her husband's elbow, and pulled him away. "Time to shmooze," she said, glancing back to where Gerald stood paralyzed.

As soon as they vanished, Gerald darted for the kitchen, pushed through the swinging metal door, and bolted for the sink. He hung over it for a minute or two, waiting for his Barry-induced nausea to subside. Turning around, he braced his backside against the counter top, grabbed a glass of champagne from a nearby tray, and downed it. As the last of the bubbles cleared his gullet, he realized that the waitress loading the tray beside him had Cleopatra hair, just like his. She was half turned away, and standing in stocking feet, her shoes close by.

Gerald nodded sympathetically. "Heels are a killer."

Without looking at Gerald, the waitress grunted, slipped on her shoes, and hoisted her tray. Gerald grabbed a couple more glasses before she moved away.

"Wow—those things must really hurt," he murmured as he watched her lumber through the metal door and into the banquet room with all the grace of a plough horse. He applied himself to knocking back the glasses of champagne, then stood staring into space as the horror of Barry's advances played over and over in his mind.

"Hey—no slacking." The catering manager stood before him. "Didn't I just see you heading to the executive suite, 'Geraldine'?"

"Hmm?" Gerald couldn't pause his mental video tape.

"Never mind. Fill your tray and get back out there."

The ceremonial drumming of the local First Nation greeted Gerald as he returned to the banquet room. His load of champagne vanished during several speeches, a fashion show, and folk songs of northern derring-do performed by men sporting plaid shirts and rubber boots. Once the glasses were gone, he ditched the tray and lurked by the stage until the master of ceremonies said: "And now, the moment you've all been waiting for—the Borealis Diamond Girl, and the North Wind."

The room went dark. A spotlight picked up Krystal at the end of the dais, wearing a silver lamé gown, pink lipstick, and a nervous smile. A golden shawl hid her neckline. With the exaggerated stroll of a model, she made her way to centre stage. Pausing, she tried to smile more broadly. She flung open her shawl. Before anyone had a chance to glimpse the North Wind, the lights went out. Krystal screamed. Gerald was knocked to the floor.

When the lights came on, Krystal lay sprawled beside him. She sat up, and Gerald noticed her throat was bare. Then he noticed his night scope lay smashed between them.

Barry pushed through the crowd. He stared at Gerald, whose glasses and wig were askew.

"You . . . you . . . you!" He took a lungful of air. "GUARD!"

Gerald was frog-marched to the executive suite, where Barry searched him.

"What's this?" Barry pulled the North Wind from Gerald's pocket and dangled it in his face.

"I didn't—"

"We'll see about that." Barry snatched back the necklace and headed into the next room. "Get those security tapes rewound!"

Body quaking, Gerald sank onto the nearest couch. Guards stood nearby as Barry reviewed the security videos. Gerald squirmed.

"Feeling guilty?" one of the guards asked.

"No—this bra is killing me."

The man stared at Gerald's chest.

Gerald crossed his arms protectively. "Men," he said. "You're all the same."

"Gotcha!" Barry marched into the room, the North Wind still dangling from his fingers. "We have you on tape, bringing a tray of drinks to the executive suite. That must be when you stole it."

"But I never came here."

"No mistaking the wig or that schnozz of yours. I'm getting rid of you once and for all, you loser."

"Hold it," Gerald said. The phrase rang a bell. He cast his mind back over the past few days. He gasped. "Krystal set me up! She said she wanted to seal my fate as a courier!"

He pulled out his recording pen, clicked a button, and Krystal's voice said, ". . . my chance to get rid of him . . . I'm sick of that loser."

"I can't believe it!" Gerald said. "I can *not* believe it! What did I ever do to her?"

Krystal's dress rustled as she entered, flanked by security guards. She was pale, and her makeup did not mask the dark circles under her eyes. "You're not the loser I was talking about, Gerald. Keep blithering, though, and I might change my mind. I was talking about Frank. He was sitting behind you that night in the bar." Seeing the necklace wound around Barry's fingers, she moved forward. "Thank heaven the North Wind is safe."

Barry clutched the necklace to his chest and retreated a step. "You said you'd dropped Frank."

There was a ruckus at the door. A security guard reappeared and pushed the other Cleopatra-coiffed waitress onto the couch beside Gerald.

"Hey there, sister-friend," Gerald said. "Feet still hurt?"

The waitress's lip curled in scorn. She took off her purple-tinted glasses and scrutinized Gerald.

"Didn't I say he looked like you, Frank?" Krystal said.

"About twenty-five years ago," the 'waitress' said in a baritone as he pulled off his wig.

"Found him lurking around the back door—with this." A security guard flashed the pastiche of the North Wind that Krystal had worn in the bar.

"It's not illegal to have a necklace like that," Frank said.

Barry inspected it. "Should be."

"Came back for the real one, didn't you?" Krystal asked.

Frank's gaze flicked toward the North Wind, still swinging from Barry's fingers. Then he shifted his weight and pulled a small object from beneath him. It was a multi-blade knife. He turned it over a couple of times.

"I used to have a model just like this," he said.

"Hey! That's my James Bond knife." Gerald grabbed at it, but a security guard intercepted.

Frank's complexion took on a greyish tinge. "What'd you call it?"

"Actually, it's my dad's James Bond knife. Musta slipped out of my pocket."

"Oh, good God. You're *that* Gerald. How did you end up in Yellowknife?"

Gerald peered at him. "Dad?"

Frank's pallor progressed into a shade of green. Gerald bounced closer on the couch.

"Dad! Look—I'm just like you. I'm James Bond."

Frank recoiled. "James Bond is a lady's man. Not a girlie-man. He never dressed like a broad."

Gerald's eyes went round. His top lip quivered.

"You're such a jerk, Frank." Krystal turned to Barry. "He's the one who came up to the suite."

"Prove it," Frank said.

Krystal pulled something from her purse.

"My wrist camera!" Gerald's eyebrows contracted for a few moments. "You took that at the coffee shop!"

"And I took your night scope in the bar, Sherlock." She pressed buttons on the tiny camera.

"Haven't lost your touch, I see," Frank said.

Barry's head snapped toward Krystal. "*What?*"

Krystal glared at Frank. He sneered back. Krystal took a deep breath. "I used to pick pockets, Barry. I was very good, but I eventually got caught."

"But your security check—"

Krystal shook her head. "I was a young offender. My records are sealed."

"You're fired."

"Just listen. Frank knew me in those days. He knew you wouldn't be thrilled to have a former thief working for you. When he heard I was going to be the Diamond Girl, he insisted I help him steal the North Wind or he'd tell you about my shady past. And that would be it for me in the diamond business."

"Some story," Frank said. "You're just ticked I dumped you."

Krystal gave the camera to Barry. "See. He's here in the executive suite. When Frank delivered the drinks, I ducked into the bathroom and wrapped the North Wind in toilet paper. The original plan was for me to tuck it into his pocket and keep my neck covered until I went downstairs. When the lights went out, I was supposed to plant the fake on Gerald—that's why I needed the night scope. Frank would make his getaway while everyone tried to figure out where the real necklace was, and how Yellowknife's favourite spy was involved. But I swapped them to keep the North Wind safe. Gerald's a flake, but he's an honest guy. Unlike you, Frank."

Frank snorted. "You are one bitter and twisted woman."

"You have to believe me, Barry. I couldn't shake Frank, and he would have tried to steal it with or without me. He had a private collector. I had to stage a fake theft to prove I'm trustworthy."

"You and Gerald were caught red-handed." Barry's eyes wandered over Krystal's silver-clad figure. "I'll miss having you around."

Krystal's head drooped. "I'm sorry, Gerald. I really was trying to help."

Shoulders hunched, Gerald was fiddling with his spy pen. "You broke it that night," he grumbled. There was a snap, then came Frank's recorded voice.

". . . better not double-cross me, you stupid cow. I don't get the North Wind, you don't get a future. Got it?"

"Dad!" Gerald said. "That's not nice."

"Stop calling me that, you freak."

Gerald's face crumpled, then abruptly smoothed itself out. His eyes narrowed. "I thought you worked for the government."

"Until I stole a couple million dollars."

"And took off with some floozie."

"Ya."

"Leaving me and mom on our own."

"So?"

Krystal's purse sat on the coffee table. Gerald grabbed it and got in three or four blows before the security guards hauled his father to safety. Barry, Krystal, and Gerald remained in the room.

"You're still fired," Barry told Krystal.

"I don't think so," she said. "What about your wandering hands, Barry? Your wife would want to know about that."

The thought of his own recent encounter with Barry's hands made Gerald shiver. He jabbed a finger in Krystal's direction. "You go, girl."

"My word against yours," Barry said.

"Oh, I think she'll believe us." Gerald rose from the couch and moved to Krystal's side. "She already suspects."

Krystal raised an eyebrow. "Us?"

A security guard returned. "Barry—everyone's waiting for the North Wind. And the RCMP phoned to see if everything's all right. They're getting calls." The guard glanced at Gerald and Krystal, then leaned close to Barry. "And your wife wants to know what you're doing up here with a couple of floozies."

Gerald squeaked. "I am not a floozie!"

Sweat glistened on Barry's forehead.

"We'll talk terms later," Krystal said as Barry relinquished the necklace to her. "One thing's for sure—the Diamond Girl needs a bodyguard." Krystal cast a glance over Gerald's uniform. "Seeing as how James Bond never dressed like a woman, you want to put on something else?"

"To hell with James Bond. But I do want to get out of these drab duds." Gerald's eyes glittered. "I brought the purple dress. It's downstairs."

"You go girl," Krystal said as Gerald ran to change.

Baneberries

"Sweets will be the death of you," Bernice said.

Vivian's arm paused halfway to the cookie plate.

"So you keep telling me." Her hand shot out and scooped up three oatmeal cookies, depositing two beside her coffee mug and one in her mouth.

"I got you something when I was in town the other day." Bernice laid a couple of brochures beside Vivian's cookies. "The heart and stroke society had a booth in the mall."

"Gee, thanks." Vivian tossed aside the brochures, then fished a racy women's magazine out of her shoulder bag.

"You should get someone else to chop and stack your wood this winter. Wouldn't want you to drop dead of a heart attack. Or maybe you could lose a few pounds," Bernice said.

"Henry always liked my figure." Vivian ran a hand over a well-rounded hip clad in leopard-print spandex. "He said a woman should look like a woman, not a broomstick. And your Walt didn't hide his admiration, either." She raised her mug to her lips, her eyes smirking over the rim.

Bernice drummed her bony fingers on the table.

"Just remember what happened to Henry after thirty years of gravy on his fries and too many beers after his shift at the mine," she said.

"Your Walt popped off almost as quick. Those rich desserts you make couldn't have been good for him."

"Walter had a *hereditary* heart condition. He was proud of the awards I won for my baking, but he knew the meaning of self-control."

"That's what you think," Vivian murmured, caressing her hip again. "It's the repressed ones who surprise us all."

Bernice stared out the window, lips pursed. Vivian nibbled another cookie.

"Speaking of handsome men, Fred says he can't plough my access road this winter," she said. "He could have warned me—it's almost September. And I don't know anyone else with a plough on their truck."

"I said it was a mistake to build your cabin so far from the main road."

"It's thirty years too late to do anything about it."

"I insisted Walter build in one of these little neighbourhoods," Bernice said. "They're nice and close to the highway. And there's people around in case you need help. Fred's still ploughing for us, but six households together can pay him properly. You should have put your foot down with Henry."

"Henry wanted to get away from it all."

"It's the Ingraham Trail, not the TransCanada Highway. People from Yellowknife going to their cottages, a few campers, a few canoeists."

"*Au contraire*—party-hearties with their beer and car stereos in the summer. Big trucks heading to the ice road and up to the mines in the winter. Henry wanted nothing to do with that racket. Besides, it's so romantic in my little spot. Henry used to say that the wind in the poplars is like a thousand people whispering something you can't quite make out.

He had the soul of a poet."

And the beer gut of a hard rock miner, Bernice thought.

"Too bad you got yourself fired from that receptionist job, otherwise you could afford to live in town and not worry about snow ploughs," she said.

"Too bad Walt got Henry to invest in that pyramid scheme. Otherwise we could both afford to live in Yellowknife and not thirty miles down some crappy little highway in the middle of nowhere," Vivian said.

Bernice lowered her eyes. "You just said you were enchanted with the romance of cottage country."

"At least Walt got out with enough money so you can pay for a satellite dish and bingo on Saturday night," Vivian added.

"Oh, yeah. A regular merry widow—that's me." Bernice shuffled into the living room, which was practically the same thing as the dining room in her tiny cabin. She grabbed the remote control from the coffee table and, squinting through half-glasses, fiddled with the buttons. "You watch plenty of TV over here, so I don't see that you should complain. And I don't get to bingo much since Selma moved to Kelowna."

"Last of your cronies?"

"Gladys is still around."

"There's hardly anyone left from the old days. Wish I could afford to move to British Columbia." Vivian finished the last cookie. "These could use more vanilla."

"Thanks for the advice, Sara Lee, but that recipe won first place at the Yellowknife Fall Fair with precisely the same amount of vanilla."

Vivian opened her magazine and ran a bright pink fingernail down a page.

"I'm going to try this cake—it's called *Ménage à trois*—'an intoxicating union of chocolate, caramel and pecans.'"

"Sounds revolting. Besides, I thought your search for your artistic voice left you no time for cooking."

"I have to go." Vivian jumped up and twirled a black cape over her shoulders.

"But the soaps . . ."

"Not today. It's my rug-hooking class. Didn't I say?" She fixed a fuchsia beret over her red curls, tilted it over one eye, and banged out of the cabin.

Bernice sat down to watch the soap operas. *General Hospital* had just ended when there was a knock on the back door.

"Buzz off, Vivian, I'm busy." She yanked it open to find not Vivian, but a slim, well-tanned man with close-cropped, curly grey hair and deep, dark eyes—beautiful, chocolate-brown eyes, just like Walter's.

"I didn't mean to bother you, ma'am. I'm moving in two doors down. Forgot to get groceries and I was wondering if I could borrow a can of Spam."

"I'm sorry . . ."

"I tried the people next door, but they're vegetarian. They offered me a pack of tofu, though."

"They would. Come in and I'll fix you a care package."

His name was Arthur. He'd been living in Inuvik, but moved south after retiring because his son lived in Yellowknife.

"I'd be pleased to meet your wife when she has a free minute," Bernice said.

"I'm divorced."

"I see." Bernice turned so he couldn't see her smile.

"Seems like a nice neighbourhood. Even with the vegetarians."

"The Ingraham Trail is lousy with them these days. I call them 'Granola Flakes.' They all have university degrees and big, important jobs with the government. When they're not working they're raising money, or public awareness, or some such thing, for causes they think are important." She grabbed items out of the cupboards and refrigerator and stuffed them into a brown paper bag. "They say they live on the trail to get in touch with 'natural values' and to avoid the 'conspicuous consumption' of city life. I personally don't see much natural value in using an outdoor privy at forty below. They're too cheap to pay Yellowknife property taxes, which is fine, if they'd just be honest enough to say so." Bernice paused to draw breath. "I'm sorry—I'm doing all the talking."

"No problem." Arthur accepted the paper bag holding a tin of Spam, some dry biscuits, half a dozen eggs, a bit of butter, and a small plastic bag half full of coffee. He drew out the coffee, and handed it back to Bernice. "I just drink tea."

"I don't have any," she said, abashed.

"No matter. This is very kind. I'll return the favour in a few days."

"Don't worry about that. I'm happy to help." Bernice stood in the doorway and watched him disappear through the spruce trees.

Not wanting to seem pushy, Bernice waited a full twenty-four hours before she baked a Cranberry Crumble Cake—a family specialty for three generations—curled her short grey hair, put on her best dress, and prepared to be neighbourly. A half-ton truck, piled high with cardboard boxes, was parked at Arthur's front door.

"I brought you a little something." She presented Arthur with the cake, then slipped past him into the cabin. "What on earth?"

The carpet was littered with dirt that had spilled out of pots of long-dead wild plants, now crawling with bugs. Bernice nudged her toe against a pile of loose fur and feathers that had drifted into a corner of the living room.

"Granola Lady next door says the last tenants tried to nurse injured animals and birds back to health," Arthur said.

"Figures. Anyone with a lick of sense would've put the poor creatures out of their misery."

"Apparently they were trying to be compassionate. You should see the cupboards."

Bernice yanked one open. A box of Cheerios lay on its side, cereal and mouse droppings scattered all over. She checked a drawer. Same scene, with a box of unsalted soda crackers in place of the cereal.

"Probably trying to feed the little woodland animals. Not very compassionate for the next person moving in. Well, we're not all Granola Flakes around here." Bernice marched out the door, returning a few minutes later dressed in slacks, a kerchief protecting her fresh curls. She was toting a bucket and a bottle of bleach.

"I have trouble with mice, too, and nothing kills germs like bleach," she said, filling the bucket with hot water. She used up the entire bottle trying to make Arthur's cabin livable, down on her knees scrubbing out the lower cupboards, climbing on a stepladder to get to the higher ones. Arthur continued to move furniture and boxes off the truck. They'd take a break from time to time to have a bit of Bernice's Cranberry Crumble Cake, and to sip some tea Arthur had found in a box.

"This is better than any dessert I've had anywhere,

even in fancy restaurants in Edmonton or Calgary." Arthur's eyes glowed just like Walter's used to when he bit into one of Bernice's creations.

"Secret ingredient. And I pick the berries myself." Bernice blushed. "Have you travelled much?"

"Not really. Worked for the Department of Wildlife for thirty-five years," Arthur said. "Spent most of my time on the land. Best job in the world in the best place in the world. How about you?"

"Just kept house for Walter. Sometimes I'd go out with the girls for bingo or a card game. Walter and I went to Vegas a couple of times, to play the slot machines and see the Elvis impersonators. That's about it."

"Sounds real nice," he said.

"If you want to watch anything on TV, just pop down." Bernice picked up her bucket. "I have the full satellite package, including all the sports channels."

Arthur did indeed pop down, that very evening. He returned the cake plate.

"You ate it all?"

"Still haven't made it into town for groceries."

"You'll give yourself sugar diabetes," Bernice scolded. She reheated some of the chili she'd cooked for supper and made fresh biscuits.

"This is great," he said around a mouthful of biscuit. "Can we watch wrestling now?"

Bernice spent the next couple of days helping Arthur get settled. In the evening he'd come to Bernice's cabin for supper and TV. When they finally unpacked everything, Arthur drove into Yellowknife to buy Bernice some beer and Chinese takeout as a thank you. She was putting away the leftover Chinese food, and Arthur was looking for a nature show on TV, when someone pounded on the door. It swung open and in waltzed Vivian. She took a good long look at Arthur before turning to Bernice.

"Bernice, I was so worried about you. You haven't been over in days—I was afraid you'd fallen and broken your hip."

"For Pete's sake, Vivian, old ladies fall and break their hips, not someone like me." Bernice didn't know who'd told Vivian about Arthur, or that Bernice had been helping him, but Vivian had obviously been practising her lines.

"I can see why you haven't had time to get together." Vivian gave Arthur a honey-coated smile. "I would have called to make sure everything was okay, but I'm not a rich widow like Bernice, and can't afford a phone all the way out here."

Bernice introduced them and went to make tea. By the time she got back, they were laughing it up like they'd been old buddies for years.

"Since when are you so refined that you serve tea?" Vivian asked.

"Arthur likes it."

"How elllegaunt," Vivian drawled in an attempt at an English accent. "They always have awwfternoon tea on the soap operas."

Bernice made a mental note that Vivian would not be watching any more of her satellite TV.

"I always had tea out on the land," Arthur said. "The native wildlife officers drink it, and I got used to it. Now I prefer it. Sometimes we'd pick Labrador tea, throw it in with the regular, and have 'bush tea.'"

"You're just like my Henry—that's my late husband," Vivian said. "He was always outside. He loved the outdoors."

Arthur said that Henry sounded like a man after his own heart. Bernice felt her Chinese supper rising in her throat. Vivian leaned toward Arthur.

"I find living in the bush to be . . . well . . . spiritual, you know?" she said.

"Cookie?" Bernice stuck the plate under Vivian's nose.

Vivian's scoop-like hand swung toward the cookies, but she stopped herself and picked up one oh-so-daintily.

"I would have thought you'd make Cranberry Crumble Cake for your new neighbour," she said.

"I've already had most of one," Arthur said. "It was great."

"Watch out—that's how she trapped her husband. Walt always said it was the reason he married her."

"Vivian!" Bernice said.

"Bernice is quite the cook, but she's not adventuresome, always sticking to the tried-and-true." Vivian fluttered her eyelashes. "I like to experiment with a little spice."

Bernice rolled her eyes.

"I'm fascinated by the treasures of our natural world," Vivian continued. "And a poor widow like me has to make her pension stretch as far as possible. I'd like to know more about the plants around here, but I'll need a guide. Not everything's safe to eat—Bernice keeps warning me about something called 'baneberries.'"

"Never heard of them," Arthur said.

Vivian laughed.

"I always figured they were just a projection of Bernice's hostility. A way to scare me out of the berry patch, which she considers her own special turf. I prefer a positive approach and I'm sure you do, too. For instance, maybe you could show me where to find this Labrador tea."

Bernice was washing dishes the next morning when she saw Arthur drive past. As he waved, she had a feeling he wasn't going into town for supplies. She was right. When he turned onto the Ingraham Trail, he headed away from Yellowknife and toward Vivian's cabin. He got home late, well past supper, and came over to offer Bernice some beer in exchange for TV time—there was an old movie he wanted to watch.

"Thirsty work." He popped open a can. "Been helping Vivian gather firewood. Have to admire a woman who'd stay in the bush all by her lonesome."

Bernice grunted.

"It's my duty to help," Arthur said. "Like you helped me when I moved in. People are so neighbourly here. Well, some people. The guy who's been ploughing her access road backed out on her. Just like that. Good thing I showed up when I did."

Bernice started to say something, but he held up a hand, his gaze fixed on the TV.

"Hang on—this is a good part."

They exchanged hardly a dozen words for the rest of the evening, which Bernice figured was just as well considering the turn the conversation had taken. Arthur's interest in wrestling, nature shows, and old movies dropped off over the next couple of weeks.

Bernice, on the other hand, had little to do but watch the soap operas. Seeing the actors and actresses hop in and out of bed made her wonder what Arthur and Vivian were up to. She told herself not to be ridiculous—he was just helping Vivian, who probably repaid him with a lot of yak about her quest for self-fulfilment through macramé. Bernice knew what men really appreciated, and kept busy in the kitchen. He'd eventually come around, just as Walter had. Thank heaven Vivian couldn't cook anything more appetizing than hamburger casserole.

Arthur never locked his door, so Bernice left her

offerings on his kitchen table. While at his cabin one day, her eyes fell on a pie plate that looked like a reject from a beginners' ceramics class, which is exactly what it was—Vivian had created it years earlier to honour the Queen on her fortieth jubilee. The pie plate carried Her Majesty's silhouette and the royal coat of arms with a shaky lion and a unicorn that looked like a cow wearing a dunce cap. Bernice examined it. There were traces of blueberry along the edge.

Her heart did an ugly little ker-thump. So Vivian had invaded the berry patch. Bernice had been leaving Arthur the usual sorts of treats, like date squares or banana loaf, but she'd also given him wild gooseberry jam and wild blueberry muffins. Her self-sufficiency in the bush was intended to prove they were kindred spirits. Not that it had much effect. As much as she hated to admit it, Arthur seemed to prefer Vivian's wheedling dependence. It was certainly a formula that had worked for her over the years. After Vivian's husband died, even Walter fell for her damsel-in-distress routine. As soon as she put a quaver in her voice and let her well-endowed chest heave a little, off he'd rush to her rescue. Bernice had never learned those wiles—she knew only one way to a man's heart. And now Vivian was stepping onto her turf. Bernice scribbled a note inviting Arthur to supper the next day.

He appeared on her doorstep in the morning.

"Thanks for the invite, but I'm busy tonight," he said. "And sorry for not coming around sooner to thank you for all the stuff. I'd like to make it up to you." He presented Bernice with a package wrapped in the previous week's edition of *News/North*. She opened it.

"Gee, thanks. Half a fish."

"It's a real northern delicacy—smoked whitefish." He puffed up his chest. "I caught it, and Viv smoked it!"

Vivian could also shove it, as far as Bernice was concerned.

"Gives me indigestion," she said.

"Turns out Viv's a real gourmet. And serious about living off the land. A few days ago she made rabbit with mustard sauce, and last night she cooked a *cassoulet* with ptarmigan she'd been keeping in the freezer."

"Yep, she's a marvel with roadkill."

Bernice moved away from the door so Arthur could enter. She set the fish on the counter, her brow puckered.

"What else has she been cooking?"

"A gooey chocolate cake. And she keeps trying these new desserts with berries. Her wild raspberry cream flan was okay, but some are just weird, like this cloudberry clafoutis thing. I think she's trying to top your Cranberry Crumble Cake."

"It'll never happen," Bernice said.

Arthur smiled. Bernice couldn't tell if he agreed, or if he was humouring her.

"Is that all you've been up to?" she asked.

"Well, Vivian's been teaching me about food presentation—it's so important, she says. She does up her table real nice, with a tablecloth covered with doilies she's crocheted herself. She uses real silverware, and has all these fancy little coffee spoons that she's bought on special occasions, like when Prince Charles married Lady Diana. And she has this special pie plate she made herself."

"I've seen it."

If this was the way the world was turning, it was clear that Bernice had to resort to Plan B. A few days without superior baking might help Arthur put his priorities in order, so Bernice went into Yellowknife to visit her friend Gladys. She returned to her cabin late one evening, to find the kitchen light shining through the thin gingham curtains. She thought she'd turned it off. The annoyance that flooded through her at the thought of wasted electricity turned into a cold jolt of fear when she saw a shadow move within. She picked up a wrench from the floor of her car and pulled open the cabin door, prepared to bean the low-life who'd rob a poor, defenceless widow. Vivian was hunched over the kitchen table, cramming cards into Bernice's recipe box.

"I didn't think you'd be back so soon," she said. "It's not like you to leave without telling me. I was worried."

"And you thought I'd left a note with my whereabouts in my recipe box?"

Vivian was silent.

"What were you looking for? As if I don't know."

"The Cranberry Crumble Cake recipe," Vivian whispered.

"It's not written down."

"I would have asked, but you left so quickly, and I didn't know when you'd be back. Arthur was saying how he loved your Cranberry Crumble Cake, better than anything I bake, and I wanted to make one before he goes on his fishing trip. He'll be gone two weeks, and that's a long time to pine for a piece of Cranberry Crumble Cake."

Bernice's face turned as red as the berries in her renowned dessert. She slapped the wrench into the palm of her hand.

"Do you have to take everything that's mine? First Walter, now this."

"I was joking about Walt." Vivian faced Bernice across the kitchen table. "Just trying to get your goat."

"Walter always denied it too." Bernice slapped the wrench into her palm again.

"Bernice . . ."

"You're the bane of my existence. You poisonous old tart."

Vivian cringed as Bernice swung the wrench upwards, then crashed it onto the table, leaving a splintered scar in the wood. The women stared at each other.

"Sorry." Bernice set down the wrench. "Just projecting my hostility, I guess."

"No kidding!"

Bernice's fingers traced the outline of the wrench, her eyes staring right through it.

"I should take a positive approach," she said. "For instance, I could bake you something. A new pie recipe."

"A new recipe? You?"

"You've inspired me. But the pastry won't turn out unless it's baked in a ceramic pie plate. Could I borrow that one you made for Queen Elizabeth's jubilee? I've always admired it, and food presentation is so important."

*****

Arthur left on his fishing trip the following morning. A couple of days later, Bernice returned to Yellowknife to visit Gladys. She was surprised when Arthur tracked her down the following day. He was calling from the hospital. He'd brought in Vivian, who was real sick, and had been asking for Bernice.

"She can talk?"

"Yes, but she isn't making a lot of sense."

The doctors were still working on Vivian when Bernice arrived at the hospital.

"I came home early from my fishing trip and found Vivian thrashing around on her bed," Arthur said. "She'd been throwing up, but was too weak to get up. I rushed her into town, but she went into shock. The doctors asked what she'd eaten, but I don't know and Vivian can't say. And you were in Yellowknife, so you couldn't help."

Arthur's voice broke off. Bernice patted his clenched hand. A doctor came out of the emergency room.

"I'm sorry," he said. "She's gone."

*****

A few days later, Arthur came to Bernice's for dessert and to watch wrestling on TV. Between mouthfuls of Cranberry Crumble Cake, he said the doctors figured Vivian died from eating a pie made from baneberries she'd mistakenly picked. With Vivian's love of sweets, she'd eaten about three-quarters of it before the poison kicked in. They found the rest of the pie sitting on the kitchen table, in the ceramic pie plate Vivian had made for the Queen's fortieth jubilee.

"I blame myself," Arthur said. "I'd been teaching her which plants were edible, and which ones to stay away from, but I'd honestly never heard of baneberries. We don't have them around Inuvik."

"It doesn't matter. She shouldn't have eaten so much at once. I tried to tell her."

"At least I got to talk to her at the end. I feel bad, Bernice, because Viv really wanted to see you. She called your name a couple of times before she went unconscious."

Bernice murmured something sympathetic as she poured Arthur another cup of tea.

Fireweed

"Come on, Rick. Get out of the truck."

Clark paused beside the gravel road, then headed into the ditch. His brother remained inside the battered orange half-ton, twisting knobs on the radio. Squeaks and static carried through the open window.

"Rick?"

"How am I supposed to get the stock market report in the freakin' middle of nowhere?" Richard thumped the dashboard, jerked himself out of the truck, and slammed the door. "What's so bloody important?"

Clark swept an arm toward a rocky clearing filled with waist-high plants—long stems bristled with narrow emerald leaves, each topped with a tower of small pink flowers. "Fireweed—isn't it beautiful?"

Richard squinted at the flowers swaying among skeletal jack pines, charred by wildfire. Some trees remained standing, tilting in all directions, while others lay scattered among mounds of grey bedrock and clusters of fireweed.

"Freakin' fabulous. Can we go back to town now? I can't believe you left your loser staff in charge of the store."

Clark wandered into the clearing, stopped beside the remains of a tree, and ran his fingers down the blackened bark. "Fireweed is the first plant to appear after a forest fire.

It brings colour and the promise of new life in the wake of utter devastation."

Following his brother, Richard came across two half-toppled trees leaning on each other for support. He karate-kicked one; they both crashed to the ground.

The manoeuvre provoked a frown from Clark. "It felt like the end of the world, when the wildfire came through. Smoke was so bad in Yellowknife, the streetlights came on at noon. Rained ash for two days. That was only a couple of years ago, and now look. It's all a part of the cycle. Death and rebirth."

Richard rolled his eyes. "Cut the flower child crap. I'll puke."

"It only seems like the end of the world, Rick."

"Losing my business, or having to work for my baby brother?"

Clark moved closer and put an arm around Richard.

A shudder shook Richard free. "When Mom told me you'd opened a hardware store, Clark, I thought you'd finally toughened up. 'Hardware—there's a man's business,' I said. But nooo, not you."

"You might take a lesson from these beautiful flowers."

"Or I might take the next flight home."

Emitting a gentle smile, Clark glided farther into the bush. Richard picked up a stick and prodded an anthill at his feet. Leaving wasn't an option—he had no home any more, not since the bank had repossessed his Ottawa brownstone, along with his Mercedes and the cottage in the Gatineau Hills.

"Is that why you made me manager of the garden centre?" he asked. "To teach me a life lesson?"

The morning sun lit Clark's brown curls as he ambled to his brother's side. "Everyone starts in the garden centre.

There's a certain Zen to working with plants, nurturing them, watching them blossom."

Richard gagged.

"Flowers first, then the whole forest grows back." Clark drifted toward the truck. "Give it a chance. You've only been at it a few days."

They rattled down the Ingraham Trail, Clark humming with the radio as they zigzagged through the boreal bush of jack pine, birch, and willow, around huge outcroppings of grey rock, and lakes fringed with reeds.

Richard glanced at his brother. People had trouble believing Clark was only a couple of years younger than he was. Clark had moved north right out of university, twenty years earlier, and had barely aged. Sun exposure had caused lines around his eyes, but years of hiking, kayaking, and skiing had kept him in great shape. Richard, on the other hand, had lost most of his hair through the stress of building—and losing—a high-tech company. He'd been a faithful gym-goer throughout his career, lest a potbelly ruin the lines of his custom-tailored suits, but in recent months he'd been unable to face the boys at the gym. His waist and jawline now sagged.

As much as he detested Clark's plant metaphors, little brother was right about the state of his life—Richard's professional reputation was in shreds; existence as he'd known it had ended. For years he'd lived for the rough and tumble of the corporate world: acquisitions, mergers, and—his favourite—hostile take-overs. There was nothing like going *mano a mano* with his own kind, battle scarred and street smart: someone who understood weakness, greed, and the need not just to win, but to obliterate the opposition; someone who could match him, move for move; someone who might, possibly, out-manoeuvre him.

Entertainment like that did not come along every day,

however. When nothing had been happening on the corporate level, he'd roam the corridors of his company. All he usually found was a whiny peon to goad into argument. He preferred a hungry up-and-comer. Those he would invite for a meal or a round of golf, then let slip some imaginary weakness—liberties with his expense account or, worse, a loss of nerve. His opponent would slink around, forming alliances with other staff, lunching with one or more of the directors. As they moved in for the kill, he'd confront them with their disloyalty and fire them.

The mere thought of it gave him a buzz. Many of Richard's cohorts reached for booze or cocaine when corporate raiding didn't provide enough of a high. Richard needed neither; the adrenaline rush of a well-fought battle was all he craved.

He'd been so enmeshed in a particular set of intrigues that he'd failed to notice a much smaller competitor buying up his company's shares. The take-over was complete almost before he realized it. For a corporate warrior, the loss of his company had been disappointingly bloodless. And now his only challenge in life was forcing his spineless brother to face facts about his own dying business. The bulldozer approach had always worked when they were growing up. Simple. Mind-numbingly simple.

The office buildings of downtown Yellowknife finally appeared amid the rocky terrain. Clark steered the truck into the city and down Franklin Avenue to the Old Town. The character of the neighbourhood had been established when Yellowknife was a mining camp, a mix of homes and commercial establishments crowded beside Great Slave Lake. Remnants of the city's original businesses—housed in tube-like Quonset huts and warehouses sided with peeling tar paper—were scattered along Franklin Avenue. Newer commercial buildings with aluminum siding had sprouted among them. Along the side streets, posh houses stood on sites originally occupied by shacks and wall tents. It was a blend of old and new, quaint and trendy, scabrous and well-heeled.

Clark's store had a foot in both camps. The building was a 1950s warehouse, which he'd attempted to gentrify with fake log siding. A narrow asphalt parking lot ran along the front. The greatest effort at beautification was the garden centre, an octagonal addition finished in natural wood, featuring several windows and a skylight. In front, gravel paths wound around raised flowerbeds shaped like dancing amoebas.

As Clark pulled into the parking lot, a dumpy brown-haired woman, the manager of the lighting section, scurried toward an ancient van. Clark parked and got out of the truck. Richard followed.

"Everything okay, Gloria?" Clark asked.

"My turn for lunch supervision at play school." Gloria opened the van door and flung her purse onto the passenger seat. With a glance at Richard, she turned to Clark and dropped her voice. "I was on the phone all morning chasing down some special fixtures. I didn't get the weekly order done, and it needs to be in by 2:30. Could you . . .?"

"Of course. Give the twins a hug for me."

Gloria climbed into the van, and Clark shut her door. She backed out of the stall, flipped the vehicle into gear, and squealed out of the parking lot.

Clark shook his head. "I keep telling her to slow down. You can't let a few light bulbs ruin your day."

"She takes advantage." Richard pushed through the glass doors ahead of his brother. "She sleeps on the job."

"She's a single mom."

"She's stealing her salary from you, just like Frankie Dolan stole your lunch money in Grade 10."

"That's ridiculous. Besides, the customers say she's indispensable."

"What customers?"

The two men stood beside the check-out counter and surveyed the store. The paint department was located on the left-hand side of the building, the lighting department on the right. General hardware occupied the centre shelves and the back wall, along with Clark's office. The garden centre opened off the lighting section on the far right.

An elderly man picked at bulk nails in galvanized holders in the centre aisle. Near the front of the paint section, a twenty-something woman with a blonde ponytail examined a handful of pink and red paint chips.

"It's lunchtime on a Tuesday in July," Clark said. "Of course it's slow."

Guitar chords floated through the store as someone strummed a folk tune. The young woman swayed to the music. A male voice sang, "If you'd ever set me free—"

The music paused, then repeated.

"If you'd ever set me free—"

Another pause. "What rhymes with 'free'?"

"Knee," the old man said. "'I would kick you in the knee.'"

Goosebumps rose on Richard's skin. *Perfect. Just the boost I need.*

"Toby!" he shouted.

A young man with stringy hair and a patchy beard appeared from one of the paint aisles.

"Yo."

Richard jerked his head toward the woman. "Customer. Remember what they are?"

Toby winced. "You've got to be kidding."

"Now, Richard—" Clark said.

Richard's blood vessels constricted, pushing up his blood pressure. Slackers were a favourite target, partly because they drained profit and partly because they fought like a demon to keep their seat on the gravy train. The old, familiar cocktail of increased blood sugar, adrenaline, and other fight-or-flight chemicals rushed through his veins. "Now!"

Toby turned to the woman. "Can I help you?"

The blonde's cheeks were well on their way to matching the deepest red in the samples she clutched. She ran out of the store.

Clark shook his head. "Was that necessary?"

"What just happened?" Richard asked.

"She's Toby's groupie. Comes in to hear him play. We leave her alone."

Richard looked at the old guy. "Anyone else just here for the music?"

Nails clattered into a bin. The geezer hobbled out.

"Hey, man. I'm writing a new song," Toby said. "Stanley likes to help."

"This is a store, not a bloody coffeehouse."

Toby squared his shoulders. "They buy stuff."

"How could anyone buy anything in this place?" Richard marched through the aisles, flicking a hand to the left, then to the right. "Completely out of fine-grain sanding blocks, only one package of sponge paint brushes, no—absolutely *no*—cans of shellac. How the hell is my brother supposed to make a profit? He counts on you, and this is how you repay him?"

Toby frowned. "The order hasn't come in—"

A glow settled over Richard as he drew a bead on his

target. "Do you value your job, at least? How's Clark supposed to pay you, if you're too slack-assed to make opening the doors worthwhile?"

Richard paused. Would Toby come right back at him, or use a more devious technique like shifting the blame?

Head down, Toby pulled a paint roller off the shelf and fidgeted with it. He shuffled his feet. He looked up and glared at Richard. Richard held his breath.

"Clark, buddy, I'm sorry. I didn't know you felt like that. I'll call the suppliers."

Richard's blood vessels went flaccid. His heartbeat dropped to normal with disappointing efficiency.

"Sure. See what you can do." Clark dragged Richard to his office and shut the door. "What is with you?"

"What's with me? This place could be a freakin' goldmine, but you have no business sense."

Clark moved behind his desk. "At least I still have a business."

"I was chief executive officer of a multi-million-dollar corporation. What do you clear in a week? A couple hundred bucks?"

"Not your problem."

Richard paced the room. "You must pay a fortune in taxes. You'd cut overhead if you moved to the industrial area."

"The industrial area is a wasteland. We're part of a community here."

"Well, fire your two deadbeat employees, at least. We can run the place together."

"They're good people who need their jobs."

"Collateral damage."

Clark planted his hands on the desk. "Like Mark Gullen was collateral damage?"

Richard stopped pacing. "Thirty years and you haven't got over that? He was lipping off. Said he'd beat you to a pulp."

"So you beat him to a pulp instead."

"Talk big, you got to back it up with your fists."

Clark leaned toward his brother. "He was a scrawny little math nerd. Frankie Dolan made him say that under threat of death, just to see what you'd do."

"So either I took a round out of him, or Frankie did. What doesn't kill you makes you stronger."

"Frankie Dolan was a bully and a thug. You didn't have to play his game."

"Sometimes you have no choice."

Clark's tone increased a notch. His face turned bright red. "Mark Gullen dropped out of school. Lost all chance of a scholarship."

"It stopped Frankie and his gang from coming after you. You stayed in school and got your scholarship. Right?"

Clark stared at the floor.

"I did it for *you*. No one picks on my brother."

Clark dropped back.

"Besides, Frankie was a worthy adversary," Richard said. "Had the smarts to keep things interesting."

"Oh well, then."

"The Zen approach doesn't work in the school yard, and it doesn't work in business," Richard said. "You'll go under."

The colour in Clark's face showed no sign of dissipating. "Focus on your own responsibilities."

Richard yawned. "It's July—no more bedding plants and everyone in Yellowknife is stocked up on sprinklers and garden gnomes."

Clark's head vibrated with tremors of anger. "The flowerbeds need tending."

"So?"

Clark kicked a metal wastepaper basket across the room. "Why do you always argue? You said you'd help with my business. That's why I let you come here. And right now I need help with the flowerbeds." Clark closed his eyes and took a deep breath.

"Gone to your happy place?"

Clark's jaw tightened. He took another deep breath and it relaxed. He opened his eyes. "Just trust me about the therapeutic effects of the garden centre. Pull a few weeds. Spread a little fertilizer. You'll be amazed."

"What amazes me, little brother, is your ability to spread fertilizer." As Richard swaggered out of the office, he looked back to find Clark holding the metal wastepaper basket, examining the dent he'd made.

Richard whistled as he rooted in the storage room for a bucket and hand rake. A full frontal assault no longer worked with Clark; he'd gained gonads in recent years. Well, if Clark wouldn't fire Toby or Gloria, he'd make one of them quit—it was necessary for the business, it would get him out of the garden centre and into the store, and it would be fun, to boot.

As he strolled into the yard, Richard's whistling choked off in mid-note. The flowerbeds were a sea of weeds dotted with islands of colour—red petunias, blue pansies, sunny marigolds. To add insult to injury, several fireweed in full bloom stood beside the flowerbed closest to the street. Trust Clark to drag him all the way into the bush just to make a point.

Turning his back on the fireweed, Richard reached for a clump of smaller offenders. The shallow roots pulled away from the soil. The next cluster also came up with a gentle rip-p-p. He tossed the weeds into the bucket. Another bunch followed, and another.

"Wanna talk about mind-numbing." He put a hand to his forehead. "Yes—the frontal lobe is definitely freezing over."

Clark, he realized, was watching from the store's front window. Richard flashed a rapturous smile and waved. Clark turned away. Richard's eyes rolled back in his head. He stood up and stretched.

He pointed at the next clump of weeds. "You are the weasel of a marketing manager whose attempts to undermine me distracted me from the hostile take-over." A flick of the finger. "Think you can push out those at the top of the food chain, the ones who really belong?" He uprooted it and lobbed it into the bucket. "So long, sucker."

He zeroed in on another weed. "You are the company president who abandoned me at the crucial moment. If you'd hung in, we could have beaten them back." Yanking up the weed, he tossed it into the air and drop-kicked it into the bucket.

Clark was right. Gardening *was* therapeutic.

Richard was squatting beside the flowerbed closest to the store, out of view, when Gloria's rusty van squealed into the parking lot. Toby appeared and nabbed her.

"He's been here a week, and the vibe's changed already."

"He looks at me like I'm dirt. He's going to tell Clark to fire me."

"Clark won't do that," Toby said. "He'll keep going with the flow."

"There's going with the flow, then there's being swept away by a major water diversion, which is what Richard is planning." Gloria's voice shook. "I'm not the greatest lighting manager in the world, but I need this job."

"There are other jobs."

"Not with the flex-time Clark gives me to deal with the kids. And who else would let you write songs when it's slow?" Gloria sniffled.

"We can't do anything about Richard."

"We can keep him in the garden centre. If he starts messing around in the store, there'll be no stopping him." Gloria sobbed.

"Okay, okay. We'll think of something." Toby put an arm around her and they went inside.

Behind the flowerbed, Richard shook with the heebie-jeebies. *Tears. Why couldn't women fight fair? Talk about a water diversion . . .*

Richard reached for a plant and felt a snap. Crap! He'd pulled up a flower. The plant he held was four inches across, with spiky leaves. This was no petunia or pansy. He carried it over to the bank of pink flowers beside the front flowerbed. Fireweed.

He tossed it into the pail, and spotted another one. A quick twist and it followed the first. "'Colour and new life after utter devastation,' my butt."

The weeds finally routed, Richard paraded around, lavishing fertilizer and water. Finally, Clark came to check. He walked among the flowerbeds, lifting leaves to see if weeds lurked beneath, occasionally sticking a finger into the soil.

"Ease up on the water," he said. "But you're doing a good job."

"Thanks, bro."

"Okay, then." As Clark turned toward the store, movement in the front window caught Richard's eye. Gloria and Toby were backing away.

Over the next few days Richard arranged and rearranged rakes and shovels, hoses and sprinklers, stepping stones and tiki torches in the garden centre. He couldn't see the rest of the store, so he made many trips to the staff washroom, conveniently located on the far side.

"Bladder condition," he told Gloria as he cut through her section for the umpteenth time.

Clark floated around, helping customers in the hardware section, which he ran in addition to acting as general manager.

Gloria, Richard noticed, spent most of her day at the lighting counter "checking inventory" on the computer, an activity that ended with her face-down on the keyboard, snoring. She only came alive when a customer needed something. No wonder she was indispensable—no one else could find anything. The 40-watt bulbs were two aisles away from the 60-watts, the night lights were hidden behind the wall sconces, and lampshades were scattered everywhere. Anyone entering the section ran a gauntlet of half-unpacked cartons of merchandise.

Toby had miraculously found paint brushes, sandpaper, a case of primer and other sundries, and had managed to restock many of the shelves. He was a good worker when motivated, sustaining momentum for several days. Richard watched, and waited.

Fewer gaps on the shelves meant fewer musical interludes in the store. Both the blonde girl and Old Stanley hung around, often leaving without hearing Toby play. And when he did, something wasn't quite right.

"Might wanna tune that guitar," Stanley said one day.

"I've been trying." Perched on a stool by the paint-mixing machine, Toby twisted a knob and ran his thumb across his guitar strings. He twisted another knob and tested the strings again. "Finally."

Toby launched into a song. His groupie tapped her toes as she sorted through a bin of masking tape. The tuning was perfect, but something else was amiss—his rhythm was off. Richard made his way to the edge of the paint section. The tension returned to his circulatory system and he braced himself for the adrenaline rush. As Toby laboured along, Richard clapped to the uneven beat. Then Toby hit a bad chord. The groupie set down a roll of tape and headed for the door.

Stanley nodded as she passed. "You're right. He sucks." He followed her out.

Guitar hanging at his side, Toby hurried to the front window as the blonde got into her car and drove off. Clark arrived and watched over Toby's shoulder as the old man shuffled out of sight. Toby shook his head and ran a hand over the neck of his guitar, a gesture both affectionate and protective.

Richard quivered. Victory was in sight. Usually he liked to prolong the frenzy of battle, playing out his stratagem until the final body blow . . . but a person could take only so much weeding. He observed from a distance as Toby turned to face Clark. Gloria dashed to join them.

"I hate to do this, buddy, but I qu—" Toby yelped as Gloria stepped on his foot.

"Could use the rest of the day off," she said.

"Absolutely," Richard said. "I'll cover for you."

"*I* will cover for him," Gloria said.

Richard regarded the disarray of the lighting section. "You have plenty to do. *I'll* cover."

Clark followed Richard's gaze. "Richard's right, Gloria. We don't want to overburden you."

Within seconds, Gloria's nose turned red, her eyes puffed up, and she started to cry. "I can handle it." She sniffled. "Are you saying I can't handle it?"

"Okay, okay," Clark said. "You can do it."

"Clark!" Richard said.

Gloria stopped crying. Her eyes narrowed as she turned to Richard. "Don't want to get you into trouble, but have you checked the flowerbeds lately?"

"Nothing out there."

"Sure about that?"

"Let's look." Richard strode into the yard, the others following. "See—you have your petunia and pansy, marigold and—" Richard's hand came to rest on a tuft of spiked green leaves. "Okay—there's one weed." He snapped it off.

Gloria smiled. "Look again."

Closer examination showed the flowerbed was full of tiny red shoots. One of the bigger ones was morphing into a tuft of spiky reddish-green leaves.

"Fireweed," Toby said. "Once it takes hold, it's a pain to get rid of."

"Kind of like Richard," Gloria muttered.

"Bummer," Clark said. "Well, Gloria and I will cover for Toby. You have your hands full out here, bro."

"But—"

Clark placed a hand on his shoulder. "Regrowth happens slowly. The flowers will let us know when you're ready to move on. Right now they need your help."

As the group retreated to the store, Gloria glanced over her shoulder. "Happy gardening."

Slouched on the wall of a raised flowerbed, Richard swatted at a piece of fluff floating past his nose, watching it twist and turn on the sudden air current. Then he noticed similar bits of fluff scattered across the flowerbed's surface. Richard scanned the yard, his gaze finally travelling to the fireweed beside the front flowerbed.

"Crap!"

It was moulting. The tiny pink blossoms had fallen

off, leaving fuschia-coloured spikes sticking out from the top of the plants. Many of these had split open and were releasing seeds attached to bits of white fluff. Once airborne, they headed straight for the flowerbeds.

"We'll see about that."

Into the garden centre Richard went, returning with the biggest, sharpest shears in stock. With open blades he moved in on the plants.

"You are the inglorious Gloria, passive-aggressive little cow." The blades snapped shut. The head of a fireweed tumbled to the ground. "And you are Toby, worse than Gloria, because you're just plain passive." Snip. Another one bit the dust.

The stand of fireweed was almost demolished when a shout interrupted his train of thought. Clark was sprinting across the parking lot. "What are you doing?"

"They're taking over the flowerbeds."

"Then deal with what's in there. Wild and cultivated can co-exist. Both bring joy."

Richard looked at the flowerbeds, at Clark, at the last remaining fireweed. A quick snip and it was beheaded.

"We cannot all co-exist in that little store. Let Toby go. I'll manage paints."

Clark relieved Richard of the shears. "You have work to do out here. Do it properly."

Had a wall been handy, Richard would have banged his head against it. Clark's business was on the skids; he was the only one who could see it. They needed to streamline operations and expand their client base. Only Richard had the drive to do it. Besides, this little role-play was getting old, real fast. He tugged a fireweed shoot, which broke off just beneath the soil's surface. Digging with the hand rake, he found the root again. The dank odour of compost and peat moss hit his nose. He scowled and gouged the soil, tracing the root down and across the flowerbed. It broke again. Blood flowed into his face; sweat formed on his forehead. His ears were ringing by the time he discovered that the root connected to a thicker one, which had several plants dividing off it. The thick root led right underneath a particularly nice clump of pansies.

"You little devil."

Richard assessed his options. He noted all the fireweed shoots poking through the soil. The situation was desperate. "Collateral damage," he told the pansies, then ripped them up. So far he had unearthed three feet of root, and was still going. It burrowed right to the bottom of the walled flowerbed, leading to the decapitated fireweed next to it.

"They seed from the top, but also invade from the bottom." Gloria stood beside the flowerbed, purse tucked under her arm.

Richard gave a nod of approval. "Sneaky."

"The roots branch like crazy, sending up runners everywhere. They're impossible to get out."

"Nothing a good herbicide can't fix."

Gloria smirked. "That's what you think. Well, I'm off to pick up the kids."

"Already?"

She lifted her chin. "It's five-fifteen. I've put in a full day."

Richard watched her go. She had more spunk that she let on—could probably put up a hell of a fight when cornered. Time to up the ante. He'd been digging for almost two hours; his once-manicured fingernails were encrusted with dirt, the flowerbed was a maze of trenches. Most of the cultivated flowers had survived, but were teetering between crevices, roots exposed. He hesitated over the gaps, aware that fireweed still lurked beneath, waiting to counterstrike.

They're just a bunch of stupid flowers. Get a grip. And get yourself off petunia detail and into that store.

He filled in the holes and went to clean up.

"What's this?" Gloria asked the next morning as Richard set a large take-out coffee on the lighting counter.

"A little thank you for clarifying the fireweed situation."

"Oh?"

Clark materialized. "Something wrong?"

"Making amends for yesterday," Richard said with a chagrined smile. "I'm not good at the 'big happy family' thing."

Clark gestured toward the coffee. "Working with the plants is clearly having the right effect."

Gloria popped off the lid. She squinted at the coffee, then took a sip. "Thanks."

Richard puttered around the garden centre, casting covert glances at Gloria. Within a half-hour, she'd tucked the phone under her chin and was debating the merits of various light switches with a supplier, clattering away on her keyboard. By mid-afternoon she'd cleared an entire aisle of packing cartons.

"Haven't felt this good since before I got pregnant, and that was four years ago," she told Toby as she dusted the display chandeliers.

Richard waited a week before he brought the next coffee, and then three or four days beyond that. Although the packing cartons soon disappeared, Gloria had not reformed her organizational system, which meant she was still the only one who could find anything. In the garden centre, Richard made sketches of the perfect self-service lighting section. If he did it right, even Clark would have to see reason.

The morning he brought her a fourth cup of coffee, Gloria's head hit the desk at 10:17 a.m. Adrenaline blasted through Richard's body. His scalp tingled. He ran for Clark.

"Passed right out, poor thing."

"Don't understand," Gloria mumbled. "Got an entire five hours of sleep last night." She cast a bleary glance at Richard. "You slip me a decaf?"

"Come on, Gloria. I'll drive you home," Clark said.

"No!" She clutched the counter. "He's been watching me. Waiting to take over."

Clark frowned. "Gloria!"

"You're taking his side."

"That's enough."

"Won't go. Won't go." Gloria's head bobbed.

"It's the drugs . . . I mean *drowsiness* talking." Richard barely suppressed a happy dance.

Gloria slumped over. Clark carried her to his truck.

The immediate implementation of Richard's plan was stymied by Toby, who kept popping into the section. After glowering at Richard for a few moments, he'd disappear. Richard practically rubbed his hands with glee. Toby was playing White Knight, and there was nothing like riding to the rescue of a damsel in distress to bring out the fighting instinct. He decided to bide his time and maintain the element of surprise.

Richard was in the garden centre when Clark made his final rounds.

"I'll lock up." He hefted a seed catalogue. "Planning for next year. This stuff is fascinating."

With a thumbs-up sign, Clark moved off. As soon as the orange half-ton pulled out of the parking lot, Richard set to work. By morning, it was perfect.

Neither Clark nor Toby noticed anything amiss. Gloria was late, arriving as a customer brought a package of light bulbs to the check-out. After ringing the customer through, Gloria made a beeline for the light bulb shelves. Clark and Toby followed her.

"Forty, sixty, a hundred watts. All together." She turned to find a new display of lampshades. "Small, medium, large. In all colours. All in one place."

"You straightened things out." Clark beamed at his brother.

"Only makes good business sense."

Clark lowered his voice. "It's a huge improvement."

"Plenty more where that came from."

"No doubt." Clark placed a hand on his brother's shoulder, turned and scanned the rest of the store. He looked past Gloria and Toby as if they weren't even there. Richard's fingers and toes started to prickle.

Gloria wobbled to her counter, her face ashen. Richard's breathing deepened. Increased blood flowed to his muscles and brain, sharpening his reflexes and intellect for the battle to come. A glance toward Toby revealed clenched hands, flared nostrils. Gloria straightened herself. Her lips quivered, but her eyes shot laser beams. Yes—it looked like he'd be taking on two at once. The pinpricks in his fingers and toes turned into zaps of electricity that ran up his arms and legs; it felt like he was floating. He braced himself for the onslaught of accusations and recriminations.

A sob broke from Gloria's mouth; tears spurted from her eyes. She ran to the staff washroom. Richard returned to earth with a crash. Toby stepped forward, rekindling hope.

"Clark, buddy, I can't deal with this vibe," he said. "It's affecting my music. I gotta split."

Richard sagged against a display of fluorescent tubes.

"But the customers love you," Clark said.

Toby shook his head. "No can do."

The three men stared at each other. Gloria returned from the washroom, sniffling and mopping her eyes.

"We'll miss you, Toby." Clark opened his arms wide. "Come on, everyone. Group hug." Gloria and Toby moved into his embrace. Clark gestured to Richard. "Come on, bro. It seems you're coming into the store. You're one of us now."

Richard remained motionless. He'd been mistaken—none of them had any fortitude. Clark would always put people before profit, Gloria would always resort to tears. Whoever replaced Toby would be of the same ilk. Richard had a sudden vision of the burned-out area where Clark had shown him the fireweed. The three of them huddled together reminded him of the dead jack pines supporting each other: one well-placed kick, and they'd topple. Not a worthy adversary among them.

Richard grabbed a pail and headed out the front doors to the yard. He stopped by a flowerbed and scanned the surface. Sure enough, over in the far corner, a red sprout poked through. The adrenaline rose in his blood once more, causing a pleasant buzz to swarm over his brain. He grinned as he reached for his hand rake. Now, *this* was a battle-worthy foe.

Roommates

Tammy was pulling up in front of her house in Yellowknife's Old Town when the regular clatter of her car's engine was drowned out by a deep, persistent thumping. She groaned. More repairs, which meant more shifts at the restaurant. Or she could put her superannuated Chevette out of its misery and walk for the rest of the winter. The thought of either option made her feet ache.

Tammy shut off the engine. She could still hear the thumping.

"Oh, no." She scrambled out of the car.

Edna, Tammy's neighbour, was outside feeding her dog team. "You got a party going on?" she called through the darkness.

"It's my new roommate."

"She should take it easy on that little stereo of yours. Don't want to blast your woofers and tweeters to smithereens."

All sound stopped.

"Like that," she said.

Tammy's pasty complexion took on the same grey hue as the full moon hanging over her little, old house.

"Trouble under the full moon—your feet will find their way home soon," her mother's voice whispered in her head.

Over my dead body, Zelda. Tammy stuck out her tongue at the offending orb and started toward the house, only to be slammed into a snowbank by something big and hairy.

Not literally, mother. And it figures you'd send my last roommate to do the dirty work. All part of your conspiracy.

"If only it were that easy, my Tamsin." Zelda's voice crept through Tammy's mind like a thickening fog. She tried to resist, but her mother's presence stole into every corner and crevice of her consciousness.

"Rosie, come back here!" Edna cried. "Leave her alone."

Ah . . . close, but not quite the same species as said roommate, Tammy thought as the weight of Edna's dog drove her face into the dry mid-winter snow, its sharp crystals scratching her skin.

Zelda's laugh reverberated through Tammy's brain, and her ears buzzed as the merriment grew. Then the voice vanished.

"Thank heaven for that." Tammy turned her attention to fending off Rosie, a Siberian husky with charcoal fur, an ivory face, and an enthusiastic tongue. Edna's square little figure, clad in navy blue winter coveralls, emerged from the darkness and scurried toward her.

"Stop struggling—you'll just wind her up."

Tammy lay still, despite her better judgement, and only after she'd covered the exposed sides of her face with her arms.

"She likes you." Edna hauled the dog off Tammy's prone figure.

"Really?"

"You'd know if she didn't."

Edna drew the sturdily built young woman to her feet

and brushed snow from her parka. The dog ran circles around them.

"Sorry about that." Edna squinted at Tammy, her eyelashes and the fur trim of her dog-musher's hat white with frost. "We just came in from a run. I was unhitching the team when Rosie escaped, little minx."

It seemed the City of Yellowknife had few rules about how many large dogs could be kept on one small lot, so Edna staked her half-dozen huskies in her front yard, where they made an unsightly mess and an unbearable racket. Rosie was the most rambunctious of the pack, always looking for a reason to bark or howl, or slip her collar and take a turn around the neighbourhood. For the moment, at least, the dog had calmed and was sitting beside Edna, her tail thumping the snow.

Edna rubbed the fur of the animal's neck. "She worked hard today. Might turn her into a lead dog yet. Things not working out with the new roommate?"

"Nope."

"Well, I hope you find the right one. Pity if you had to move out so soon. That's a nice place you got."

Tammy raised her eyebrows. The little white house had been built in the 1940s, shortly after gold had been discovered in the area and Yellowknife was just a northern Canadian shanty town. Despite a few renovations, it retained what her landlord called its "frontier charm."

"Much better than living in the suburbs, like you were doing," Edna said. "The Old Town's the soul of the city. Sheer magic—the stars in the sky, the frost in the air . . ."

"The junkyard across the street."

Edna's eyes went round with mystification as she followed Tammy's gaze to a house kitty-corner from where they stood. Its lot served as a graveyard for a crumbling dog sled, several decomposing snowmobiles, a partially dismantled bombardier, and huge, rusty gears from a local gold mine. One of the Old Town's few streetlights cast a yellow glow on the outer surfaces of the rubble, plunging the rest into shadow. Edna gave Tammy's sleeve a playful pinch.

"That's an installation piece, you goose. Harold got a grant. He calls it 'Ghosts of Yellowknife Past.'"

Tammy snorted. If this was the soul of the city, then Yellowknife had been consigned to everlasting purgatory. The area had the ambience of a rundown trailer park, a subject on which Tammy was an expert. Over the years, she and her mother had hop-scotched through dozens in British Columbia, staying put only as long as her mother's charm impressed the landlord. When the desire for months of back rent became more pressing than the urge for drinks with an exotic woman—and vague promises of something more—they'd be off again. They usually departed around midnight.

Tammy shifted her weight on her tired feet as she watched a shadow glide back and forth in Harold's junk pile. Edna beamed at her.

"That's old man St. Germaine."

Tammy looked Edna in the eye.

"I don't see anything."

"Most people don't get the full experience of the piece, but you obviously do. Old man St. Germaine died fourteen years ago. A couple of other ones sometimes show up."

"I don't see anything!"

"He's a strong presence—in more ways than one." Edna flapped a hand before her face. "Them that can't see 'em can still smell 'em, I've noticed. Yesterday a lady slapped a mitt over her nose and took off across the street—didn't realize Jordie St. Germaine was leanin' up against his old bombardier. There was no running water down here in the

'40s, you know. Guys like Jordie got pretty ripe before their Saturday bath."

"I-do-not-know-what-you're-talking-about."

"Whatever you say." Edna winked at her. "Want to go for a dog sled ride tomorrow? Rosie'd love to have you along."

There were few things Tammy liked less than roommates, but dogs were on the list, along with cats and small children.

"I work tomorrow," Tammy said.

"What time?"

"Four o'clock."

"Fine—we can go for a couple of hours in the morning."

Tammy sighed. Taking a lesson from her encounter with Rosie, she decided to stop struggling.

"Sure. Thanks. Well, time for Janice to face the music—or the lack thereof."

Tammy dumped her coat and boots in the mud room tacked onto the side of the house, and made her way through the kitchen into the living room. Janice was sprawled in an overstuffed chair in the far corner, leafing through a fashion magazine. The glare of a reading lamp bounced off her long blonde hair, making Tammy squint. The rest of the room was lit by a dying fire in the wood stove and scattered candles, which cast a glow on the cheap wood panelling, installed circa 1970, and the dingy carpet.

"What happened to the stereo?"

"Hmm?"

"I was standing in the yard. What happened?"

"I turned it off. I know you don't like my music."

Tammy twisted a knob on the amplifier. Nothing. She clicked another one back and forth. Still nothing. Janice shrugged.

"It's old and rickety. Buy a new one."

"I can't afford a new one."

Janice sneered. "I'll tell Daddy to give you a raise."

Janice's father owned the restaurant where Tammy worked. Carl had also been her landlord for the past three months, ever since she'd moved into his newly purchased rental property. Just as Tammy was disposing of her previous roommate a few weeks earlier, Janice had returned from college. When Carl had suggested that his daughter move in, Tammy had given little thought to why Janice had left school in the middle of the semester, or why her parents didn't take her back.

As Tammy considered how to handle Janice, her eyes fell on a Ouija board set out on the coffee table. It was hers, sure enough—the corner was broken from the time she and Debbie Lambert had tried to summon Jack the Ripper when they were thirteen years old. Tammy had paid the little boy next door to let loose with a maniacal laugh at the crucial moment. Not only did Debbie hit the ceiling and break the board, she never again spoke to Tammy.

"What did you expect?" Zelda's disembodied voice whispered. Tammy shook her head.

"Last I saw, this was in the storage closet at the back of the house," she said to Janice. "The one I told you was out of bounds."

"I had a friend over. We were trying to get in touch with the spirits of the house." Janice sneezed. "This is a heritage building, as you know."

A rhythmic picking sound erupted on the other side of the living room, in a dark corner near the wood stove. Both women stared. As Tammy approached the spot, the sound stopped.

"Probably just the wood stove cooling down," she

said doubtfully. It sometimes popped and pinged as it cooled, but never in such a vigorous way.

Janice reopened her magazine and sneezed again.

"Catching a cold?" Tammy tried to keep the satisfaction out of her voice.

"Probably. It's draughty in this place, even with an oil furnace and a wood stove." Janice pulled her sweater around her. "Or maybe it's those fancy foot-soaking salts you have. I had to pull the plug after two minutes, they made me wheeze so badly."

"You didn't get into that?"

"You don't use it."

"It's expensive. I use it as a treat—usually after a twelve-hour shift. Ever worked one of those?"

Janice rolled her eyes. "You shouldn't have stuff like that in the house. You know I'm allergic."

Tammy retreated to her room, put on her flannel nightie, climbed into bed, and pulled the covers over her head.

The decision to flee north a year earlier had liberated Tammy from her feckless mother, but low wages shackled her to a series of roommates just like Zelda. Some were drunks, others rowdies; none had any respect for her privacy or her property. They borrowed and broke her belongings, and raided the groceries without paying their share. Janice was the worst, a virtual clone of Zelda, whose long career as a sponger had seen her kicked out of who-knows-how-many communes in the '60s for being a little too communal, freely helping herself to the group's homemade wine, other people's cigarettes, other women's boyfriends. Between the roommates and the never-ending dialogue in her head, it seemed her mother had found a way to haunt her while she was still alive. Figured.

When Tammy had hinted to Carl that his daughter might be more comfortable elsewhere, he'd replied that Janice's presence in the house was now a condition of the lease. Further, the opportunity to rent the house was a perk of the job and it would be sad to see Tammy lose both through lack of care and attention to public health issues.

"The tables in your section are filthy—wipe them again," he'd said. Tammy had sullenly rinsed a cloth and gone to polish the spotless tables.

Tammy eventually fell asleep, waking only once to hear Janice banging around in the kitchen.

She found Janice seated at the kitchen table the next morning, eating breakfast in the midst of mass destruction. Tammy's brand-new pottery canisters had been knocked off the kitchen counter—tea, coffee, sugar, and flour were strewn across the scarred pine floor. The tea canister was broken. Tammy picked up the pieces and tried to fit them together.

"Daddy's right—you do have the temper to go with that red hair," Janice said. "I didn't know you felt so strongly about bath products."

"You're saying I did this?" Tammy asked.

"I certainly didn't."

"Someone did."

"Then we have a poltergeist." Janice sneezed sharply.

I'll say we do. And she's sitting at the kitchen table eating the last of the strawberry jam.

"I'm going shopping." Janice stood, brushed toast crumbs from her lap onto the kitchen floor, and put on her coat.

"That's my scarf!" Tammy said, but Janice had already slammed out of the house.

Tammy rummaged in the mud room until she found the dustpan. One moment she was stomping back into the kitchen, the next she was flying through the air. She landed on all fours smack in the middle of the mess. The air had been knocked out of her; she took a moment to assess herself. Her knees hurt. Arrows of pain shot from her wrists into her shoulders. She'd be sore for a couple of days, but there was no serious damage. As she waited for the hurt to subside, a single tear dropped into a pile of flour. Tammy pushed herself onto a clean bit of floor. She sat with her fingers pressed over her eyelids.

The cost of replacing the stuff her roommates lost, "borrowed," or broke had always kept Tammy's skimpy finances teetering on the edge, but Janice had put her over—she'd had to ask Carl for an advance on her salary. There seemed no way to get ahead. That meant only one thing.

"Your feet *will* find their way home soon," Zelda murmured.

The sting of tears finally stopped. Tammy opened her eyes and looked toward the door to see what had brought her down, but it seemed she'd tripped on thin air.

After cleaning up the mess, Tammy poured a bowl of cereal and made her way to the breakfast nook, a recent addition to the back of the house. She stared out the picture window, noticing neither the squad of ptarmigan nibbling at the willows in her back yard, nor the expanse of Back Bay that opened a few yards beyond them. All she could see was a vision of her mother, "The Amazing Zelda," in full fortune teller regalia—tiered skirt, head scarf, and fringed shawl—flouncing through the downtown of any one of the places they had passed through.

"Marketing, dahlink," she'd purr in a fake Russian accent whenever Tammy complained she was making herself unduly conspicuous. And Zelda, whose real name was Nancy, was right. Those who shunned them by day would flock to their trailer at night to have their tarot cards read or to contact long-lost loved ones at a seance. Sometimes her mother made the effort to do the job properly, but usually she just strung together a bunch of plausible lies. In her mind's eye, Tammy trailed a few yards behind Zelda, whose wavy auburn hair rippled in the wind. Her mother turned and beckoned, her smile smug.

Tammy's eyes came into focus and she realized that Edna had already set her sled on the snow of Back Bay, and was bringing the dogs from the front of the house, one by one, and hitching them in two rows. As Tammy prepared to join them, she could hear them yip and bark.

Tammy arrived just as Edna was fastening Rosie in one of the lead positions. Rosie's tail started wagging when she saw Tammy, but as she came closer, the bark of welcome became a snap and a snarl. Tammy froze.

"Settle down!" Edna grabbed Rosie's collar and shook her. Rosie bared her teeth at Tammy and emitted a long, low growl. Tammy's knees turned to water. Edna yanked the dog toward her house and tied her to the back fence. Tammy sank into the snow.

"What the hell was that?" she asked when Edna returned.

"Don't know. Only time I seen her go off like that is when that cat from your place used to come around. Before your time. Belonged to my friend Minnie. Used to parade up and down on the fence. Most of the team ignored it, but it got right up Rosie's nose. You ain't been around a cat, have you?"

Tammy twisted around, scanning the snow for feline interlopers.

"Not that I've seen."

"Horrible creature. Spent most of the time asleep in the back closet. Best place for it. When it came out, it was pure malice," Edna said. "I'd be having tea with Minnie, and the damned thing would be shredding the living room carpet or strolling across the kitchen table. Saw it push a tea cup off the counter once. Disappeared a couple of years ago. Good riddance."

Tammy's knees had stopped shaking, so she struggled to her feet. The two women gazed down Back Bay as they waited for Rosie to regain her composure. Snow-covered hills of rock, bristling with jack pine, sloped to the shore on the left-hand side. On the right stood the edge of the city, a combination of shacks dating from Yellowknife's early days and huge new houses built by the North's *nouveaux riches*.

"That's what I like about Yellowknife. Rich and poor got the same view," Edna said. "Bay's quiet right now, but you wait 'til summer—sailboats drifting, kayakers paddling, float planes coming and going. Sheer magic."

"Sure better than the view from the front of my house."

Edna shrugged.

"Good, bad. It's a matter of perspective."

Edna went to check on Rosie, but the dog still could not abide being close to Tammy.

"Don't know what's up, but I have to work her today," Edna said. "Mind taking a rain check?"

"Of course not." Tammy was surprised at how disappointed she actually was.

Not yet ready to return indoors, Tammy wandered around the neighbourhood. Passing Harold's installation piece, she almost gagged on the stench of body odour and axle grease. Old man St. Germaine, taking a break from his perpetual scavenging, sat on the cracked vinyl seat of a snowmobile. He tipped his filth-encrusted ball cap at Tammy, who snapped her head in the opposite direction and marched past. A pang made her turn back to the ghost, who was still watching her. She realized that Harold's artwork had an interesting symmetry when viewed from this angle. Tammy smiled. The old man nodded in reply. Tammy went into her house.

She made a cup of tea, took it into the living room, and sat on the couch. The Ouija board still lay on the coffee table; Tammy leaned forward and traced the jagged edge with a forefinger. Debbie Lambert had been one of Tammy's few friends during the lonely trailer park years—until she'd asked for the seance, that is. Tammy had always refused to participate in the family business, preferring respectable work like raking leaves for neighbours, or waitressing when she was old enough. She'd been furious to discover that her so-called friend was just another creep attracted by Zelda's seedy mystique. A lousy judge of character, Tammy would have used her psychic gifts to screen prospective friends or roommates. This was the one area, sadly, where they failed her—she often wondered if her mother was somehow blocking her intuition. What she needed was a fool-proof way of testing people.

"There's only one way for the likes of us, my Tamsin," Zelda whispered in her ear.

It's "Tammy." Please.

"Don't be so conventional. Come home."

No.

"Join the family firm."

So you can sit on your butt?

"Easy money, my Tamsin. If you can't beat 'em, might as well join 'em."

Tammy sank into the cushions and closed her eyes. Her head ached. Her feet hurt. And it *was* easy money.

"Stop struggling," Zelda whispered. "Join the club."

A cackle rippled through Tammy's brain. It was the same one her mother used on her clients when she was about to utter a fabulous, but false, prediction; it was the sound of her mother's delight at swindling yet another sucker. She saw Zelda leaning over the crystal ball she used for show, her black lace shawl hanging from outstretched arms like an eagle swooping down on its prey.

Tammy's eyes popped open.

The picking noise from the previous night resumed by the wood stove. The carpet was lifting as something pulled at it.

"Hey!" Tammy shouted.

A shadow fled along the wall toward the back of the house.

Tammy went to the door of the kitchen.

"Here kitty, kitty." Something invisible brushed against her leg. There was a pause and then she felt it again. "Nice kitty, kitty."

Tammy smiled.

"Sure, mom," she said. "I'll join the club."

Tammy returned home from work that evening to find Janice propped on the living room couch, sneezing like a pop-gun stuck on fast-forward.

"Caught a cold after all?"

"I tink id's judst a twendy-four-hour ding," Janice snuffled.

"That's the spirit," Tammy replied.

Janice sneezed again. As the explosion subsided, the rhythmic scratching sound echoed through the room.

"Hey!" Tammy shouted.

"Wha?" Janice looked around, bewildered.

"Pardon?"

"Whad was dat noid?"

"I didn't hear any noid. Your ears must be acting up. Try to get some rest."

"Den why did you—"

Tammy exited, leaving Janice on the couch, a box of tissues and a wastepaper basket beside her. She fell asleep to a soothing symphony of sneezes streaming from the living room.

Janice was no better twenty-four hours later.

"Your wastepaper basket runneth over." Tammy kicked damp and crumpled tissues out of the way as she examined the patient's progress.

"If I didn't know bedder, I'd say by allergies were ack-ding ub." Janice pulled another tissue from the almost-empty box and dabbed a runny eye before blowing her nose. "Mudst be someding in de houze. You're nod hiding a cad, aw you?"

"A cad? Some of the neighbours are a little dysfunctional, but I wouldn't call any of them a cad."

Janice meowed huskily.

"Oh, a cat! Good heavens! Do you see a cat?"

Janice shook her head as she groped for a new tissue.

"You know as well as I do that there are no cats living in this house."

Janice's doctor confirmed that she was suffering from an allergic reaction. Tammy gave her foot-soaking salts to Edna, but it made no difference. Janice and her father searched the house, but could not find the problem.

Tammy waved from the front window as they drove off in Carl's half-ton, Janice's belongings piled in the back. Once they disappeared, Tammy went out to her car and pulled a small bag of catnip from the glove compartment. She took it into the house.

"Here kitty, kitty," she called, sprinkling some on the living room floor. Something brushed against her leg.

"Come on," she coaxed, using the catnip to lure the little ghost to the back storage closet. She tossed in the bag of catnip and slammed the door. Then she opened the windows as much as the winter air would allow, vacuumed thoroughly, and washed her clothes. She called Edna to collect on her rain check.

The following weekend, Tammy waited until Edna had the team hitched to the sled before she approached. The dogs were so intent on the excitement of a run that they didn't see her coming. Tammy was almost within lunging distance before Rosie noticed her. The dog wagged her tail.

"You're back in her good books. Hop in," Edna said.

As Edna carried out final preparations, Tammy settled into the bottom of the sled, stretching her legs and wiggling her toes.

Now that the little ghost was back in the closet, Tammy was betting that it would stay there until someone disturbed it. If it didn't, a quick incantation would probably do the trick. Considering the speed and severity of Janice's allergic reaction, Tammy was willing to bet others would be happy to put down a decent deposit for the privilege of staying in a clean environment. Tammy would, of course, warn new roommates not to open the door. Anyone who was well-behaved would be just fine. Anyone who wasn't would leave quickly enough, forfeiting their deposit and padding Tammy's bank account.

"Marketing, dahlink," she told her mother. The fact that Zelda had been keeping a sulky silence for the past few days told her she was on the right track.

Tammy started writing the newspaper ad in her head: "Attention, allergy sufferers! Seeking a roommate? Smoke-free, cat-free environment . . ."

Edna climbed onto the back of the sled. "Hike!" she

called to the team, and they slipped from shore onto the snow-covered ice of Back Bay.

As Tammy felt her muscles relax, she realized that Edna was right—this place was sheer magic.

Sand Trap

The wind whistled past Todd's ears; grit flew into his eyes and crunched between his teeth. But he did not shrink from the assault of sand and air—he welcomed its bite. He defied the fate that had brought him to this godforsaken place, this patch of desolation in the garden of life, this lonely desert of broken dreams, this—

"Buddy. Hey, buddy. You okay?"

Todd stopped flailing his pitching wedge through the sand trap on the second hole of the Yellowknife golf course and blinked toward the voice. His surroundings wavered into focus—his bag full of custom-made clubs, reclining on its pull-cart, and the black-haired man who stood beside them, his eyes shaded by the visor of a red ball cap.

"What?" Todd said.

"Just wondering if you're okay. You were kicking up a lot of sand."

"That's because I'm in a sand trap. A sand trap! What kind of twisted mind puts a sand trap in this bloody wasteland?" Todd gestured down the fairway. There, where one could reasonably expect a manicured carpet of green, lay choppy stretches of sand, interspersed with stands of scraggy jack pine.

"You forgot your grass." The man held out a rubber mat, about the size of a book, with green plastic turf sprouting from one side.

"Thanks." Todd scanned the man's black T-shirt, jeans, and grubby runners as he accepted the mat, his hand reflexively straightening the collar of his own immaculate white golf shirt. The man's lack of style betrayed him as local; his coffee-and-cream complexion revealed him to be First Nations. Turning, Todd noticed a lumpy golf bag lying halfway down the fairway. "I didn't see you coming."

"Guess not. My name is Alphonse. Want to join me?"

Todd couldn't help staring at the man's attire. He tried not to flinch. "No thanks. I'm new on the course—I'd slow you down."

"Doesn't matter. Not much traffic on a Tuesday morning. And there's no other place I need to be."

Todd thought about his closet-sized law office in one of Yellowknife's more decrepit downtown buildings. There was no other place he needed to be, either, but that was beside the point. "Really—I wouldn't think of it. I'll putt out, then you can play through."

"You want to know how to handle the sand? You'll have to modify your swing."

"No thanks. I've been taught by the best."

"Oh." Alphonse's gaze strayed toward the crater Todd had dug in the sand trap.

Todd adjusted his collar again, flashing the logo over the breast pocket. "Windermere Country Club in Calgary," he said. "Excellent golf pro."

Alphonse stared at the smudge Todd's fingers had left on his collar, then shrugged and headed off. While Alphonse's back was turned, Todd tossed the ball onto the patch of plastic grass that constituted the green. By the time Alphonse reached his bag, Todd had sunk the ball and repaired the hole in the sand trap.

Todd plunked himself onto a bench to wait. It was a warm day for mid-June in the Northwest Territories. Puffy clouds floated through a blue sky, and a breeze kept the mosquitoes and blackflies at bay. Bits of conversation floated toward him from a neighbouring fairway. Taking out his golf towel, Todd polished the ball he had been using, taking care to ensure no grit marred the imprint of a windswept tree perched on an ocean cliff—the logo of California's renowned Pebble Beach Golf Course. This, Todd assured himself, was his true destiny—enjoying quality golf and upward mobility by schmoozing with the upper echelons of the law firm of White, Pratt and Underhill on the world's finest golf links. His current exile to this grotesque parody was no more than a temporary setback. After all, it was the firm's chairman, J.P. White, who'd given him the Pebble Beach ball.

As the tension flowed out of Todd's body, a shadow flickered across his chest. Squinting upwards, he spotted a scruffy raven landing in a nearby tree. The bird gave him the once-over. Todd scowled; the raven responded with a series of screeches that made his flesh crawl and every one of his newly relaxed muscles clamp tight. Alphonse wandered past, his bag of clubs clattering on his shoulder. He gave a quick salute. Todd nodded in reply.

Todd waited until Alphonse was safely out of sight before starting the next hole. He'd learned that the first shot on this moonscape of a course was not the issue—you stuck a tee in the plastic grass of the tee box and swung, as usual. The real problem came after. Todd's ball sailed into the air, landing on the fairway in a puff of dust. Trudging to the spot, he placed it on the plastic grass of the little mat Alphonse had retrieved for him.

Todd visualized his swing, which was not just technically perfect—years of practice in his parents' back yard, with one eye on his reflection in the patio doors, had lent it a grace that turned heads every time. J.P. had been particularly impressed.

"Appearances pay off, my boy, especially in our business. Never let 'em see you sweat."

Now shifting his weight in the sand of the Yellowknife golf course, Todd pulled his damp shirt away from his chest. He swung to the place instinct told him the ball should lie. His club slammed into the back edge of the rubber mat. Shock waves quivered up the shaft, into his wrists and shoulders. Todd shook off the pain and replaced the ball. He'd need a little less club, obviously. He swung again, topping the ball, which dribbled onto the sand. Todd stifled a scream. He was about to try again when a chill shot down his spine and the back of his neck felt creepy-crawly, as though invisible fingers were running over the flesh with a feathery touch. Turning, he found two sets of black eyes watching through the trees from an adjacent fairway—an almond-shaped pair belonging to Alphonse, and a beady set belonging to the bedraggled raven, who sat on a branch close by.

Todd straightened his shoulders and concentrated on the Pebble Beach logo staring up at him. He imagined playing that glorious course: lush fairways, stunning sea views, immaculate greens devoid of plastic grass. The sweet spot of the club was heading directly for its target when a metallic trill broke the silence. The ball flew into a stand of trees. Todd grabbed his cell phone.

"What?"

A guffaw greeted him. "Practising your bunker shot? Did you rent an electric cart, or a camel?" The guffaws degenerated into string of snorts.

"As a matter of fact, I am hard at work." Todd slid his

club into his bag and headed toward the trees. "Setting up the firm's new northern office is a huge responsibility."

"Sure. I can hear the tell-tale clank of all those papers you're shuffling."

Todd stopped moving; his clubs stopped rattling.

"Don't let me interfere," Bradley said. "Gotta amuse yourself somehow, since you won't be going to Pebble Beach this year."

"Don't spend too much time polishing your golf shoes, Bradley. I'm not out of the running yet." Todd glanced down to find the white leather of his own shoes coated with fine dirt. He swiped at one of them. The shoe was no cleaner, but now his hand was dirty.

"Cling to that delusion if it gets you through the day. J.P. and I were on the course yesterday. He gave me some pointers on my back swing. Really helped."

"There's nothing wrong with your back swing," Todd said.

"I mean it really helped my career prospects."

"As if."

"Speaking of career prospects, have you entered the Tournament of the Midnight Sun?" Bradley asked.

"Stay up until midnight on the summer solstice to play eighteen holes in a sand pit in the semi-dark? Why?"

"To make it back to civilization. Rumour has it you have to either win the tournament or make a strategic corporate alliance."

"Like you'd have half a clue," Todd said.

Truth be told, Bradley had two-thirds of a clue. J.P., his face red with repressed fury, had given Todd another alternative: he could return to Calgary if he hit a hole-in-one on the Yellowknife course. Given the unkempt look of the denizens of Yellowknife, there was not one power broker among them, so a strategic corporate alliance was out of the question. Todd would have to take his chances on the golf course.

"Look—I've gotta run," Todd said. It was only after he'd cut off Bradley in mid-laugh that he noticed the ragged raven sitting on a nearby tree stump. It burbled at him, then flew off.

Todd found the Pebble Beach ball quickly, but then again, he always did; it had never strayed far since J.P. had given it to him a few weeks earlier. Aware of the importance of networking on the golf links—and certain that an invitation from anyone high up in the firm would not be forthcoming—Todd, Bradley, and two other new staff had contrived to get the tee time at Windermere right before J.P. and three of the partners.

Networking was Todd's only hope for success—he'd barely started his law career, but it was already swirling down the toilet. An expensive suit and smart haircut had got him through the door, but his inability to grasp the shifting details of oil and gas acquisitions and divestitures, joint venture and partnership structures, and co-generation facilities agreements would soon put him back out on the street.

That morning on the Windermere course, however, hope had lurched through Todd's veins when he saw J.P.'s white coiffure towering above his golf partners. The two groups waved in acknowledgement, then Todd had teed off.

"See that swing?" J.P. had said. "That's the quality of staff our firm attracts."

Todd's heart had swelled with anticipation.

"Quality?" one of the partners said. "He's botched the Badlands Oil and Gas file."

Todd's heart had deflated in despair.

"Those Badlands guys wouldn't know quality law work if they tripped over it," J.P. had said. "Todd just needs someone to take him under their wing. Anyone can learn the details of our trade, but personal style can't be taught. Our clients expect a lawyer who looks the part—dresses with style, speaks with confidence, swings a golf club with class."

"I remember another protégé who swung a golf club with class."

"Don't be ridiculous. Todd's a team player," J.P. had said.

"He'll need to be," someone added as the younger men moved off.

J.P.'s nods of approval had lasted until Todd landed in a sand trap on the sixteenth hole. Within two minutes, he'd gone from having the best score of the foursome to the worst. He'd been banging his club into the sand when a scowling J.P. cruised up on his electric cart.

"You're slowing everyone down, my boy. What's worse, you're making a spectacle of yourself."

"Sorry." Todd had run his hand across his damp forehead, leaving his bangs oddly spiked. "Once I get into a bunker, I can't get out."

"So I see."

"Sand and I have never gotten along. Can't keep my balance."

J.P. had stared at Todd's red face and erratic hairdo. Todd had held his breath. J.P. continued his appraisal, noting Todd's tasteful clothing, his athletic build, his expensive clubs. Then he'd smiled, hoisted himself from his golf cart and appropriated Todd's sand wedge. With an easy, one-handed swing, he'd put the ball within inches of the hole.

"Try again with this." He'd tossed Todd a ball imprinted with a windswept tree. "You might find it lucky."

"Pebble Beach," Todd murmured.

"Every year the partners hold a little competition

there. We always take the most promising new recruit. Come to think of it, all the partners were taken to Pebble Beach in their early years," J.P. had said with a wink.

Todd had started breathing again.

Indeed, the ball went farther and straighter than any other. It sailed over water traps. On the rare occasions it went into the rough, it never strayed far. It even got him out of sand traps in short order. Todd realized the ball was not just lucky—it was the symbol of his future. Until the day of the staff tournament, that is. That's when the magic disappeared.

Emerging from the bush on the Yellowknife course, Todd ensured the coast was clear before continuing to hack away, arms aching and legs weary. He arrived at a mercifully short hole. Todd popped the Pebble Beach ball onto a tee and swung.

It was a beautiful shot. The ball arced up against the cerulean sky, over the accursed patch of sand, and landed with a thud on the green. It rolled slowly, deliberately, toward the hole. Todd punched his fist into the air in a victory salute. His first time on the course, and he was already headed for a hole-in-one. Even if he didn't have the requisite witnesses, surely this was a sign that superior golf skills and a lucky ball would soon deliver him from his current hell. The ball was within inches of its goal when the mangy raven swooped down, lifted it in its beak, and flew away. Todd shrieked.

"No penalty assessed when ball carried off by raven."

Todd whipped around. Alphonse was sitting on a bench in the shade, drinking a can of pop.

"What?"

"'No penalty assessed when ball carried off by raven.' The sign by the clubhouse says so." Alphonse drained the can, and placed it in a plastic bin by the bench.

"I thought that was a joke."

"Nope. Play another."

"There's no point," Todd shouted. "That damned bird stole my lucky ball."

"Luck never made a man wise."

"What's that? Ancient tribal wisdom?"

"No—Seneca," Alphonse said. "Roman statesman and philosopher."

"Oh."

"Let me guess—a windswept tree on an ocean cliff."

The creepy-crawly feeling returned to the back of his neck. "How—?"

"A little bird told me."

Todd glanced toward the green. Beyond the fluttering flag, a black shape lurked high in a jack pine, Todd's golf ball wedged in its beak.

"Her name's Gert," Alphonse said.

"You named her?"

"We're old friends, Gertie and me. She used to steal my golf balls all the time."

A string of yodels reverberated across the course.

"That'll be Edna. Come on." Alphonse grabbed his bag and headed off.

"But—" Todd gazed down the fairway he was supposed to play. Gert rose from her perch and flapped toward Alphonse, the stolen golf ball gleaming in the sun. Todd tore after her.

The yodels were coming from a square little woman halfway up a nearby fairway. Clothed in a well-worn black golf shirt and ragged black shorts, she was sitting on the back of an electric cart, swinging her feet.

"Alphonse Bean—my hero," she cooed as the two men approached.

"Stuck again?" Alphonse asked redundantly as he inspected the rear tires, bogged in deep sand. Edna hopped down and stood clear. Alphonse took the front, one hand on a pole that supported the canopy, the other on the accelerator pedal. Todd took the back end, lifting as Alphonse pushed the accelerator. The cart moved. It hit firmer ground and sprang forward, spraying Todd with sand. He gasped as he brushed grime from the logo of the Windermere Country Club.

"Perhaps you should ease up on the off-road driving," he snapped.

Edna smiled, dark eyes crinkling under blunt-cut grey bangs. "I know I should leave the cart on the path and walk out to my ball, but the sand pulls at my old feet something fierce. Besides, there's always a handsome young man around who needs some extra exercise. Why don't you two gentlemen join me? That way you won't have to come running if I get stuck again."

"Thanks, but as I've already explained to Alphonse here, I'm new—"

"That's okay—I'm not embarrassed to be seen with you."

Todd's assessment of Edna's tattered clothing started with her shapeless shirt and shorts, ran past dimpled knees and dirty white knee-socks to her feet, which were encased in grimy golf shoes. He looked up to find Edna carrying out a similar review of his clothing. There was pity in her eyes. Todd looked down. His light-coloured ensemble was filthy. He cringed.

"If you've caught Gert's eye, you shouldn't golf alone," Alphonse said. "She's persistent when she takes a shine to someone."

"A shine? She stole my lucky ball."

"She's trying to get your attention." Edna fondled the corner of Todd's collar. "Every now and then she likes to take a young man under her wing."

Todd reclaimed his shirt from Edna's chubby fingers. "She seems to have disappeared, anyway."

"She's never far away," she said.

The trio stood in silence as Todd scanned the trees. He couldn't locate the bird, but a chill crept down his back again.

"Okay—I'm with you," he said.

Edna chose a club, grabbed her mat, and headed out to her ball. Raising her shoulders in an exaggerated shrug, she twitched her rump twice, then swung with a slow, scooping motion, like she was ladling soup out of a giant cauldron.

Todd clapped a hand to his forehead. "She golfs like a little old lady."

"She *is* a little old lady," Alphonse said.

Edna's club connected with a satisfyingly hollow "whack," landing the ball not far from the green.

"Ha! Gonna birdie this one. See you at the next tee." Edna hopped into her cart and hit the gas.

Misery enveloped Todd as they hop-scotched down the course, Alphonse and Edna making respectably long shots, then waiting for Todd to catch up. Edna's unique style made Todd cringe, but Alphonse's grace rivalled his own former elegance. Todd hooked and sliced, balls flying to the left and right. Most of them disappeared into the bush, never to be seen again.

The little group made a sad contrast to the image of J.P. and Bradley on the verdant fairways of Windermere. Todd had no doubt that Bradley had also usurped his place in the leather visitor's chair in J.P.'s office. It was the invitations into the inner sanctum for pep talks about the law and discourses on golf that finally quelled the hallway whispers about Todd's professional prowess. During his first visit, Todd had noticed a large trophy in a display case.

"A little token from our staff tournament," J.P. had said. "It's coming up again."

Todd examined the bright brass tags bolted to the wooden base. "You've won every year."

"Since I became chairman." J.P. swivelled his chair toward Todd and leaned back, smile on his face, hands clasped across his belly. "As elder statesman, I have to set an example, be a leader. Good for the team, you know."

"Hold it. Who's Al Le . . . something?" Todd squinted at a tarnished tag toward the back.

J.P.'s smile vanished as he twisted away. "Someone who used to work here. Gone on to greater glory." The chairman selected a piece of paper from his desktop and proceeded to peruse it.

"What kind of glory?" Todd asked.

J.P. examined the paper in deliberate silence. After several moments, Todd retreated.

The staff tournament certainly hadn't led Todd to greater glory, he thought as he plodded through the sand beside Alphonse. It should have sealed his invitation to Pebble Beach—instead, it secured his exile to Yellowknife. Delighted to be part of J.P.'s elite foursome, Todd did well right from the start. J.P., however, seemed ill—early in the game his complexion took on a greyish hue; by the halfway mark, he was mopping his forehead with a handkerchief. As J.P.'s game slipped, Todd's soared.

Then he got stuck in a sand trap on the last hole. He'd tried to plant his feet firmly, but somewhere between his back swing and his follow-through his stance would shift just enough to send his club into the sand. As cloud after cloud of grit filled the air, people congregated around the edge of the bunker to watch. Bradley was giggling non-stop, and even J.P. seemed amused: he was smiling for the first time since the round had started. Molten rage shot through Todd's body. Finally connecting with the ball, he sent it onto the green, his club flying after it, connecting with Bradley's knee with a satisfying "whump." Todd's score was still good enough to win the tournament, but J.P. had been furious. Todd insisted that sweaty palms, and not bad temper, had been the reason for the runaway golf club, but J.P. was not assuaged.

"Absolute lack of self-control," the chairman had shouted. "Team player? You think of no one but yourself."

And now Todd was golfing on a course moulded out of the Yellowknife sand pits. He took a half-hearted swing and duffed another ball into the underbrush.

"Getting worn down?" Alphonse asked as Edna pulled up.

"Guilty as charged, Your Honour," Todd replied.

Alphonse raised his eyebrows.

"I'm a lawyer," Todd said.

"Oh. I know lots of lawyers."

Suspicion rose in Todd's mind. A knowledge of lawyers and a lot of leisure time on weekday mornings usually meant one thing. "What do you do for a living?"

"I'm between jobs right now. Mostly I try to stay on the right side of the law."

"I'll bet." Todd handed Alphonse a business card. "I don't usually do criminal work, but I'd make an exception for a fellow golfer."

Alphonse tucked the card into his back pocket without looking at it. "To make a living, craftiness is better than learnedness."

"Another lesson from Seneca?"

"No—*The Marriage of Figaro*. Not familiar with French drama?"

Todd grimaced.

"If you're going to make it back to Calgary, you'll have to get crafty with that swing of yours. Hole-in-one or win the Tournament of the Midnight Sun, right?" Alphonse said.

Todd shuddered. "You're creeping me out, pal. You psychic, or something?"

Alphonse smiled.

"Little bird?" Todd searched the treetops for Gert, who was still absent.

Edna leaned into the conversation. "Little bird says that if you loosen up and fix your swing, you'll achieve your destiny."

"Actually, I was about to leave. Just lost my last ball."

A flick of Edna's wrist, and a zipper on her golf bag opened. Balls spilled out like silver dollars from a slot machine. "Take as many as you want. I get them for free from a friend who collects strays."

"Thanks, but there's nothing wrong with my stroke," Todd said. "I've been known to win tournaments."

"Like the White, Pratt and Underhill staff tournament?" Alphonse asked.

A full blown case of chills gripped Todd. "I sense that I'm fighting the inevitable. Okay—teach me what you know."

"Not me," Alphonse said. "Edna."

"Edna?"

Edna pinched Alphonse's cheek. "He was such a fast learner. And I have high hopes for you, too. I can help you compensate for the shifting sand."

Checking to make sure no one was watching, Todd followed Edna through several shoulder-shrugging, hip-twitching, club-scooping gyrations. Alphonse joined in for moral support. Todd felt trapped in the line dance from hell.

"Try it for real," Edna said. "Hole's around that clump of trees."

Todd executed Edna's choreography—and sent the ball sailing around the trees. Moments later, they heard a "ping." Edna jumped into her cart and beetled away.

"A hole-in-one! A hole-in-one!"

Todd dropped to his knees and kissed the fairway. "And I have witnesses this time! It's official!"

He scrambled to his feet and ran toward the green, spitting out grit as he went. He'd survived the humiliation of banishment, the desecration of his beautiful golf swing, the ruin of his favourite golf shirt. J.P. may have expected him to dig himself a hole so deep he'd never escape, but he'd already proven himself worthy of White, Pratt and Underhill.

Todd streaked past Edna, who was standing in the middle of the fairway staring into a gleaming white toilet. He charged up to the flag and looked into the hole. It was empty. He searched the green. Alphonse whistled and Todd turned to find him scooping a ball out of the toilet. Todd's shoulders slumped. He retraced his steps.

"It's yours," Alphonse said.

"I said you'd achieve your destiny," Edna said. "It's a sign."

"Oh, it's definitely a sign." Todd accepted the ball between his thumb and forefinger, held it at arm's length, and winced.

"The toilet's usually for tournaments," Edna said. "They put it in a different spot each time, and them that hits closest wins a prize. I never seen anyone hit a hole-in-one before."

"There's no tournament today."

"But the Tournament of the Midnight Sun is on Saturday," Edna said. "It's booked solid. Alphonse and I have a couple of spots on our team. There's lots who want to play, so to be fair, we asked the pro to put out the toilet, and whoever shot closest could join us. Congratulations!"

"Oh, no—"

"Look how well you're doing with the new stroke. You're going home!"

The air stirred. Todd looked up to see Gert flying overhead, a golf ball clutched in her beak. Somehow, he knew it was his Pebble Beach ball, receding ever farther. He sank to his knees and rested his forehead against the toilet's tank. "I am never going home," he said.

"Well, if you can't beat us, might as well join us." Edna beamed at him.

*****

Shortly before midnight on June 21, Todd found himself among the throng inside the white frame clubhouse at the Yellowknife golf course. Unwilling to sacrifice another of his expensive golf shirts to the grime of the sand fairways, he had followed the lead of the locals and dressed in the oldest, darkest clothes in his closet. He camouflaged his face with a low-hanging ball cap. He handed a form to a man behind the registration desk.

"Your team starts at the thirteenth hole," the man said.

"Figures."

"When you hear the gunshot, start swinging."

Todd turned away, only to come face to face with a familiar, white-haired figure.

"J.P.!"

"Todd."

"What—?"

"I'm here to see how you're doing. I've heard stories, and I have the reputation of the firm to consider."

"Stories?" Todd scanned the room from beneath the protection of his ball cap. "Who are you golfing with?"

"You, of course. And a former protégé."

A sudden vision of the toilet in the fairway—the very reason he was here tonight—flashed before Todd's eyes. Edna had said it was a sign, and Todd could already hear the sucking sound of his career going down the drain. Success in this overgrown sandbox meant the sacrifice of his celebrated swing. Even if he did win the tournament, J.P. would be too horrified by his loss of style to take him back to Calgary. He'd just started his dash for the door when Edna and Alphonse emerged from the crowd. Edna grabbed Todd's arm. J.P. stuck out his hand.

"Long time no see, Al," he said. "Thanks for inviting me up."

"Alphonse!" Todd hissed.

"Al LeFebvre." J.P.'s eyes grew misty. "Years since I've seen that swing."

Todd shook his head. "This is Alphonse Bean."

"We live in a country full of bilingual food labels, and you don't know *fève* is French for 'bean'?" Edna said.

J.P. put his arm around Todd's shoulder. "You should have told me you'd made a strategic corporate alliance with Al LeFebvre. Expert litigator in the energy sector. You should see him handle royalty obligations, fiduciary duties, right of first refusal."

"We're still negotiating," Alphonse said.

J.P. nodded. "Haven't seen you since you disappeared to Toronto."

"You don't live here?" Todd asked.

"I spent some time here when I was a young lawyer. Now I come up for a couple of weeks every June," Alphonse said.

The man behind the registration desk shouted instructions, and the golfers headed for their tees. Edna and J.P. set out in an electric cart, Edna driving. The cart bounced over tree roots in the dirt parking lot, swerving to avoid pedestrians, as Todd and Alphonse followed on foot.

"'Mostly I try to stay on the right side of the law'?" Todd said.

"That's what I call winning in court—'staying on the right side of the law.'"

"'I'm between jobs'?"

Alphonse shrugged. "I've been on hiatus. The law can be pretty intense. A person can take it all too seriously."

"Al LeSomething. I couldn't read your name on the trophy because of the tarnish."

"I don't imagine that particular tag has been kept polished. Nor will yours."

"But I won fair and square. There was only the one lapse of decorum." Todd stopped walking. He slapped a hand to his forehead. "That's what I did wrong? I *won* the staff tournament?"

Alphonse paused beside him. "What did you think?"

"How'd you escape? Hole-in-one? Win the Tournament of the Midnight Sun?"

"Nope. Quit and found another job. Not the easiest thing, given J.P.'s influence in the oil patch."

The two men continued on.

"At least you have talent," Todd said.

Alphonse shrugged.

"You've known about me all along?" Todd asked.

"Yep. Got a call from a buddy in Calgary."

"Oh." Todd peered at Alphonse through the twilight. "That raven doesn't really talk to you, does she?"

Alphonse smiled.

"I don't understand why you're helping me," Todd said.

"If your brother is lost and wandering in the woods, give him your hand and lead him to the light."

"*The Marriage of Figaro*?" Todd asked.

"No. Ancient tribal wisdom. But it doesn't hurt to remember Figaro, either."

The gun sounded as Alphonse and Todd arrived at the thirteenth tee. Halfway down the fairway, J.P. approached Todd.

"Good job with Al. Been trying to figure out how to get him back into the fold. Left in a bit of a snit—not really a team player in the old days. What the hell happened to your swing?"

"I'm learning to compensate for the shifting sand."

J.P. frowned. "Hope the damage isn't permanent."

A thud sounded at Todd's feet. A golf ball lay inches from his toe. He picked it up. It was marked with a windswept tree.

"I think I'll recover my style if I get back to Calgary soon. But my distance is probably gone for good."

The chairman nodded in commiseration, patted Todd on the back, and moved off.

Gert cackled from a nearby tree. Todd pocketed his lucky ball and followed J.P.

The Dog Island Floating Film Festival

When the wailing began in her front yard, Marge put on her headphones. When a wave of answering howls blew across Yellowknife Bay, she turned up the volume. When someone started pounding on her front door, she waited until the thumps reverberated right down into her guts before ripping off the headphones, yanking open the door, and staring into the darkness. Her neighbour Freddy danced in anger at the bottom of the steps, a small figure in greasy coveralls quick-stepping amongst discarded tires and assorted snowmobile parts.

"If your butt-ugly mutt doesn't stick a sock in it, I'll do it for him."

Hubcap, the mutt in question, took exception to either the description of his visage or the general sentiment, and lunged at Freddy's leg. The rope he was tied to left him a couple of inches short of his goal. His keening rose an octave, the pitch soon matched by the dog team a quarter-mile away.

"It's bad enough I have to listen to this racket," Freddy said, "but now Melvin's on the phone telling me to get your damned dog to shut up. Seems your phone is off the hook, Marge."

"I'm watching movies, if you don't mind."

"And so's Melvin. He's screening the out-of-town entries for the film festival and needs to concentrate."

Despite the January cold, Marge lumbered down the front steps of her Quonset hut and around the side of the tube-like building. She peered across the moonlit roofs of the lop-sided shanties of her neighbourhood, part of Yellowknife's Old Town, where they sloped down to Great Slave Lake. In the distance was the little island in Yellowknife Bay where the howls originated. Next to it sat Melvin's wooden frame houseboat, frozen into the ice. The windows glowed with light. Marge tipped back her head and bayed. The dog team staked next to the houseboat answered.

Freddy appeared beside her. "Stop that."

"They're his dogs. Can't he get them to shut up?"

"They're high-strung. They're—"

"Inbred?"

Freddy scowled. "Pedigree. The point is: *your* dog is a troublemaker. And every time Melvin calls, it interrupts my script writing. I need to start story-boarding next week."

"You didn't finish Grade 10. No way you're winning any film festival."

"It's not about winning, as you well know."

There was a lot riding on the Dog Island Floating Film Festival, brainchild of Melvin Popoff, impresario of the Old Town. Its goal was nothing less than the salvation of the city's oldest and most unconventional neighbourhood. The jumble of shacks that spread before Marge dated from the 1930s and 1940s, Yellowknife's early years as a mining camp. Most were built of boards salvaged from packing crates, leftover plywood, and whatever else could be scavenged by the poor and desperate, attracted north by Yellowknife's gold mines. The original owners had long since moved on, but the shacks had been continually occupied by young adventurers, middle-aged flower children, and drifters. Many shacks had decayed beyond repair over the years and had been replaced with modern housing. Although the newer homes were upscale and well maintained, their residents harboured a nostalgic feeling for their down-at-heel neighbours, fading symbols of Yellowknife's frontier past.

Not everyone shared the sentiment, however: there was a move afoot to speed the gentrification of the neighbourhood. Many of the shacks squatted on public property, which also happened to be prime real estate. Rumour had it that an unnamed developer was pressuring City Hall to evict the residents, tear down the buildings, and put the land up for sale. The developer, it was said, had pointed out to the City that it could be liable if the shacks caught fire and someone was hurt. It was only public support for the area's heritage value that had slowed the plan.

Melvin's solution of a floating film festival appealed to the community's Bohemian sensibility. It would be held in the fall, once the northern nights brought darkness again. A projector would be set up on Dog Island, a piece of rock on which Melvin kept his dog team, and the films would be projected onto the side of his rickety little houseboat. Spectators would watch from their boats. Professional short films celebrating the heritage of the North would be shown, but the main event would be a competition of local films, emphasizing the unique character of the Old Town. Melvin would engage the services of a celebrity judge, raising the event's profile and ensuring its success.

"Collective action is essential," Melvin had warned residents at a community meeting. "The shacks are just the beginning. The Old Town turns into some fancy development area, we're all at risk. Many older places aren't up to code. Someone doesn't like the look of your house, all they got to do is call an inspector. And some Old Town landscaping is an acquired taste."

"What's that supposed to mean?" Freddy had asked.

"It means those derelict cars in your yard would be deemed an eyesore, Freddy. You'd have to get rid of them."

"I'd like to see 'em try," Freddy said, flecks of spit lighting on his bushy beard.

"If you don't comply with a clean-up order, they can fine you. If you don't pay, they can foreclose and evict you."

Freddy's mouth dropped open. "But the Old Town's always looked like that. Why should we have to change?"

"You seen that black SUV that's been creeping around the neighbourhood?" someone said. "That's owned by one of the big developers. Scoping out the place."

"Marge's yard looks like a spare parts dealer," said Sadie James, owner of a newer home. "With the taxes we pay, you'd think she'd put her property to better use."

"You're the one that's ruining the neighbourhood," Marge said, "with your stupid garden and twenty varieties of pink flowers. Yeesh."

"Twenty-seven varieties." Sadie's white curls shook and her voice rose. "Some of us are on a pension. Our house is the only equity we have, so property value matters."

Melvin held up his hands. "People! This is exactly what they want. Divide and conquer. I discussed this very issue just a few months ago with Francis Ford Coppola when I was down at that film festival in L.A. Bumped into him at the opening reception, and over some excellent canapés—crab puffs with brie—he told me, 'Art is a unifying force. Culture builds community.' So let's take Frank Coppola's advice and pull together, draw attention to our plight, and get the Powers That Be to leave us alone."

The meeting broke up soon after. People hurried home to dig through their closets for long-forgotten video cameras.

*****

Marge had been one of few dissenters at the meeting. Now, as she stood in her yard in the January cold and surveyed the buildings before her, the idea seemed just as futile.

"No stupid film festival is going to keep the bulldozers from rolling on the shacks. And City Hall isn't going to make you, or me, or anyone else clean up unless someone in the neighbourhood complains, and no one's going to do that. Melvin's just roping you into another artsy fartsy scheme. He wants to drop names and act like a big shot."

"No need for sour grapes, just because you got no poetry in *your* soul," Freddy said. "The rest of them's planning little more than home videos. Mine'll be a real film, a northern epic: man against nature, lots of snow, lots of dogs. And I got the backing and the buzz to make it happen."

Marge's reply was obliterated by the stereo booming from a rattle-trap car that bounced past and skidded to a stop at the Anderson house at the end of the road. An impressive number of teenaged boys exited the car and entered the garage. A couple of them carried guitar cases.

Marge groaned. "Rehearsal night for Bug Gutz. What's the deal with Tommy Anderson and heavy metal? It's like he had a personality transplant."

"Those boys are trained musicians," Freddy said. "They write their own lyrics."

"They sound like three-year-olds banging pots and pans. What's worse, Tommy's let his odd job business slide."

Freddy smirked. "He's kept his preferred customers. Like me."

Marge flicked her greying ponytail over her shoulder and turned to re-enter her home. Hubcap's squealing resumed. Freddy froze in mid-step. The howling across the frozen lake gathered strength. They could hear the phone ringing at Freddy's place.

"Hubcap—shut it," Marge said.

The dog closed his mouth. He cocked a squinty eye at her. The ringing across the road stopped.

"For Pete's sake." Marge unhooked the dog's collar and he made a beeline for the Quonset hut. By the time she huffed in behind him, he was sprawled on the Naugahyde couch, snout in a bowl of popcorn, chewing briskly. Marge hit the "play" button and Robert Redford appeared on screen. Hubcap pointed his rat-like nose at the ceiling and unleashed a series of shrieks.

"It's my turn! I haven't watched one Robert Redford movie all week."

The screeches crescendoed. Marge had just got rid of Freddy; if the racket continued, he'd be back. Jaw set, she popped the movie out of the VCR and slid in a battered cassette. Lassie bounded across the screen, tail wagging, the wind tossing her great collie ruff. Hubcap dropped his head between outstretched paws and locked his eyes onto the TV, oblivious to the musical stylings of Bug Gutz, which banged and crashed through the corrugated metal siding of the hut. Marge picked through the bowl of popcorn. Unable to find any kernels that weren't soggy, she set it aside.

She checked her watch. Surely Hubcap would get bored and fall asleep—then she could watch Robert Redford in peace. Hours later she awoke, a cramp in her neck and her alarm clock screaming from the bedroom. Bug Gutz was silent; Hubcap was snoring. Marge rewound the Lassie tape and got ready for work.

*****

Minus thirty temperatures kept the Powers That Be occupied elsewhere for most of January—there had been no further sightings of the mysterious SUV, and no eviction notices were received by the shack dwellers. A freelance land surveyor, Marge took only the occasional job in mid-winter, which left her plenty of time to watch videos. She supplemented her main diet of action films and Robert Redford movies with classics from Ingmar Bergman and Louis Malle. Sadly, the members of Bug Gutz seemed to have little to do outside of school hours, and spent their evenings and weekends rehearsing. Marge offered Tommy Anderson ten per cent over his regular rate for a load of the firewood he harvested in the bush south of Yellowknife—partly because she was willing to pay for a reprieve from the music, and partly because she really did need the fuel.

"I'm only taking on essential tasks," he said.

"It's January. My furnace can't keep up. It *is* essential."

"Other people sell firewood."

"Other people didn't play in my yard as a six-year-old. Other people didn't hitch rides to school in my truck."

"I can't."

"Can't?" Marge said, but he'd already hung up.

The following day, Marge was ensconced on her couch, afghan on her lap, Hubcap by her side. The dog snored gently, sated with a bowl of popcorn and two Lassie movies.

"That Robert Redford is one fine-looking man," Marge murmured as banging started across the road. She pulled aside the front curtain and squinted into the glare of sun bouncing off snow. Tommy Anderson was performing the non-essential task of rearranging car parts in the yard surrounding the decrepit garage that served as Freddy's home and workshop. A fellow band member unloaded firewood.

"We'll see about that." She dropped the curtain and put on her parka. Hubcap followed her outside. After answering a call of nature, he headed for his doghouse. Marge headed across the road.

Freddy's continual one-upmanship was getting on her nerves. He taunted her about having no poetry in her soul, but Freddy himself had thwarted her artistic ambitions almost a year earlier. Marge had been a contender to win Yellowknife's annual Ugly Truck and Dog Contest, thanks largely to the years of decay gracing her truck. It was her adoption of Hubcap, however, that made her a shoo-in: his asymmetrical features, disproportionately small head, and patchy fur were awe-inspiringly repulsive. During one of Marge's absences, however, Freddy had orchestrated a covert make-over for both Hubcap and the truck. The dog quickly reverted to his prize-winning self, but the truck's restoration had been permanent. It now squatted in the back yard like some old tart wearing too much rouge.

Tommy had completed his original task of moving a pile of rusting car radiators from one end of the yard to the other, setting them along a peeling wooden fence next to the shell of a '56 Ford Fairlane and a rust-pocked '73 Mustang, perched on a set of blocks. He'd just loaded his arms with stove-lengths of firewood and was turning toward Freddy's house when he ran into Marge. His blue eyes went wide with alarm; his round cheeks, already red with cold, burned a couple of degrees brighter.

"If you can deliver wood to Freddy, you can deliver to me. I'll expect you and your associate—"

"Snake," the associate said.

Marge surveyed the boy's sallow face and scraggy black hair. "I'll expect you and 'Snake' when you're done here."

"Can't," said Snake. "Got rehearsal."

"Cry me a river, kid."

"Look lady, we have a deal with Freddy," Snake said.

Marge eyed Tommy. "A deal that excludes other valued customers?"

Tommy studied the toes of his boots.

"Half a cord," she said, then departed.

The rhythmic "thunk" of wood being piled against Marge's house began a few minutes later, but stopped far too soon. Marge looked out the window. Hubcap blinked sleepily in the door of his doghouse. Snake was standing a few feet in front of the dog.

"Holy crap! Ugly sucker, or what?"

Tommy scratched Hubcap's ears. "Marge found him at the junkyard."

Snake flicked his scarf at Hubcap. "Bad dog."

Hubcap yipped.

Snake snapped the scarf again. "Bad dog!"

Hubcap barked.

Marge stepped outside, hands on broad hips.

"Whaddya mean, bad dog?"

Tommy glanced at Snake and shifted from foot to foot. "It's the name of one of our songs."

"I'll bet. That's enough for now." She paid them, and watched Tommy follow his associate down the road.

"He used to be such a nice boy," she said.

*****

It was a sunny day in March when Marge poured a mug of tea and sat on her top step to watch the auditions in Freddy's yard. He'd been right about his film's "buzz." The line-up of people and dogs would have stretched around the block, if there'd been such a thing in the Old Town—as it was, it ran down the road and past the Andersons' garage, which was mercifully silent. Marge snorted. Most days, the people lingering on the spring snow would cross the street to avoid Freddy.

"There's Sadie James and her poodle, for Pete's sake," Marge said to Hubcap, who lolled on the roof of his house. "When was the last time you saw a poodle on a dog team?"

Tommy and Snake kept order among the throng until adequate anticipation had built up. Then Freddy swept out of his dwelling, bushy beard trimmed into a goatee, a minuscule pair of dark-rimmed glasses perched on his nose. Marge almost spit out her tea. Freddy paraded up and down the line of hopefuls, his own dumpy dog, Troy, wandering behind.

"Listen up," he bellowed. "I'm looking for extras and supporting actors, but most of all, I'm looking for a star. I'm looking for courage, verve, charisma."

Marge wished Bug Gutz would start playing.

Snake placed a director's chair near the shack. As Freddy assumed the place of honour, Tommy handed him a large cappuccino. Freddy slurped at the mound of foam that rose above the top of the paper cup and auditions began. Marge smirked and giggled through two hours of dogs sitting, playing dead, rolling over, shaking a paw. The dance performance of Sadie's poodle Maximo, pink bow bobbing in his topknot, had been a highlight. Her guffaws carried across the street, earning her a poisonous look from Sadie. Marge was wiping away tears when she noticed a wad of papers crammed between her steps and the front wall of her Quonset hut.

She extracted the lump and smoothed the pages. They included a clean-up notice from the City dated weeks earlier, as well as a second notice. One more, and she would be fined. Disbelief seized Marge. She stood and scanned her treasures, harvested over the years from the dump, friends, and neighbours: parts for snowmobiles (tracks, windshields and skis, in all sizes); parts for trucks (wheel rims, axles, and miscellaneous tires); and a collection of carburetors, pistons, and assorted gas tanks. Sometimes she'd sell the parts to make extra cash, but usually she just gave them away. Like last spring, when Old Man LaRue had split the track on his little snow machine in heavy slush and thought he'd have to cough up seven hundred bucks for a new one. Marge had dug through her inventory and found exactly what he needed. Installed it too. Old Man LaRue had been a trapper all his life, and wasn't exactly flush with cash. The look of relief on his face when Marge showed up with the right part had been all the payment she'd needed.

Anger shot through Marge's body; it felt like the top of her head was going to blow off. Bad enough she'd been ordered to get rid of her stuff, but who had shoved the notices out of sight? Her gaze roamed the line of auditioners. It lit on Freddy, who was trying to put his own dog through his paces. Troy was lying on the dirty snow, staring morosely at the great director.

Marge stumped down the steps and across the road, Hubcap trotting after her. She shook the papers under Freddy's nose. "You'd go this far the get rid of me?"

"Take it someplace else, Marge. We're busy here." Freddy prodded Troy with his toe.

"Not as busy as you're going to be when I—" Marge said, just as Melvin's truck rolled into the yard. He hopped out.

"Not too late, I hope," he said.

"Just in time," said Freddy, turning away from Marge.

Tommy Anderson dropped the tailgate and the crowd watched half a dozen sled dogs—lean and long-legged—swarm out and mill around the yard. Then a high-pitched bark issued from the back of the truck. Everyone turned to see a collie poised on the tailgate, face to the sun, wind playing with her ruff. Marge recognized the dog as Melvin's house pet—it was common for dog team owners to have one animal that did not live the rough outdoor life of a working dog, but led a pampered existence inside. Hubcap stared at the collie.

"Meet our female lead," said Freddy. "Melvin's Tiffany. The hero's love interest."

Tiffany jumped from the tailgate and slipped on a patch of ice. Hubcap charged up to her. She cringed.

Snake swung a stick. "Buzz off, you ugly mutt."

Hubcap ducked the blow, but refused to move away from the collie.

Marge sighed. "You've got as much chance with her as I do with Robert Redford."

Hubcap wagged his tail.

Melvin's head snapped toward Marge. "What do you know about Robert Redford?"

A note of tension in his voice made Marge pause. Had she stumbled onto something?

"I know he's got a soft spot for independent films," she said. "Runs his own festival. Sundance."

Melvin moved closer. "Who's been talking?"

"You'd be amazed what I know." Marge watched Melvin fidget. So Robert Redford was the big name judge for the Dog Island Floating Festival. "By the way—Hubcap's auditioning."

"Over my dead body," Freddy said.

"Might be in your best interests to consider him." Melvin laid a finger beside his nose and winked.

Freddy frowned. "What's his piece?"

Hubcap ran through the entire repertoire of the other dogs: rolling on the snow, flopping on his back, offering a muddy paw to Melvin. Then he pulled back his lips to expose a full—if crooked—set of teeth. He growled, then snapped, then broke into a string of shrill barks.

Melvin blanched. “What the hell is that?”

“That’s Hubcap guarding the junkyard,” Marge said. “Kept away lots of bad guys over the years. Very courageous.”

“And very convincing.” Melvin used the thumb and forefinger of each hand to make a rectangle, and peered at Hubcap through it. “You can shoot around the face, Freddy.”

“No way.”

The assembled auditioners were studying Hubcap, considering the limited options for shooting him at his best, when their contemplation was broken by the crunch of wheels on gravel. The crunch was quickly swallowed by the roar of an overpowered engine as a huge black SUV approached and rolled past. A collective shiver gripped the crowd.

“Hubcap’s better than Troy,” someone yelled. “Make sure this film doesn’t totally suck.”

As Freddy scowled at Hubcap, a large dog strolled into the yard. He was good-looking: salt-and-pepper fur covered the top half of his body and formed a mask over his eyes. The darker fur faded into ivory, which covered his lower half—chin, throat, belly, and legs. The other dogs slipped between the legs of their owners, who stirred with curiosity.

“Whose animal is that?”

“Stray, I think.”

“Bigger than your average Old Town mix.”

“Malamute,” someone muttered.

“Wolf,” Sadie James hissed, clutching Maximo to her bosom.

“Archie Beasley’s dog was killed by wolves last winter, out at his cabin,” someone said. “Dog was tied up—didn’t stand a chance.”

“What’s worse is when they lure a dog into the woods by being all friendly, make the poor thing think it’s one of the pack, then turn on it, tear it limb from limb,” Sadie said.

Everyone stared at the newcomer. Hubcap released a volley of yips at the animal. Growling, he circled the new dog.

“Stop it,” Marge said.

Hubcap’s growl deepened; he circled closer. The crowd edged away.

“I said ‘stop it’!” Marge threw snow in his face. Hubcap shook his head.

“All you can expect from a junkyard dog,” sniffed Sadie James.

Freddy turned his attention to the new animal. “This one’s got the right look. And he’s no wolf. Wolfs is sneaky things, like Sadie said, and this guy walked straight into a group of people.” Freddy patted the animal’s head. The dog licked Freddy’s hand. “See. He’s friendly—” Freddy broke off in a choke—the dog had tried an experimental nibble, and now had Freddy’s hand clamped between his teeth. Freddy pried open the animal’s mouth, and examined the dents in his skin. The dog wandered around the yard, sniffing.

Tiffany approached and lowered her head. The big dog licked her left ear. Then he licked it again.

“We’ve found our leading man,” said Freddy. “I’ll call him ‘Rex.’”

“Hey! What about Hubcap?” Marge said.

“He can guard the camp while we’re shooting,” said Freddy. “Maybe have a bit part.”

Hubcap growled. Rex lifted his lip, exposing sturdy white fangs. Hubcap snarled.

"Enough!" Freddy pointed at Hubcap. "As of this minute, Marge, he is on probation—one false step and he is off the set. We'll be watching." He nodded to Snake and Tommy.

Rex sauntered to the edge of the yard and glanced over the crowd, his eye pausing on Maximo. Then he turned and loped away.

Marge and Hubcap watched him go. Both had seen the drool running from the corner of his mouth.

*****

A few days later, filming began on a snow-covered lake not far from town, encircled by stands of bent jack pines and the white skeletons of birch trees. On a rock outcropping overlooking the scene, a string of trailers was set up as a camp where the actors—canine and human—were made up, watered, and fed. The pool of extra dogs was housed in a temporary enclosure; only Hubcap was at liberty to roam. Marge was busy working elsewhere, but Hubcap's experience in the junkyard meant he needed no supervision as a security guard, protecting the camp against vandals, thieves, and freeloaders from town drawn by the lavish buffet Freddy had organized. As cast and crew banged in and out of the trailers preparing for the day's shoot, Hubcap patrolled the camp, his surveillance focusing chiefly on Tiffany. All the humans and the handful of canines required for the first scene finally moved down to the lake. The security guard pranced around the dog enclosure, ensuring its remaining inmates took note of his freedom, and whipped them into a frenzy of yowls and yelps. When Freddy's curses reached his mismatched ears, Hubcap flipped his stumpy tail and continued on his rounds.

An hour later, Hubcap was yipping at a squirrel, who pelted him with pine cones. Despite the rodent's chatter, Hubcap heard the snap of a breaking branch. He froze, hackles rising, and squinted into the trees. A pine cone hit his head. He snapped at the squirrel, who fell silent. Then it was back—the crack of a frozen tree, the rustle of someone moving through the bush. Hubcap paced, snarling. Something smacked his head again, and he flinched. It was no pine cone this time; an egg-sized stone lay beside his front paw. His voice rose to an outraged shriek as he rushed into the bush.

"Holy crap, let's get out of here."

Two figures rose from the snow. Hubcap broke off as he recognized Tommy Anderson. Tommy stared for a moment before following Snake, who dodged through the trees, video camera dangling from one hand.

Marge dropped by the camp at lunchtime. She surveyed the enormous buffet set out for the human cast and crew. "Quite a spread you got here."

"I told you—I got backers," Freddy said. "With deep pockets."

"Deep enough to drive around in shiny black SUVs? Like the one that's parked about a mile down the road?"

"As if." Freddy moved toward the buffet.

If Freddy was working with the developers to run Marge off her lot, the film festival had bought her a reprieve. Melvin had convinced City Hall that not one rock, tree or piece of scrap metal in the Old Town could be disturbed while residents were making their films.

"Had a word with Mayor Plunkett," he said with a wink. "With an election coming up, he's decided to cooperate."

Hubcap roamed the perimeter of the dog enclosure. Tommy and Snake hauled in a sack of dog food and proceeded to fill bowls, starting with Tiffany and Rex, who lounged together. Tiffany nibbled at her kibble while Rex stared into his bowl of pellets. He reached over and nipped Tiffany's neck. She licked Rex's snout. Hubcap growled.

Each morning, Freddy strolled through the enclosure, deciding which dogs to use as extras. Every dog who auditioned got a turn down on the lake, except for Hubcap. As filming progressed he became more subdued.

"You'll get to show your stuff," Marge told him. "Don't worry."

The day came when Hubcap found himself guarding an empty camp. He wandered the row of silent trailers and stared at the vacant dog pen. A tour of the nearby bush turned up not one squirrel to divert his attention. Hubcap plopped flat onto the snow beside the last trailer, watching the action down on the lake. The eventual bustle of the lunch crowd had no effect on the guard dog, who remained inert, even when Tommy set a bowl of kibble beside him. Then a familiar thump carried through the air and resonated in Hubcap's chest. Marge's truck chugged into the parking lot.

"No wonder you're bummed, if this is what they're feeding you. I brought your favourite." Marge kicked aside the bowl and dropped a frozen jackfish in front of Hubcap. His tail beat the ground. He'd just gnawed off a fin when Rex appeared beside him and stared at the fish.

"Hard to believe any self-respecting dog would eat like that, but that's the company we're keeping," Sadie said, helping herself to a plate of sushi.

Melvin strolled over to the guard dog. "You should use him, Freddy. His look is pure Old Town. Raw, but with an ethereal quality. Federico would approve. Very Fellini-esque."

Sadie snorted. "Is that what you call it?"

"Fellini was a great director," Marge said. "Just like Robert Redford."

"Hubcap is on probation," Freddy said. "Doesn't play well with others."

"He's got a grip on himself. Don't you, boy?" Melvin reached for Hubcap's forehead, but stopped short of actually touching him.

Cast and crew were focused on their own lunches when Rex made a grab for Hubcap's fish. Hubcap launched himself at the other dog, aiming for the throat. Rex side-stepped the attack and the adversaries circled each other, growling. Marge looked up to find Tommy and Snake video-taping the altercation.

"Still working for Freddy?" Marge yelled. "Collecting evidence to make sure Hubcap never makes it into the film?"

"No taped evidence needed," Freddy said. "Get him out of here."

"Takes two to tango, Freddy, and Rex started it. Notice how well he handles himself in a fight?"

"Rex is not the issue."

Marge saw Rex's hackles go up. His eyes took on a predatory gleam and he appeared to be assessing the best way to break Hubcap's neck.

"Good God. He *is* a wolf."

"You will say anything, won't you? He's a malamute. Now get your damned dog out of here, Marge. For good."

*****

Life in the Old Town was quiet as filming continued. Even Bug Gutz was silent. Hubcap spent his days slumped on the roof of his doghouse, or slumped on the couch beside Marge. He refused to watch Lassie movies.

"Doesn't matter we're not in the film festival," Marge said. "Even if I was introduced to Robert Redford, he wouldn't look twice at an old thing like me."

Hubcap licked her chin.

Out in her yard, Marge began stacking her treasures for their eventual removal to the dump. Since she was not part of a film project, it seemed Melvin's influence with City Hall no longer protected her. Unable to pay the fine she faced, she had no choice but to comply with the Powers That Be.

When Hubcap started yipping and howling a few days later, Marge was relieved to hear him sounding like his old—albeit shrill—self. She peeked out through the curtains, but her smile evaporated when she saw Snake taunting the dog, while Tommy videotaped him, holding the camera high, squatting down, twisting it at odd angles.

Marge burst outside, shaking her fist. "Get out before I put the boots to you!"

Tommy aimed the camera at her until she came within arm's reach, then bolted down the street.

"He used to be such a nice boy," she said.

*****

Summer passed, and autumn brought with it the Dog Island Floating Film Festival. As darkness fell, the northern lights streaked the sky above Yellowknife Bay and swirled, green and pink, over Melvin's houseboat.

From her back yard, Marge could see the giant torch Melvin had lit on the island to guide people to the film festival. She and Hubcap traipsed the short distance from their home down to the shore and climbed into Marge's big freighter canoe. They motored into the bay and toward Dog Island, Yellowknife's houseboat community bobbing on one side of them, Jolliffe Island rising beyond it. On the other side stretched Great Slave Lake, from which blew a wintry breeze. Hubcap was prostrate on the canoe's front bench, his body bouncing with each wave.

Boats were assembling; everyone in the Old Town and their dog, literally, had shown up. Marge squeezed between a dinghy and a kayak, about twenty yards away from the screen. The audience was buzzing as people chatted from boat to boat, and passed mugs of mulled wine or chunks of napkin-wrapped banana bread and other snacks to their neighbours. On Dog Island, Melvin and other festival organizers arranged films and tested the projector. The light bounced against the houseboat, silhouetting Tiffany as she wandered its platform. Hubcap raised his head and wagged his tail.

A yacht elbowed into the jam on the water, pushing several smaller boats out of the way. From its deck came the pop of a champagne cork and the clink of glasses. Marge recognized it as one of the extravagant toys that moored in the Yellowknife marina.

"That must be the boat that Robert Redford's on," she told Hubcap, fumbling with gloved fingers to pour herself hot chocolate. She offered Hubcap a handful of popcorn; he pushed around the kernels with his nose before drooping back onto the seat.

Melvin welcomed the crowd. First came a series of National Film Board shorts. Various narrators intoned the history of the Northwest Territories, the accompanying footage abundant with images of float planes, canoes, mosquitoes, ice, and snow. The films seemed old-fashioned at first because they were grainy, but once Marge looked past that, she was pleasantly reminded that things in the North had changed very little. People were still flying the same bush planes they had in the '40s and '50s, and the aluminum boats used for fishing and travel across Great Slave Lake were pretty much the same. Granted, the world had seen the invention of Gore-Tex in the intervening years, and the younger people in the audience—those in their 20s, 30s and 40s—couldn't step two feet from their front door without swathing themselves in it and other high-priced wilderness gear. Still, many wore jeans and plaid shirts underneath their modern accoutrements. And the older Dene ladies in the films wore exactly the same uniform they did today—heavy stockings, pleated polyester skirts, windbreakers, kerchiefs.

The old documentaries soon ended, and Marge was plunged into the sad reality of her neighbours' film-making efforts. Tommy Anderson's father and a buddy stumbled through a demonstration of the best technique for catching jackfish, smiling stiffly at the camera while holding stringers of the long-jawed monsters. Neighbourhood toddlers rode circles on their tricycles, their monotonous and unrelenting circuits going on for so long Marge had an attack of vertigo. Sadie James enumerated every single flower in her front yard before marshalling the camera through the murk of her carport and repeating the torment in her back garden.

Marge's brain was almost numb when something spurred her back to consciousness. She searched the screen. "Something's not right about that video, Hubcap. Other than the twenty-seven varieties of pink flowers."

Then the clang and clash of heavy metal rent the air. Bug Gutz flashed onto the screen. The lyrics of the song they sang were indecipherable, except for the occasional shriek of "Bad dog! Bad dog!" Marge gasped. Hubcap raised his head to be confronted by his own face, twisted in rage, as he paced the snow by the film camp. Next came a clip of Marge shaking her fist at the camera. The crowd howled with laughter. Marge and Hubcap sank lower in their seats as shots of an increasingly vicious Hubcap flicked across the screen, interspersed with Marge's fist. The crowd screamed "Bad dog!

Bad dog!" along with the band. Only Marge heard Hubcap's whimper from the front of the canoe.

The jumpy shots and clumsy acting of Freddy's painfully long film passed in a blur for Marge. As images from the Bug Gutz video replayed in her mind she glanced toward the yacht, but she could see nothing in the darkness. So she did get "introduced" to Robert Redford, after all. Hubcap lay with his head on the canoe's gunnel, awaiting a glimpse of Tiffany in the flesh or on the screen.

What appeared instead was a shape moving through the waters of Yellowknife Bay then climbing onto the dark side of the deck of Melvin's houseboat. The shape shook itself. Rex.

Hubcap yipped. Several people turned toward him.

"Shh!"

"Quiet!"

"Bad dog!"

"Shut up yourself," Marge said.

Tiffany joined Rex on the houseboat's deck. Rex slipped back into the lake. Tiffany hesitated, then followed Rex into the water. They swam across the bay toward Jolliffe Island, a small, rocky lump wooded with birch, white spruce, and willow, and dotted with squatters' cabins.

As the movie ended, Hubcap leapt over the neighbouring kayak and into a canoe, then barrelled across a motorboat and into the lake, a chorus of "bad dog!" following him.

The film festival volunteers trained the light from the projector on Melvin. "And now, to render the verdict, our celebrity judge—Mayor Plunkett."

"Hey! Where's Robert Redford?" Marge said.

A short, balding man stepped into the spotlight to scattered applause. Despite the cold breeze, he blotted his forehead with a handkerchief. "Let me start by saying that it's difficult to choose among so many fine voters . . . I mean *film-makers*. I think you'll agree, however, that it's good to encourage our youth. And so the winner of the Dog Island Floating Film Festival is . . . 'Bad Dog' by Bug Gutz."

Freddy's shout of "say what?" was lost in the general cheering. Tommy Anderson and Snake bounced forward.

"Thanks for, like, not giving the award to one of those crappy films," Snake said.

A dog screamed from Jolliffe Island. The crowd froze. Pet owners checked their boats. A film festival volunteer did a nose count of Melvin's dogs.

"Tiffany's missing," he called.

Marge arrived at Jolliffe Island just before the others, who armed themselves with paddles and flashlights. Sadie James stepped ashore, Maximo in one arm, an empty champagne bottle in the other. Freddy came face to face with Tommy and Snake.

"Traitors," said Freddy. "You were supposed to be working for me."

"And Bug Gutz was supposed to be in your film, but nooo, you changed your mind," said Snake. "Didn't fit with your artistic vision! Double-crosser."

The group followed the sounds of fighting dogs into a clearing. A flashlight's beam showed Tiffany lying on her side, the white fur of her throat stained red. Hubcap stood over her, growling, blood running down his face.

Sadie threw her champagne bottle at Hubcap. It bounced onto the grass beside him. "I always said he was no good. You see? You see?"

Tommy trained his light farther into the bush. Rex stood gnashing reddened teeth; blood matted the fur around his mouth. Sadie's shrieks has drawn his attention. Maximo cowered in her arms; Rex catapulted himself at the small dog. Hubcap intercepted and pulled him to the ground. Rex snapped at his neck. Marge entered the fray, swinging a canoe paddle. The edge connected with Rex's head. He backed off and surveyed the row of people, weapons raised, moving toward him. Then he turned and ran, splashing into the lake on the far side of the island.

"Told you he was a wolf." Marge dropped the paddle and examined Hubcap's forehead. "Just a cut—you'll live."

Tiffany whimpered as Melvin probed her neck. "Skin's torn. She'll need stitches."

Hubcap returned to Tiffany's side and lowered his head. Her tongue flicked toward him.

"Not such a bad dog after all." Marge wrapped an arm around Hubcap and glared at Tommy.

"We couldn't tell you, Marge," Tommy said. "You had to be sincere. You saw how phoney all the other films were."

"No kidding." Marge frowned at the champagne bottle lying beside Hubcap. "That's expensive stuff you're drinking, Sadie. Thought you were a poor pensioner."

"She was on the big boat," said Tommy. "The one owned by the property developer with the SUV."

Marge's fingers itched with a sudden urge to clamp themselves around Sadie's windpipe. "*You're* the one trying to run me off my property. I know what was wrong with your film. There was a shot of the SUV parked in the shadows of your carport. Had your buddy the property developer over for tea and conspiracy?"

"The City's glad I complained. They've been wanting you to clean up for years."

"Ya, well, I've put off the trip to the dump so far, Sadie," Marge said.

"Nothing will be changing in Marge's yard any time soon." Melvin looked up from his examination of Tiffany. "I'll be taking the Bug Gutz video to my next networking opportunity—a seminar of film-festival organizers down at Sundance. Bob Redford will love it."

Marge groaned.

Tiffany yelped as Melvin hefted her into his arms. "Mayor Plunkett understands that the images in the video are archetypes of our city's heritage." Melvin started across the clearing, Hubcap sidling beside him. "Bob's into salt-of-the-earth types. He's gonna love you, Marge."

It was Sadie's turn to groan.

The crowd followed Melvin down to the shore. Freddy hauled off and kicked a tree stump.

"No need for sour grapes," Marge said. "So who were your backers, big shot, if not the guy with the black truck?"

"Melvin, mostly, but he got donations from businesses in town. There had to be at least one feature-length film in the festival for him to qualify for this Robert Redford thing."

"Beat out by a music video."

"I told you—those boys are trained musicians."

"And me and Hubcap are archetypes."

"As if."

From the shore came the yips and howls of dogs being harassed by one of their own. People were shouting "bad dog." Marge turned her back on Freddy, and went to find Hubcap.

Old Town Bait and Tackle

"You're sure that's the place?" Howard squinted into the morning mist rising from Great Slave Lake.

"Yep, that's it. Old Town Bait and Tackle." The burly man operating the canoe rental shack didn't bother to follow Howard's glance toward the lime green houseboat bobbing in Yellowknife Bay. Turning his back to the shack's open door, he rummaged through a pile of life jackets, extracted one, then lifted a couple of paddles off the wall.

"Marty Malone really lives there?" Howard asked.

"For the third time, yes. Trust me, buddy, I know. I take Marty his groceries once a week." The man nodded at a cardboard carton holding cans of beans, boxes of macaroni and cheese, bottles of tequila, and a couple of fishing magazines.

"Just seems an inconvenient location for a business . . . um . . . Earl," Howard said, noticing the name on a chipped coffee mug.

Earl snorted and dumped the paddles and life jacket into a large red canoe beside the shack. "Marty caters to a select clientele. They find him no matter what."

A cold breeze blew in from the lake. Across a narrow channel, on Jolliffe Island, autumn leaves rattled. Howard shivered. This was the season to be settling back into the civilization of the big city, not undertaking a northern fishing expedition. He picked up the life jacket. "How deep's the bay?"

"Deep enough. But it's not like you need a life jacket paddling a tank like this—you'd have to be a complete incompetent to flip it." Earl kicked the canoe. The tough plastic bent inward, then flexed back into place. Howard hitched his pants and followed suit. His brand new hiking boot bounced off without making a dent. He hobbled in a circle until the pain subsided.

Earl cast an eye over Howard's round face, bulky waistline, and soft hands. "On second thought, let me buckle you in." In a sequence of movements that bespoke a background in professional wrestling, Earl flipped Howard into the life jacket, and with a twist and turn, incarcerated him in the device.

He slapped Howard on the back. "Perfect."

Howard could barely breathe.

Earl carried the canoe to the water's edge and dropped it in. He squatted to steady it, but Howard waved him away.

"I'm an old hand."

Earl smirked, but after double-checking the buckles on Howard's life jacket, he retreated to the canoe shack.

Howard climbed in, trying to keep low, just as "Margarita Marty" had taught him at Lake Muskinongy, all those summers ago. The canoe drifted as Howard struggled to reacquaint himself with the use of a paddle, working his way through the J-stroke, the sweep, and the pry. One overly enthusiastic draw caused the canoe to tilt violently. Heart pounding, Howard forced himself to sit still until the boat steadied. Earl, he realized, was sitting atop an outcrop of rock, sipping coffee and keeping watch.

Howard fought the breeze as he zig-zagged into the bay, his shoulders tiring after only a couple of minutes. The knowledge that Earl's eyes followed him—and that making up lost ground would be twice as painful—kept his arms moving: reach, dip, pull; reach, dip, pull.

Howard wished, for the umpteenth time, that he'd developed some brawn. But that was his own fault, as his father liked to remind him—since childhood he'd squandered his spare time reading comic books, when he could have been fishing.

An advertising executive, his father Charlie would make his sales pitch. "Fishing develops the physique and tempers the nerve. You need look no farther than your closest lake to learn the secret of success. Even the smallest minnow knows it's a fish-eat-fish world." He'd propel Howard into the family room, and plant him in front of a massive muskie hanging on the wall. "Old Fred, your grandpa's biggest catch ever. I'll never forget that day—breeze in our hair, picnic lunch in the boat, lots of laughs. 'Big fish, big man,' he'd say. They still talk about him at Muskinongy Lodge."

Howard had grown up in Toronto, but his family spent summers at their cabin on Lake Muskinongy in northern Ontario, where the quarry consisted of perch, pickerel, walleye and anything else that had fins and moved. The prize, however, was the species for which the lake was named—a creature the Ojibway people had astutely dubbed "maskinonge" or "ugly fish"—a serpentine beast whose elongated jaw, menacing teeth, and audacious disposition made it unsurpassed as both predator and prey. Charlie often said that pursuing muskie was like playing the slot machines in Las Vegas.

"Takes some luck, sure," he'd tell his cronies at Muskinongy Lodge. "But skill, persistence, that's what really matters. Only the most devoted of anglers pay their dues and collect their prize."

Unless Howard was in the boat, then it was like hitting the jackpot every time.

Howard had barely been out of diapers the first time Charlie thrust a fishing rod into his hands. His mother, who had been sitting next to him in the boat, shook her head.

"He's too young."

Charlie rolled his eyes.

Little Howard had dangled his lure in the lake for only a few minutes before a long shadow appeared beside the boat. The fish jumped—a huge muskie, his bottom lip decorated with lures snapped from the lines of unworthy fishermen clattering like a witch doctor's rattle. Howard shrieked.

The fish grabbed Howard's lure and took off. The line tangled and broke.

"Yes!" Charlie punched his fist into the air, then hugged his son. "The Rattler—on his first ever cast!"

"But now his lure is stuck in the Rattler's lip," said Howard's mom, pulling her son close. "And you know what that means."

"You don't believe the old wives' tale about the C-U-R-S-E? No one who's gone a round with the Rattler has been seriously injured."

"Except the poodle."

"But what if Howard caught the Rattler?" said Charlie. "Talk about carrying on the family legacy!"

Both adults stared at the boy. Howard's stomach lurched.

Minutes later, Howard's mother caught a muskie, then Charlie did. Even now, Howard's nightmares were haunted by the vision of those prehistoric predators, jaws snapping as they slithered across the floor of the boat. Little Howard had cowered in the far corner while Charlie flailed at each beast's head. The stench of fish slime and the repeated thwack of Charlie's club had been too much—Howard had heaved up his lunch into the lake's pristine waters.

Those two muskies and Old Fred still glared at him from the family room wall. But the biggest thing on the wall was the space allotted for Howard's fish: a space big enough for the Rattler.

Howard had tried to accept his destiny. Throughout the summers of his childhood, his father would cajole him into fishing.

"Trust me boy, it'll be fun," Charlie would say, his angular form bent toward his son. He'd try to keep his tone light, but the tension in his jaw would distort his voice and a dark gleam in his eyes would give his face a malevolent cast.

Suppressing a shudder, Howard would give in. His father only wanted what was best for him, after all. To catch the Rattler would confer on him a level of prestige that would be hard to reach by other means. Members of the Muskinongy Lodge held key positions in the Toronto business community; a long and successful career was assured. It was the cruellest of cosmic jokes, however, that Howard was terrified of the water and everything in it—as he prepared to join Charlie on the lake, memories of previous fishing trips would lead to shaky hands, graduate into body tremors, and end in full-blown hysterics. His infuriated father would grab his fishing rod and picnic lunch and stomp down to his boat alone. When Howard was eight or nine, Charlie lost patience once and for all.

"Howard the Coward. Go read your damned comic books—you'll never amount to anything, anyway."

"Enough!" Howard's mother pointed a finger at Charlie. "I know the real reason you want him along. It's your own fault you can't catch anything. Even Howard can't help you."

Charlie did catch a couple more trophy muskie over the years and added them to the collection, despite Howard's inability to contribute to the family honour.

Now here he was, Howard the Coward, alone in a canoe on Yellowknife Bay. The bay itself was bad enough, but what lay beyond its mouth was worse: a lake the size of Belgium, its waters teeming with who-knew-what kind of creatures. Howard slowed his stroke. The sun lit up the dozen or so houseboats in Yellowknife Bay, ranging from the rusty hulk of a derelict barge to a perky cedar-sided hut on a wooden platform. Most were wooden frame houses painted vibrant shades: turquoise, sunflower, fuchsia. A cold breeze rocked the canoe. The baby toe on Howard's left foot tingled. Then it began to itch. He wiggled his toes, which only made it worse. Howard peered into the lake. A shadow stretched half the length of the canoe. His eyes snapped shut, the canoe wobbling beneath him.

It can't be. I'm too far north.

Howard opened his eyes. The shape had vanished. He released a shaky breath and glanced back at the shoreline. Time was wasting, and there was only one person who could help him: "Margarita" Marty Malone, his old mentor and Canada's top fishing guide three years running in the '80s. Howard fixed his eyes on Old Town Bait and Tackle, and thrust his paddle into the lake.

While the other houseboats were solidly built with state-of-the-art flotation, Marty's weathered shack teetered on old oil drums. The platform was littered with deck chairs and debris, including a pile of laundry, which had apparently blown off the line. Another gust, and it would be swept into the lake. Howard paddled faster and bumped his canoe against the platform. Just as he stretched out a hand to grab the clothes, they sat up. Grimy jeans, a rumpled Hawaiian shirt, and a stained windbreaker hung from the frame of a skinny, hatchet-faced man, his skin baked brown by the twenty-four-hour daylight of the northern summer. He straightened his mirror-lensed sunglasses and aimed them at Howard.

"Sorry," Howard said. "I was looking for Marty Malone."

"No refunds, pal."

The man yawned, revealing an uneven set of yellow teeth. Then he slapped a dirty lime green ball cap on his head; it read "Margarita Marty."

"Marty! It's great to see you again."

Marty stared at Howard.

"It's Howard Tuddy," he said.

Marty's face remained immobile, except for his eyebrows, which contracted in concentration.

"You saved my life. Lake Muskinongy. Summer of 1979."

Marty's eyebrows rose in recognition.

"Oh, yeah. Howie. You fell outta my canoe."

Howard trembled. The canoe in which he currently sat swayed as he remembered his descent toward the bottom of Lake Muskinongy, the water getting colder with every foot he dropped, the light from the surface growing ever dimmer.

"Sank like a stone," Marty said.

The canoe rocked.

"Who'd believe it with a build like yours?"

Howard clung, white-knuckled, to the platform. "Can I get out?"

"Sure. Whatever."

Howard heaved himself onto the deck and collapsed, twitching with panic.

"I know what you need. Follow me." Marty disappeared inside.

As soon as he stopped shaking, Howard secured the canoe and lurched after his host.

"How'd you find me?" Marty bustled around in semi-darkness. He'd removed his sunglasses, but the faded green hat remained upon his head.

"Through your website."

"Pretty snazzy, eh? Image counts in this business. Only way to 'reel' in customers, heh, heh."

"Business must be good, then." Howard stepped inside.

The room was an indoor junkyard. An unmade cot lolled in the far corner. Closer to the door squatted a well-worn couch and chair. A rough wooden counter with an aluminum sink ran along a side wall. The sink's silver belly dipped into open shelving below, where cans and boxes of food surrounded it.

Marty grabbed an ice pick, opened a battered propane-powered freezer and chiselled a chunk of ice from a block inside. He flipped it into the sink. Several more followed. Then he dumped the chunks into a blender, adding lime juice and tequila.

The sole sign of Marty's livelihood—paraphernalia for tying flies and making lures—was strewn across the coffee table. Howard poked a tuft of feathers sitting beside a pile of little gold hooks. Dislodging a hook, he noticed that everything was coated with dust. He picked up a fly and examined it. "If it hadn't been for the website, I wouldn't have found you. The Northwest Territories are a long way from Ontario."

"Ain't far enough, some days." Marty spooned sugar into the blender, leaving a trail of crystals across the counter.

"But Great Slave Lake is much bigger than Muskinongy. Guess it's full of monster fish."

"Guess so."

Howard's little toe began to prickle. He set down the lure, turned, and came face to face with glassy eyes and a long jaw lined with vicious teeth. Lures in a variety of shapes and sizes dangled from the creature's mouth. Howard stumbled backwards, knocking over the coffee table just as Marty pulled a ripcord on the blender. The clash and clatter of the blender resolved itself into a hum as the ice disintegrated. Marty cut the motor.

"Gas powered. Goes like stink. Same motor as those weed trimmer thingies. Got it for free, in return for promotional considerations on my TV show." He slopped green slush into two glasses. "They sold thousands when I was on the air. On a clear night you could hear those little motors buzzing all around Lake Muskinongy."

Howard righted the coffee table and gathered the hooks from the floor. *Margarita Marty's Good Fishin' Show* had only lasted two seasons, but Howard watched every week. "You always had a glass in your hand and that hat on your head," he said, moving a safe distance from the stuffed fish.

"My lucky hat. Was wearing it when I caught that guy." Marty gulped his green slush. He pressed a thumb to his forehead and winced.

"You okay?"

"Ice cream headache." Marty held out a glass for Howard, but he shook his head. "A bit early for me. Have any iced tea?"

After some rummaging, Marty presented Howard with a Mason jar containing amber liquid and a lump of ice. Howard plopped onto the couch, removed his left shoe and sock, and scratched ferociously. Marty slid into the easy chair.

"Need some medicated powder?" Marty searched underneath the chair's cushion. "Think I got some around here."

"It's my toe. Remember?" Howard held up his foot, a perfectly formed size six, except for the stump where the little toe should be. "It's the phantom itching I get whenever—"

Marty jerked upright. "But there's no muskie up here. Too far north."

"It's probably that guy." Howard flapped his sock at the monster mounted on the wall.

Marty relaxed. "Must be. Specially since he's the one who took your toe in the first place."

Howard had been ten years old the afternoon Charlie lured him to the lakeshore with promises of ice cream. The ice cream stand was next to the town dock, where Charlie wanted to fish. As Charlie stood casting, he encouraged Howard—who was preoccupied with his treat—to dangle his bare feet in the lake. In no time, Charlie had hooked a fish. Howard was drawing his foot from the water when something latched on and pulled so hard he'd almost been dragged into the lake. The pressure released; a cloud of red formed in the water and the pain registered. Just before he passed out, Howard heard a splash and an all-too-familiar rattle.

Sitting in Marty's shack, Howard inspected his mutilated foot.

"Gotta give yourself credit for pursuing the guy, after he did that to you," Marty said.

"If I wasn't able to catch the Rattler, I'm glad you were." Howard cast a nervous glance at the huge fish hanging on the wall. "You deserved it, after saving my life."

Marty wandered back to the blender and refilled his glass. "Some thanks I got from your father."

"He was just surprised anyone got me into a boat."

"He accused me of using you as muskie bait." Marty sloshed in extra tequila and stirred the concoction with his finger. "After I took you under my wing, taught you everything I know."

"And I'm grateful. You never gave up on me, even when you had to force me onto the lake."

Marty glanced sideways at Howard. "You ever remember what happened the time you fell in?"

"Just what you told me—I leaned too far out of your canoe. Ruined your chance of catching the Rattler."

"Should've been wearing a life jacket."

Howard frowned. "You said it would restrict my movements."

"The prize of Lake Muskinongy, big bounty on his head, just feet away. Catching him would have changed my life."

"Well, you did catch him—eventually. And it did change your life."

It was a couple of years after Howard's near-drowning that Marty caught the Rattler. The notoriety of landing the local version of the Loch Ness Monster and the twelve-thousand-dollar bounty—which he used to buy a decent motorboat—were all Marty needed to launch himself onto the professional fishing circuit.

Marty gulped his drink. "We didn't know that at the time. But did Charlie appreciate my efforts to get you onto the lake, make you a man? No, sir. He and his big city buddies at Muskinongy Lodge saw to it that my few guiding jobs dried up—almost finished my fishing career before it got started. Had to work in my brother's taxidermy shop to make ends meet. How is Charlie, by the way?"

"Dying."

"Oh."

Something in his own glass caught Howard's attention. He wiped his fingers on his pants and extracted a grey strip about three inches long. With a shriek, he flung the object from him. Marty picked it up.

"A minnow. Damn. I've been using the wrong ice again. One block is for drinks, the other block holds the frozen bait that I'm supposed to be selling. Think I can remember which is which?"

Howard set his iced tea on the floor.

Marty tossed the minnow through a window, into the lake. Moments later, an answering splash sounded from alongside the houseboat.

"Was that a fish?" Howard asked.

"Have to be a honking big fish to make a noise like that."

Marty knocked back his margarita. Howard's complexion turned the same green hue as the slush that disappeared down Marty's gullet.

"So there are a few minnows in the margaritas," Marty said. "Extra protein. Means I don't have to eat lunch. So if Daddy's dying, I can guess why you're here."

"It's the least I can do for him."

"You know there's no muskie this far north?"

Howard's foot twitched. "Since you caught the Rattler, there's not much point in going after muskie."

"True enough."

"A big fish is a big fish. Dad'll have to be satisfied with that."

Howard pulled a piece of paper from his back pocket and smoothed the folds. It was a website photo of a much-less-haggard Marty and another man, a satisfied client, holding up a huge lake trout. The fish was plump and goggle-eyed, cherubic compared to a muskie. Still, Howard shuddered. "They don't have much in the way of teeth, do they?"

"Never heard of anyone losing a toe to one."

"Great. Can we go out tomorrow?"

Marty shook his head. "No can do. I'm fully booked for the next couple of weeks, then it's freeze-up. It'll have to be next spring."

Howard gasped. "Dad won't make it to spring."

Marty shrugged.

Howard scratched at his missing toe and put on his sock. "Are you sure there's no way?"

For the first time since Howard arrived, Marty smiled. "Tell you what. For old time's sake, I'll cancel my existing gig, but you'll have to pay my cancellation fee for the other party."

"Of course."

"That's five hundred bucks, plus my regular fee of three hundred a day. You supply the boat and the lunch. Be here at five a.m. tomorrow. And bring cash."

*****

"You're twenty bucks short."

It was noon the following day. Marty was slouched on his sofa counting a pile of bills, his lucky hat pulled low over his eyes.

"I'll make it up. Apparently Earl has a twenty-dollar early morning pick-up charge he forgot to mention. Too bad you've been under the weather since five a.m. I could have stayed ashore until Earl's regular opening time and saved some money."

Marty waved toward a stack of fishing magazines. "Stayed ashore? What's the problem? You got caught up on your reading. By the way, I forgot to add the price of tackle. I only use Marty Malone lures on my expeditions. They're precision engineered. Expensive, but worth it. I'll add it to your tab." Marty stuffed the bills into a battered cookie tin, popped a couple aspirins into his mouth, and washed them down with the dregs of a margarita. He shoved a crumpled paper bag at Howard. It held a tangle of lures in all shapes and sizes. Howard pulled one out.

"Looks like a two-dollar lure from the hardware store."

"To the untrained eye. We'll fish in the bay today." Marty donned his sunglasses, shuffled outside, and sprawled in a lawn chair. As Howard disentangled a rod from a pile beside the front door, a faint buzzing reached their ears. Down the bay, not far from Earl's canoe rental shack, a little motorboat pulled away from shore. Marty watched it for a moment.

"So how do you make a living, Howie?"

"I'm the night clerk at a video store."

"Bet Charlie's thrilled about that."

"He's not the only one." Howard's lack of confidence left him ill suited for most workplaces—at the age of thirty-seven, he still lived in his parents' basement. If the measure of a man was the size of his trophy fish, as family tradition held to be true, Howard feared he could expect little from life.

He teetered on the edge of the platform, feet shoulder-width apart, knees bent. The lake water seemed glossier than usual, the languid waves almost viscous. "Does the water look funny to you?"

Marty leaned forward. "Yep. It's thickening up. Going to freeze soon."

"Then we better see what I remember." Howard flipped a metal gate on the reel, and whipped the rod toward the lake. The lure flew through the air.

"Not bad," Marty said.

The line snarled and the lure stopped short, flopping just above the water.

"Not great, either," his mentor added.

Howard untangled the line, reeled in the excess, then flipped the rod over his shoulder again. As he tossed it forward, there was a loud "snap" and Howard found himself staring at the bottom half of the rod. Turning, he found his line, lure, and the top half of the rod wrapped around a decaying snowmobile slumped beside the front door.

"That's another hundred bucks," Marty said. "That rod was a precision instrument."

The little motorboat approached. A man was standing in the stern shouting and shaking his fist.

Howard squinted. "Isn't he the guy off your website? The one holding up the big fish?"

Marty pulled his lucky hat lower on his face and sipped his drink, while Howard strained to hear over the outboard motor.

"Did he say something about fraud?"

"No—'frog.' Has no idea what kind of bait to use. Loser."

"But he caught that big fish."

"Stop wasting time. Remember your sick daddy."

Howard sorted through the rods for a new weapon. Re-armed, he cast again, the lure entering the lake with a satisfying plop. While he was retrieving, the rod dipped toward the water. Then it bent double. Wracked by the heebie-jeebies, Howard concentrated on his technique. His reward was the tell-tale clicking of a reel that had just engaged with a fish.

"It's huge!" He shuffled a victory dance. "It's a monster, it's the trophy fish to end all trophy fish, it's—"

"A rock." Marty whipped out a jack knife and cut the

line. Howard stumbled backwards, the lure-less end of his line fluttering in the breeze. Reluctantly attaching another piece of his expensive tackle, he resumed casting. The wind rose, riffling Howard's hair. It lifted Marty's hat and swept it into the lake.

"Damn!" Marty said.

The hat started to sink. Howard shot his lure toward it, hitting the water just beyond. Reeling slowly, he pulled up sharply just as the hook reached the hat. He snagged it.

"Nice set," Marty said as Howard retrieved the hat. When it was a few feet from the houseboat, the water around it started to boil. A huge, snake-like fish shot straight up from the lake, Marty's hat balanced between its jutting jaws. The jaws clamped shut, and with a twist of its head, the fish broke the line and carried its prize to the depths of Great Slave Lake.

"Muskie!" Howard shrieked.

"Oh, man. You lost my lucky hat!"

"Muskie!"

"Shut up. There-is-no-muskie."

Howard crumpled onto the deck. "He's a demon and he's going to pursue me to the ends of the earth."

"You still believe that fairytale? 'The Revenge of the Rattler'? Out there wreaking vengeance on those who've left a lure in his lip?"

"What about the chunk he took out of Frank Billingsley's hand? What about Old Man Warner's poodle? One minute it's taking a dip at the end of the dock, the next it's pulled under. Whoosh. Never to be seen again." Howard was becoming shrill. "What about my toe?"

"What about my hat, doofus? That and the blender were the only things I had left from my show."

The two men stared at each other.

"The Rattler is hanging on the wall inside," Marty said.

"Ever heard of reincarnation?"

"Get a grip."

"It's been stalking me since I got here."

"Lesson's over." Marty stomped into his house. The freezer banged open, and ice clanked into the sink.

Howard stuck his head in the door and watched Marty drain a bottle of tequila into the blender. "Can we go out on the lake tomorrow?"

His mentor stood with one hand on the blender, the other running over his hatless head.

"Marty?"

Marty pulled the cord and the blender roared. Howard waited, but Marty just kept crushing ice. Howard got into his canoe and paddled away.

*****

Over the next few days, Howard was unable to persuade Marty onto the deck of his houseboat—let alone the lake—without his lucky hat. If Howard was going to catch the big one, he'd have to resort to Plan B.

He'd heard Earl-from-the-canoe-shack talking about a path littered with fishing spots that led from Con Mine, on the edge of Yellowknife, down the shore of Great Slave Lake. Howard took a cab to the mine, found the trail, and followed it into the bush. After a few minutes of walking, he emerged onto the rock that bordered the lake—grey mounds of granite punctuated by beds of frothy lichen or stands of scrubby jack pine and yellowing birch. He found a nice little cliff and started casting, throwing his lure wide of the crust of ice forming along the shoreline. Meeting with no success, he continued on. Over a small rise, sitting on a sheet of rock that sloped into the lake, he found Earl fishing and sipping coffee.

"Mind if I join you?"

Earl shrugged.

"Any luck?" Howard asked.

Earl held up a couple of grayling.

"Wow—they're small," Howard said.

Earl shook his head. "You people are all alike. They're three pounds each. Absolutely the right size for grayling. *You* caught anything?"

"Nope, but I'm going after trout."

"So Marty tells me. Lotsa luck." Earl moved a few steps down the shore to a place where the bedrock dropped into the water.

Howard attached a lure to his line and started casting. After another unsuccessful half-hour, he paused to rub his numb hands. "Wow, this is weird. Usually fish won't leave me alone. Maybe there aren't any in this lake, after all."

"Some of us have no problem." Earl tilted his ear into the breeze. Moments later, Howard heard the putter of an outboard motor. A boat approached and Howard recognized the man from Marty's website, the one who'd passed the houseboat a few days earlier.

"Greedy swine," Earl said.

"He's not too happy with Marty."

"Him and a gazillion of Marty's former fans," Earl said. "I told you Marty appealed to a select group—the greedy and the shallow. That one's already caught his trophy fish, but he wants more."

"Lots of people catch more than one trophy fish."

Earl snorted. "Not as many as you'd think. And it ain't going to happen for this guy."

"Why not?"

"Because of the Cosmic Law of Fishing."

"Of course." Howard unzipped his jacket and stuck

his hands in his armpits. He rocked back and forth on his heels.

"You don't know what I'm talking about, do you?"

"Not exactly."

Earl leaned toward Howard. "The main principle of The Law is that the worse you want to catch a fish, the less likely you are to do it. Greed repels fish. Used to see it all the time with Marty's groupies. Thankfully, fewer are showing up as the years go by. Haven't seen a bloodsucker for ages. Present company excepted."

"Hey! I'm here for my father, not myself."

"If your cause is so noble, how come you can't catch anything? That in itself speaks volumes."

"Your luck seems to have run out, too."

"It's not me." Earl studied the water. "Something's spooked the grayling."

"Says you." Howard cast his lure into the lake. Something big and heavy grabbed it. "So much for your cosmic law," he gasped.

Howard cranked and cranked. A muscle throbbed in his temple, sweat gathered on his upper lip. The fish drew toward shore, then flipped its tail and flashed its white belly before speeding away, the line unwinding at rocket speed. When it slowed, Howard resumed reeling, beleaguered arms shaking, missing toe prickling.

He eventually pulled the fish up onto the rocky shore, but instead of the rounded body and dainty pout of a lake trout, there lay a sinister, serpentine shape. Howard screamed.

Earl moved closer. "Holy crap. That's got to be fifty pounds."

Howard dropped the rod.

The fish flopped toward the water. The rod caught on

a rock, the line snapped, and the fish disappeared into Great Slave Lake.

"I'll be damned." Earl sat down with a thump.

"M-m-muskie."

Earl shook his head. "That's a lake snake, a slough shark, a jackfish. Officially known as a Great Northern Pike, although I've yet to figure out what's so great about them. They're the muskie's idiot cousin. Whereas your muskie is a cunning fish, your jack is a thug. Your muskie is reclusive, your jack wears out his welcome. No wonder the grayling vamoosed."

Howard pulled off his boot and sock and raked at his toe. "But you saw it—Marty tried to pretend it wasn't there."

"That thing's been hanging around Marty?" Earl rubbed a hand over his face.

"Actually, it's been hanging around *me*."

Earl spotted Howard's foot. His eyes grew round. "You're the guy with the missing toe?"

"Marty told you about me?"

"Yeah. One night. But it was really the tequila talking." Earl stared at Howard's foot. "You gotta keep Marty off the lake. It's not safe."

"He lives on a houseboat."

"You know what I mean. No more fishing."

"But my father—"

"*Your* father? To hell with him." Earl slammed shut his tackle box, rose, and disappeared over the rock.

*****

The phone woke Howard in his hotel room the next morning.

"Dad is slipping," his mother said. "Come home."

"A couple more days."

"Sweetie, please. He needs to go to the hospital, but won't budge. He just sits in the family room and stares at Old Fred and the other fish on the wall."

And that big blank space. "One more try," he said.

Howard hurried down to the canoe shack, muttered an excuse to Earl, and headed for the lime green houseboat. When he arrived, Marty was asleep in a deck chair outside, a ratty sleeping bag pulled around him. An empty glass tilted in one hand; a fishing rod sagged in the other. Howard climbed out of the canoe and secured it to the platform. Marty stirred.

"Hey, Howie."

"Time we went fishing."

"I don't know, man." The rod and glass slipped to the deck. Howard pulled a wad of cash from his pocket. Marty sat up straighter.

"Brought you a new hat." Howard flashed a floures-cent green ball cap at Marty, the words "Old Town Bait and Tackle" emblazoned on the front. "There's not much I can do about your Margarita Marty hat, but I thought you'd like a memento of your current business."

Marty took the hat, examined it, and set it aside.

"And I have sandwiches," Howard added.

"What kind of sandwiches?" Marty struggled out of the chair. He was soon into a roast beef on whole wheat, while Howard packed the canoe with fishing gear, a cooler of margarita supplies, and Marty's blender.

"I'm the guide—I'll take the stern," Marty announced when the canoe was ready. He installed himself in the rear, blender between his feet, his new cap lying beside it.

They bobbed away from the houseboat community, a cold wind in their faces. Howard's toe was acting up; he kept an eye on the water, but they seemed to be travelling alone.

The waterfront homes off the School Draw slipped by, then the industrial buildings and houses of the Con Mine camp. The orange top of Con Mine's Robertson headframe soon receded and, with it, any signs of human occupation. They approached the mouth of Yellowknife Bay, where Great Slave Lake opened up: sky and water joined in blue nothingness, stretching into infinity. Marty directed Howard into the void, and told him to stay about a half-mile offshore. Panic formed in Howard's stomach; cold fear shot along his arms and legs. Then he remembered his mother's phone call, and he willed himself to keep moving: reach, dip, pull; reach, dip, pull.

The canoe felt heavy, like Howard was dragging it along on his own. Turning, he found Marty reclining and eating another sandwich. Howard rubbed his aching arms, sighed, and resumed paddling. After an eternity, Marty told him to stop.

"Give it a go here. It's nice and deep—fifty or sixty feet." Marty tossed him a diamond-shaped lump of metal. "Start jigging."

Fifty or sixty feet. Howard's head spun as he attached the lure to his line and let it fall deep into the lake. Just as Marty had taught him to do at Lake Muskinongy, he slowly and smoothly raised and lowered his fishing rod. Marty settled back and ate another sandwich. Soon he was snoring, the Old Town Bait and Tackle hat pulled over his face.

Howard continued jigging, willing all the big fish in the vicinity to come and get it. Staring into the water, he saw his father's face, grey and pinched from chemotherapy and continuous pain. Howard reeled in. He glanced at his watch. He looked toward the horizon. He picked the peeling paint off his precision-engineered Marty Malone lure. He frowned.

"Marty."

"Wah?"

"Can we try another spot?"

Marty settled lower in the boat. "No way, José. There's fish all over here."

"But they're not going for my lure. You want to try?"

Marty's lip curled. "I can only bring you to the fish. I can't catch them for you—that's cheating."

"That's not what I meant."

Marty groaned and sat up, pulling his new hat onto his head. "Oh, all right. Move over to those rocks along the shore."

Howard splashed toward a set of boulders cascading down an outcrop of rock and into the lake. Shadows prowled the boulders about twenty feet down. As Howard lowered his lure into the water, the fish congregated around it. Marty shifted, jerking the boat. The fish scattered. After a minute or two, they regrouped. As Marty dug in his cooler, one tapped Howard's lure. Howard held his breath. The tap became a tug. Howard snapped the rod upward just as Marty pulled the ripcord on the blender. The fish bolted. Howard clung to the swaying canoe, his breath coming in bursts around clenched teeth.

"Know why you're not catching fish?" Marty asked.

"Because you're making too much noise?"

"Nah—because you want it too bad. Why do you think you were such a muskie magnet in Ontario?"

"Because of the Cosmic Law of Fishing?"

"Exactly." Marty poured himself a margarita and set the blender jar back in its base, which now sat atop the cooler. "The fish sensed you were no threat. You wanted to avoid them, in fact. Our finny little friends have a perverse streak, and like to bite the lures of the reluctant for a bit of fun. Problem with an arch-predator like the muskie is that if they sense weakness, then *you* turn into the prey. End up losing a toe, your pet poodle, whatever. So you need to learn to relax without succumbing to your usual wimpy ways."

"That's quite an insight from someone who hasn't caught a fish in years." Howard turned to face Marty. "When was the last time you had a client? Because you weren't really booked when I showed up, were you?"

"What's it to you?"

"I'm not going to get what I came for, am I?"

Marty sneered. "You going to cut and run? Like you did after falling into Lake Muskinongy?"

Howard's foot twitched. "It's time to go home. Dad doesn't have long."

"You can't go back without a fish."

"I can't wait any longer. And I've nothing left to lose when it comes to my dad."

"We all got something left to lose."

The boat shook and silver flashed as a massive fish jumped. Howard jerked away, jarring the canoe. Marty's prized blender slid across the top of the cooler and followed the fish into the drink.

White-faced, Marty stared after the blender as it sank from view. "You freaking dork." He raised his gaze to Howard's face. "That was all I had left from the old days."

"It's not my fault! That fish won't leave me alone."

Marty yanked off the Old Town Bait and Tackle hat and flung it into the lake. "Howard the Coward. Maybe you should run back to Toronto."

*****

Early the next morning, Howard made his way to the Old Town for the last time. The temperature had plummeted overnight; frost rimed the grass and made the streets slick. Upon arriving at the canoe shack, Howard found that the cold had also transformed Yellowknife Bay into a field of ice, imprisoning each houseboat for the winter.

Earl was chopping at the shore ice with a paddle. “I should take this to your backside after the stunt you pulled yesterday. I told you the lake wasn’t safe for him. First his hat, now his blender.”

“It’s not like he was maimed for life.”

Earl stopped hacking. “That’s what you think. All you’re missing is a toe.”

“I’m sorry about the blender. I’ll buy him a new one.”

“You don’t understand the danger he’s in, do you? The minute I saw that mangled foot of yours and that big ugly fish, I knew it was time for Marty’s big payback. It’s the Cosmic Law of Fishing made manifest.”

Earl’s eyes took on a disconcerting gleam. He moved toward Howard.

“Fish are sensitive creatures,” he continued. “For centuries they’ve been a symbol of the human unconscious, our unacknowledged thoughts and feelings swimming just under the surface.”

“Okay.” Howard edged away.

Earl continued his slow march into Howard’s personal space, the volume of his tirade increasing with each step. “Usually the Cosmic Law of Fishing lacks menace—just a matter of not getting what you want. In extreme cases, though, the shadows of a man’s soul gather together, find a physical body, and literally pursue the victim.”

“Right.” Howard took another step backwards. He was standing on the edge of the lake.

“Leave Marty alone. He’s made some mistakes, but don’t you think he’s paid enough? What do you suppose is next?”

“Nothing’s next. I’m leaving on the five-thirty plane.”

Howard stepped onto the frozen expanse. "I'm just going to say goodbye."

"Stop!"

"Oh, for Pete's sake. Quit telling me what to do, and stop trying to spook me with all your big talk about the Cosmic Law of Fishing made manifest. I'm sick of it." Howard flapped a hand at Earl and kept going.

"I'm serious. Do not take another step toward that houseboat."

They both heard a dry tinkling sound, like glass shattering in slow motion. Cracks formed around Howard's feet.

"Oops," he said.

"Tried to tell you."

Howard turned and shuffled back to shore.

The wind had gone out of Earl. He stood with shoulders slumped, arms hanging, head turned toward Old Town Bait and Tackle. "I guess there's no avoiding this. Here's how you get to the houseboat." He slid a canoe onto the ice. "Put one knee in the boat. Push it along the ice with the other leg. If your free foot goes through the ice, it doesn't matter because most of you is in the canoe. Got it?"

Howard donned a life jacket and slid-shuffled the canoe across Yellowknife Bay, the ice crackling under him as he went. As he reached Old Town Bait and Tackle, Howard saw the black water of the open lake just a hundred feet beyond, lapping at the edge of the ice. Marty was asleep inside the shack; the stench of tequila pervaded the atmosphere. Previous experience had taught him that waking Marty was not a pleasant experience, so Howard found a fishing magazine and sat down.

The Rattler caught his eye from across the room. His foot twitched. After his father died, he'd probably never fish again. It was time to come to terms with his persecutor. He stood, toe tingling, and inched toward the Rattler. The row of lures beckoned; he ran a finger along them, foot afire with pins and needles. He tried to look into a glassy eye.

"Let's get something straight, buddy boy. You're dead and I'm not."

The burning in his foot eased. Howard regarded the fish. There was little light in the shack, so he lifted the Rattler off the wall and carried him into the fall sunshine. "If you think you can bully me by reincarnating yourself as some garden-variety jackfish and following me around, scaring me with your ugly mug, reminding me of my failures, stopping me from catching even one little fish, you are sadly mistaken." He ogled his adversary.

"What the hell are you doing?" Marty stood in the doorway behind him.

Howard jumped; the fish fell onto the platform of the houseboat and broke into three. The middle section, with the wooden mount still attached, bounced onto the ice a few feet from the houseboat, then skittered several yards toward the open lake.

"Marty, I am so sorry." Howard picked up a piece that rested at his feet.

He examined the edges of the taxidermied head, which had broken cleanly from the body. So cleanly that the edges were sharp. A decaying piece of duct tape clung to the inside edge. Howard found the tail section—same thing.

"This fish has been glued together," he said.

Marty's glare made the Rattler's expression look benign. Howard's foot was alight again. The memory of sinking in Lake Muskinongy washed over him: terror, paralysis, the certainty of his death. Then he remembered what happened right before he hit the water.

"You dumped me! You *were* using me as muskie bait."

"So what? Catching the Rattler and collecting the reward was the only way to launch my fishing career." Marty eased himself onto the frozen lake, the ice creaking. "I thought that if he went after you again, I could bonk him on the head and haul him in. How could I have known you'd sink like a stone, with all your blubber?"

"No wonder my father hated you."

"That's not why." Marty squinted up at Howard. "You think this guy's the first cut-and-paste job I ever did? When I worked in the taxidermy shop, I did plenty of 'special jobs' for Muskinongy's finest fishermen. Often glued together two or three fish to make one big one."

Howard's jaw dropped open. "Which finest fishermen?"

"All of them. And yes, some of my work is hanging on your parents' wall. No surprise, considering how competitive your father is." The ice groaned as Marty edged toward the piece of dismembered fish. "When I went for the whole enchilada and faked catching the Rattler, it really got up his nose—him and all the rest of them. But they couldn't say anything, or I'd bust them. Imagine the shame. *Persona non grata* for all time among his buddies at Muskinongy Lodge and the high-flyers of Toronto."

Howard frowned. "And Rattler never showed himself in all these years?"

"Of course he did. Two or three times. Couple of guys from the States said they saw him. Old Man Warner damn near landed him ten years ago. Each time it was chalked up to too much beer and an obsessive mind. Old coot never did get over the loss of that dog."

A breeze swept dead leaves from Jolliffe Island across the ice. Each one that rattled past carried a memory of Charlie's rants, his insults, the sacrifice of Howard's toe. Howard watched them scramble toward open water.

"Yep, Charlie and all the power brokers of Muskinongy Lodge had to keep my secret—they were such easy marks." A web of cracks materialized around Marty as he crept along the ice. "The bigger they are, the harder they fall."

The ice snapped and popped, cracks shooting out around him. Then it gave way and the lake swallowed him.

"Marty!"

Marty splashed up through the hole. He flung his arms onto the thin ice. The edge broke off and he sank again.

Howard clawed through the piles of fishing rods and assorted junk on the deck of the houseboat. He grabbed a sturdy rope and was about to slide onto the ice, when he spotted a grappling hook. Fingers shaking, he tied it to the rope.

Marty's head popped up. "He's got me!" He disappeared.

The ice groaned as Howard crawled to the hole. Marty's hands were thrashing four or five feet under the surface. Howard flung the hook toward the far side, let it sink, then pulled. As soon as the hook bumped against something, Howard jerked upward, then slid backwards, heaving as he went. He'd snagged Marty's collar, as it turned out, and his head soon reappeared. Onto the houseboat platform Howard climbed, yanking all the while.

Marty emerged from the water, half-crawled onto the ice, and lay still. Then an enormous jackfish shimmied onto the ice after him. The fish grabbed Marty's pant leg and tried to flop back to the hole. Howard tugged at the rope. The fish strained on his end. They remained at a stalemate for a full minute, then the fish let go. One splash and it disappeared into the murk of the bay. Howard inched Marty across the ice and hauled him onto the deck and inside the shack, where he stripped off Marty's wet clothes, wrapped him in a blanket, and stoked up the wood stove.

Marty's teeth finally stopped chattering. "Didn't know you could ice-fish."

"Me neither."

"Now you know the Rattler's still around, you could hit Lake Muskinongy in winter. Once the ice is good and thick, you won't have to worry about falling in."

Howard re-examined the head of the stuffed fish. "I've always wondered—what happened to your show?"

"You think that guy out there's the first to start tailing me? Didn't matter which lake I went on, some big, ugly monster would show up and scare away the other fish. Went as far from Muskinongy as I could and I'm still not free. Might be no muskie up here, but the cosmos has found a substitute—my retribution's been off-loaded onto a pike, the village idiot of the fishing world." Marty shook his head. "Any dimwit can catch one of those, so you can't make a career out of that."

"The Cosmic Law of Fishing." Howard ran his finger along the lures in the fish's mouth. His foot no longer itched. He shook it—there wasn't a twinge. "How much do you weigh?"

"About one-fifty."

"Beats any of my dad's catches," he said.

Howard gathered the pieces of the stuffed fish, put them in the canoe, and slid-shuffled to the hole in the lake. He threw in the pieces and waited until they sank. Then he continued toward shore.

Leaving Yellowknife

Angela kicked the deflated front tire of her 1986 Grand Am. Then she kicked it again.

"Bloody stupid idiotic imbecilic useless piece of—"

Her commentary choked off in a shriek as a semi rattled by on the gravel highway, well soaked from the melting snow of the northern spring. The truck produced a mist of mud that settled on both her and the Grand Am. Her beautiful red sports car was already beyond hope, coated with a layer of filth accumulated from an hour's trek south from Yellowknife. Her hand automatically brushed at the grime on the sleeve of her suede jacket, but instead of sweeping it away, only ground it in deeper. She flapped her arms in frustration.

It figured. It bloody figured.

Angela reached into the vehicle and pulled the keys from the ignition, slammed the door, and marched around to the back, her high-heeled boots squishing and sliding in the mud of the highway shoulder. She opened the trunk and stared inside at the cardboard boxes and plastic bags that held half her worldly possessions—the other half being crammed inside the car, rising above the top of the back seat and spilling off the front passenger seat onto the floor. With staccato movements, she yanked the boxes and bags from the trunk and stacked them in the mud as she excavated her way to the chamber that held the spare tire.

She should have known her getaway from Yellowknife would not be easy. She should have realized that the North would make the most of the last few hours it held her in its clutches, taunting and toying with her, holding the possibility of escape before her—tantalizingly close—then snatching it away. Well ha, ha, she was on the road out and nothing was going to stop her. The flat tire would cost her an hour, maybe two, but she had more than enough time to make it to the ice crossing at Fort Providence before it closed for the season.

As she heaved aside her belongings, Angela had to admit that she should have been better prepared. If she'd had time to think, she would have foreseen that she'd get a flat on this, one of the Northwest Territories' prehistoric "highways," and would have strapped the spare tire to the car's roof, like the more cautious tourists who ventured up this godforsaken road. She would have foreseen it because the same thing had happened when she drove up two years earlier.

*****

Then it had been high summer. She'd started in southern Saskatchewan, travelling up to Saskatoon. There she picked up the Yellowhead Highway and followed it northwest, beyond Edmonton. A quick right turn onto the Mackenzie Highway, and she was headed straight north. In Alberta, the highway had been a dream: smooth blacktop, little traffic. She and her beautiful red car had cruised along for hours. Then they'd hit the 60th parallel, Alberta's border with the N.W.T., and the highway degenerated into a goat trail. Fifty or sixty miles in, a side road offered the respite of the towns of Enterprise and Hay River, but on the main road itself there was no sign of human habitation, just two lanes of dirt cutting through the northern bush. There was a blip of humanity at the Mackenzie River, where a ferry carried vehicles across to meet up with the road on the far shore in the summer, and an ice road connected the highway in the winter. The access road for the community of Fort Providence flashed past, then nothing for three hours as the "highway" curved west and north around Great Slave Lake.

The whump-whump-whump of a flat tire started at some point after she passed Fort Providence. She should have taken it as a sign of things to come that she'd not been lucky enough to break down in a "dust-free passing zone"—sporadically spaced stretches of road where the Department of Transportation sprinkled calcium chloride to keep the dust under control. This allowed people who had actual lives to lead to pass the vehicles that dawdled—usually geriatric tourists in motorhomes or penniless university grads crawling north in some beater of a car to make their fortune.

She'd had to chew dust for an hour until a Native couple stopped to help her. The man had given the Grand Am the once-over before setting to work. "Nice car."

"Thanks." Angela frowned as the couple's dog, a beast of undetermined breed and doubtful hygiene, sniffed around the vehicle. With one eye on the animal, Angela admired her car for the umpteenth time: the sweep of the hood, the curve of the windshield and the sleek line of the roof that dropped sharply, framing the little opera windows at the back seat, then dropped again to form the chunky little trunk. Sporty, but reminiscent of a luxury car. Perfect for someone like her—a hip up-and-comer who would someday be in a position of prestige. She reached forward and patted the hood.

"It's a couple of years old, but the '86s have such an elegant look," she said.

"Very elegant," said the man's wife.

The dog stopped beside the front tire and lifted a leg.

Angela narrowed her eyes. "Don't even think about it."

The dog paused, then lowered its leg and wandered off. The woman handed Angela a can of pop she'd extracted from a cooler. "A vehicle like that's not very practical for the North. You'll have to drive more slowly. This road can do some serious damage."

Angela glanced at their half-ton, with its chipped and pitted paint, the windshield criss-crossed with cracks. Clearly, this woman had no business giving Angela advice. She peered at the proffered can of pop and shook her head. "I only drink diet."

The woman shrugged, wiped the top with the sleeve of her sweatshirt, and popped it open.

"Just saying."

As Angela gave the woman a tight smile, the scruffy dog ambled up to her, gave her shoes a thorough sniff, then leaned against her, covering the leg of her designer jeans with hair, dust, and dandruff. As she tried to brush away the mess, Angela looked up to find the Native woman hiding a grin behind her can of pop.

"Almost done?" Angela called to the husband.

It was well and good to tell Angela to drive slowly, but it had been the road itself that had creeped her out, forcing her foot down, down, down on the gas pedal. Ruts and soft spots littered the road like land mines, waiting to roll Angela and her car into the ditch, leaving her as roadkill and her vehicle a scrap heap. The farther they travelled, the scrawnier the trees became, and the more bent and gnarled. All would be well if she could just get to Yellowknife, she'd told herself, her foot drilling down on the accelerator. She dodged slower vehicles, whether she was in a dust-free passing zone or not, and refused to slow down and pull onto the shoulder when semis rumbled toward her, creating dust storms of Saharan proportions. It was not until a rock from one of those trucks hit her windshield and left a huge crack that she realized the Native woman had been right—her beloved car could sustain permanent damage if she didn't ease up. As her beleaguered vehicle bumped and jolted along the highway, Angela had promised herself everything would be better once she got to Yellowknife, capital city of the Northwest Territories, seat of government, home to industry. Civilization.

Ha.

*****

Angela took a break from the task of unpacking her trunk to brush aside her bangs, damp from her exertion in the spring sun. She removed her jacket and placed it on the pile of boxes. She checked her new silk shirt—sweat stains were forming under her arms. Damn it. She shouldn't have put on nice clothes until she was well clear of the N.W.T. border, but she'd been so excited at the prospect of rejoining the real world—the one where culture and style actually mattered—that she just couldn't help herself.

As she opened the compartment that held the spare tire, Angela held her breath. Fact was, she'd left Yellowknife in such a rush that she'd forgotten to check the air pressure in the spare. She peeked in. It looked okay. She pressed it with a forefinger. It had more give than made her comfortable, but it would have to do. She needed to get to the Mackenzie River crossing and she needed to get there before noon tomorrow, when the ice road was due to close.

Twice a year, during freeze-up in the fall and break-up in the spring, Yellowknife was inaccessible by road for several weeks. For those who wanted to get in or out—and either couldn't afford to fly, or didn't want to—it put a definite kink into travel plans. How ironic that she'd frozen her butt during two endless northern winters but now that she wanted the cold—*needed* the cold—to escape, the weather decided to be cheerful. In this heat, the ice road would quickly disintegrate into slush and deep ruts. Semis could still make it over, but vehicles with low clearance, like her car, would become mired.

She was trying to loosen the wheel that held the flat, struggling with both the tire iron and the challenge of kneeling in a tight skirt, when a chopping noise, reminiscent of a sewing machine in need of a lube job, caught her attention. She straightened to find a little orange hatchback approaching from the direction of the ice crossing. Angela recognized it as the very type of tin can on wheels she had sped past on her trip north two years earlier. The car was dented and rusty, outrigged with a couple of spare tires and jerry cans galore. The driver was cautious, methodical. The tin can slowed and pulled over.

The man who emerged was young and good-looking in a long-haired, blue-jeaned sort of way. Angela hoped he could change a tire faster than he drove.

The man treated himself to a leisurely stretch, then leaned on the open door of his car and regarded Angela. She gave him a well-practised smile, and waited for the inevitable. Seconds later, a large, mud-coloured mutt scrambled out and followed his friend's lead in stretching the kinks from his body—first by stiffening his forelegs and pushing his butt into the air, then heaving forward and stretching his hind legs. He made a beeline for Angela and sniffed the hem of her skirt. The man ambled over.

"Need some help?"

"You're very kind." Angela handed him the tire iron, while discreetly kicking away the dog. "Moving north?"

"For the summer. How'd you know?"

Angela glanced at the dog. "Just a guess. They must issue those at the border."

"Pardon?"

"Dogs. Everyone in the North seems to have one."

"Makes sense. I hear northerners are good people. And dogs are good people."

The animal returned and continued his investigation of Angela's skirt.

"He likes you." The man nodded in approval and squatted to assess the flat.

Angela hiked up her skirt and kneed the dog in the chest. He skittered away. Only a few more hours, she promised herself, and she'd be free of mud and latter-day hippies, but mostly she'd be free of dogs, dogs, dogs. She closed her eyes and felt the sun on her face. She thought about her new job. Her dream job. Waiting down in southern Manitoba.

The young man loosened the lug nuts and removed the flat, then retrieved the spare tire from the trunk. He held it upright and dropped it on the ground. It didn't bounce.

"You can't drive on this."

"Oh yes I can. I have to keep moving—the ice crossing is going to close at noon tomorrow."

He set the spare on the edge of the trunk and traced a finger over the treads. "Actually, the ice road's going to close in just a few hours."

Angela felt the blood drain from her head and pool somewhere around her ankles. It was only her form-fitting fashion boots that kept it from collecting in her feet. "Then get a move on."

"Here's the problem." The man picked at something with his fingernail. "There's a little screw embedded."

"Well don't—"

"Oops."

The screw flew out, followed by a wheeze of escaping air. Angela sprinted after the tiny piece of hardware, only to see the dog move into her path at the last minute.

When she came to, she was sitting in the mud with her back propped against the rear wheel of her car. The dog licked her face as the young man slapped her hand with increasing violence.

"Stop that." She pulled her hand free and used it to push aside the dog.

"Wow. You went down like a sack of potatoes. My dog found the screw, though. I should be able to stick it back in and plug the hole. You rest here, I'm going to get the air compressor to reinflate that tire."

Angela touched the side of her face. The skin was raw and smeared with mud. The world twirled around her. "Where? Fort Providence?"

"No—my car. Compressor's portable—just plug it into the lighter socket." He paused. "You smell that?"

Angela sniffed. "Unwashed dog? Burnt toast?"

"No. Gasoline."

Angela dropped her head into her hands and willed the twirling to stop.

*****

Her decision to move north had been sheer desperation. Eight months out of journalism school, and she'd been unable to get a job. None of her classmates had had trouble: all were employed, one had already been promoted. And then there was Tanya Armbruster—she of the bad haircut and tragic fashion choices—who was working for national TV news, of all things. Angela had to swallow a black lump of jealousy every time she saw Tanya file a report from yet another exotic clime. But Angela's time was coming. She'd spend hours in front of the bathroom mirror: "From Cairo, this is Angela Binnie reporting. In Helsinki, I'm Angela Binnie."

Newspapers were well down on her list of employment options, given their lack of a glamour quotient. But *The Yellowknife Weekly Spectator* had been the only place to respond to the flood of résumés she'd sent out. When the job offer had come, she'd convinced herself Yellowknife wouldn't be so bad. The city had amenities: a pool, a cultural centre, the territorial museum. A few months in the boonies, and she'd parlay the experience into something bigger and better in the real world.

If her trip up the highway had not taught her to heed her instinct to flee, her first day at the newspaper should have. She'd been told to report at nine o'clock sharp, to get her marching orders from Ramona, the news editor. After spending the night in an over-priced and under-clean hotel, she was informed by the front desk clerk that the newspaper office was located in the far end of town. She hopped in her car and navigated the streets of downtown Yellowknife.

The town was hardly an architectural splendour. Except for a tatty hotel and couple of ten-storey office towers, few of the buildings were higher than two or three floors. For some incomprehensible reason, many were faced with the type of gaudy faux stonework that was popular for suburban rec rooms in the early '70s. Fred Flintstone would have loved the place; it made Angela cringe.

Okay, okay, she told herself. Maybe it's not London or New York, or even Saskatoon, but you're here now and you're going to make the best of it—absolutely *soak* up the local colour. She rolled down her window to expedite the soaking-up process.

She made her way down the main street, out of downtown, past a ballpark and the CBC building (also faced with some unfortunate stonework), past a trailer park and the city's sole suburb, before lurching down a bumpy little road into the "industrial" area. Judging from the businesses that sprawled alongside, Yellowknife's main industries were totalling vehicles and growing weeds. She went around a bend and pulled up short, partly because the road ended abruptly and partly because of the stench.

On her left was a tract of bald earth, surrounded by a chain-link fence. Inside were three rows of wooden boxes that looked like upturned apple crates. Staked beside each were the skinniest, ugliest hell hounds Angela had ever seen. Straw, faeces, half-devoured fish, and metal bowls were scattered everywhere. There were probably thirty dogs in total, and they were all staring at Angela. She rolled up her window.

She must have missed the newspaper office on her first pass. She consulted her directions. She glanced up at the small industrial trailer sitting behind the rows of dog boxes. Sure enough, there was a small sign beside the door: *The Yellowknife Weekly Spectator*. Angela groaned and swung her vehicle around. Her foot hovered over the accelerator—it was only nine-hundred and forty-seven miles back to Edmonton, after all. The image of Tanya Armbruster cavorting around Lisbon and Madrid, bad hair and all, floated before her eyes. She parked.

"Show time," she muttered.

Sixty dog eyes watched as she strode over to the gate, located in the centre of the fence. Her hand reached for the latch; the moment it made contact, pandemonium erupted.

The dogs jumped and strained on their ropes. Some struggled in her direction, others ran circles around their stakes. In the far corner, two beasts lunged at each other. Their ropes were short enough to keep them apart and prevent the fight they clearly wanted to start. The noise almost brought Angela to her knees—a racket of howling and screeching so sharp it would send a banshee scurrying for ear plugs.

The trailer door popped open as Angela was backing away. A dumpy woman with grey curls beckoned. Angela shook her head. The woman gestured with added animation. Angela returned to the gate and opened it. The dogs upped the frenzy a notch.

Hands over her ears, she tiptoed down a path that led between the doghouses. One of the creatures pitched itself at her; she jumped away only to be butted on the other side. The woman in the doorway made a vertical movement with her hand. Angela realized that if she stayed in the exact middle of the path, none of the dogs could reach her. She sprinted the last few feet and dove inside. The woman swung the door shut.

"Not bad for your first time," she said. "I'm Doreen."

Angela stood, one hand braced against the reception counter, the other plastered to her pounding chest.

"That the only way in?"

"Yep."

"Are they always like that?"

"With everyone but Ramona."

"What about clients? Advertisers? Interviewees?"

Doreen shrugged. "Most phone their stuff in. We're kind off the beaten, anyway."

"No kidding."

"Guess you're the new reporter."

"Afraid so."

As Angela straightened up, she noticed a strip of something translucent shining on the hip of her brand-new skirt. She twisted around.

"Oh, gross—dog snot. Give me something. Quick, quick!"

Doreen pulled a rumpled tissue from the pocket of her polyester pants and handed it over. Angela hesitated only a second before grabbing it and swiping at the trail of slime.

"You got worse things to worry about." Doreen stared at Angela's designer pumps. "Looks like you stepped on a land mine."

Following Doreen's directions, Angela hot-footed it to the washroom, located on the left side of the trailer. The dog doody cleaned from her shoe, she re-entered the office and assessed her surroundings.

Right next to the washroom was a kitchenette. Directly in front of her were a typesetting computer and large drafting table, used for pasting together the pages of the *Weekly Spectator*. Strips of news copy, black and white photos, and ad proofs were clothes-pinned to strings looping down from the ceiling. Beyond that, right beside the door, was Doreen's reception counter and chair, both raised so that she was at eye-level with anyone foolish enough to come in to do business. The other half of the trailer was demarcated by a battered metal desk that was now Angela's, and some dented filing cabinets. At the far end was Ramona's tiny office, barricaded from the rest of the trailer by a pre-fab wall and flimsy door.

"Ramona's going to be late," Doreen announced. "You're to read the newspaper until she gets here."

Angela settled at her desk with a copy of the *Weekly Spectator*. Doreen, perched directly across, studied the new recruit's well-coiffed shoulder-length hair and silk blouse. Angela raised the newspaper before her face like a shield.

"Last one only stayed two weeks, you know."

Angela lowered a corner of the paper. "Pardon?"

"The last reporter. Thought she was too good for us. Got a better job down south, so off she went."

"Ya, well. You can count on me sticking around."

"No one down south wants to hire you, eh?"

"No!" Angela dropped her arms, the newspaper crumpling onto the desk. "I just thought Yellowknife would be interesting. An adventure."

Doreen snorted. Angela raised the newspaper back into place. Doreen started shuffling papers and tapping on an adding machine.

By nine forty-five Angela had read three weeks' worth of newspapers, twice. She paced to a window and contemplated the skinny, leggy dogs sprawled in the yard. They had surprisingly short coats—hardly enough hair to fluff up with a shampoo and blow-dry. Not that it would improve their looks.

"Aren't sled dogs supposed to be furry? And sturdy?"

Doreen looked up from her work. "You're thinking of the endurance dogs they got in the Eastern Arctic. These are sprinters."

"Oh."

The beasts seemed to be asleep. Maybe a walk was in order. Angela tiptoed to the door and opened it. All thirty animals snapped to attention, their gaze trained on her. She slammed the door and leaned against it.

"It's a freaking siege," she said. "How do we get food?"

"I'm ordering in," Doreen said. "The Fried Chicken Palace delivers."

"Oh, boy."

Doreen was lunching in the kitchenette and Angela

was trying to copy a hair style from a movie magazine when a thin woman sporting scruffy coveralls and a bad perm strolled in. A mangy dog and the scent of stale wine followed in her wake.

Angela, seated behind her desk and holding a hank of hair, glanced at the woman. “Apparently you failed to notice that dogs stay outside.” She turned back to her magazine. “The receptionist will be here in a minute to take your classified ad or whatever.”

The animal, clearly in its dotage, hobbled toward Angela.

“Get away,” she hissed.

The dog came closer, and placed its head in Angela’s lap. With a squeal, she abandoned her styling session and turned to the woman to protest. The woman simply raised her severely plucked eyebrows. Angela’s head snapped toward the window. She’d just realized that the woman’s arrival had not provoked the least reaction among the dogs in the yard.

Doreen returned, sucking chicken grease off her plump fingers.

“See you’ve met Ramona. And Wilbur.”

Wilbur’s nose drilled into Angela’s lap. Her hands shook with the effort required to curb the urge to slap him.

“My former lead dog. Now retired. Who has the run of the newspaper office in return for services rendered.” Ramona snapped up the movie magazine. “Unlike you, who have rendered no service whatsoever. Follow me.”

Ramona strolled toward her office. Angela gave her a head start, then smacked Wilbur on the nose. “Fresh!”

The dog squinted at her. Angela rose and followed Ramona.

*****

"It's over, it's over. It's all in the past," Angela told herself as she sat in the mud beside her car. Her head was clearing. Someday this would all be colourful fodder for her memoirs, but right now she wanted plenty of space between herself and Yellowknife. The nice young man would soon have her on the road.

"Uh-oh." The nice man should have been tightening the spare, but was peering underneath the car instead.

Angela groaned. The dizziness returned. "Now what?"

"I was right about smelling gas. Your tank is punctured."

"But I can still drive it, right?" Angela glanced at the orange hatchback and the row of jerry cans fastened to the roof. "You can sell me some gas. I can still make it to Fort Providence."

The guy contemplated the patch of fuel spreading across the wet mud. "Doubt it. Hole's too big."

Angela thumped a heel onto the wet ground. "It's not fair! How come a junker like yours can make it over this bloody road, but *my* car breaks down?"

"Pays to take precautions—I have a rubber bath mat strapped over the bottom of the gas tank so the rocks will bounce off."

"Of course you do."

The man nodded at the polar-bear-shaped licence plate on her car. "If you live in the North, you should know that." He stood and wiped his hands on his jeans. "There's no point in staying here. Hop in. I'll take you to Yellowknife."

"No, no—I'm heading the other way."

"We're closer to Yellowknife. You don't want your car towed too far over this road—it'll damage the frame, the paint."

Angela staggered to her feet. “Not going back.”

“I can’t leave you here. You might have a concussion.” He tried to catch her elbow. Angela dodged. The dog danced over and jumped at her. She kneed it in the chest, hard this time. The dog yelped.

“Hey! No need for that.”

The man moved toward her again. Angela picked up the tire iron and swung it.

“Get out of here. Scoot. Shoo. And your little dog, too.”

The man crossed to his vehicle, and ushered the dog inside. He stared over at Angela, then got in, shut the door, and started the engine. The car chugged along the shoulder until it reached cruising speed, then pulled out onto the road.

Angela re-packed the trunk, scraping mud from the bottom of the boxes and bags with a rock, and with tissues from a packet that quickly ran out. She heaved shut the trunk and flopped against vehicle. There was no sign of life on the road for a good half-hour, then a distant rumble announced the approach of an older-model, baby blue half-ton. Angela stuck out her thumb.

The mud-splattered truck slowed, rolled past, and pulled onto the shoulder. A large woman clad in jeans and a plaid shirt got out, her work boots making sucking sounds in the mud as she approached. She stopped a few feet off and scrutinized the dirt-encrusted Angela.

“Whoa, girlie. What happened to you?”

“Flat. And a punctured gas tank. I need to get to Fort Providence.”

The woman shook her head. “This time of year, the garage in Fort P. is going to be over-loaded. And they might not have the right parts. You should go back to Yellowknife.”

The ache in Angela's head tightened into a knot. She faced the woman squarely, fists at her sides, jaw set. "Trust me lady, you don't want to have *that* conversation with me."

The woman shrugged. "Whatever. I'm heading to Fort Providence for a surveying job. You can catch a lift."

Angela relaxed, sucking in a great stream of air. "Thank you."

After grabbing her purse and jacket, she locked up her car. She opened the passenger side door of the truck and hoisted herself toward the seat, but paused halfway, her butt suspended in mid-air. Although the truck's exterior was dent-free and smooth, the interior was a shambles. The vinyl bench of the front seat had been slashed in several places. Angela was afraid she'd snag her skirt.

"Oh right—just a second." The big woman rummaged in the back seat until she found a newspaper. "Don't want you getting mud all over my truck." As the woman spread the newspaper on the passenger seat, Angela's photo was unmistakeable. It was a mug shot, positioned next to a column called "The Dog Sled Report." A nanosecond's hesitation, and Angela planted her muddy butt precisely on the photo.

The woman studied Angela's face. "You might want to do something about . . . um . . ." She wiggled her fingers beside her own face. Popping open the glove compartment, she sifted through the debris within until she located a packet containing a wet towelette, which bore the logo of Yellowknife's Fried Chicken Palace. She presented it to Angela, then twisted the rear-view mirror toward her passenger.

Angela gasped. Not only was the side of her face scraped and bleeding from her fall, a massive bruise was forming underneath the red archipelago of wounds. As she wiped away the dirt, though, the bright light of the midday sun revealed something more alarming: lines forming at the corners of her eyes. Two northern winters and she was already damaged. She twisted the mirror back into place.

"Let's get the hell out of here," she said.

As they drove off, Angela turned and gazed over her left shoulder at her vehicle. Huddled by the side of the road, it looked forlorn. When she'd been in journalism school, she'd been told to dress and act like she already had her dream job because it would help potential employers visualize her in the role. Her car was an extension of that thinking. But then she'd brought it here, and every day its beauty—its *élan*—was buried deeper and deeper by the grime and detritus of its surroundings. She watched until it disappeared from view.

As Angela turned to face front, she realized that on the back of the seat, on her other side, rested the head of a particularly hideous dog. It shifted closer and placed its head on her shoulder. Angela froze.

"That's Hubcap. He's harmless. Well, as long as he's happy. Left him in the truck one night, and see what he did to the upholstery." The driver pointed to the gashes in the front seat. "I'm Marge. You know, if you're going to drive that kind of princess car on northern highways, you should strap a rubber bath mat over the gas tank."

"So I'm told."

"You leaving Yellowknife?"

"How'd you know?"

"Well, first, your car's riding low. Probably got everything you own in there. Second, you got that look in your eye. Desperate. But you'll be back."

"Why?"

Marge laughed. "Desperate ones always come back. Have to."

Angela shuddered. Ramona had pretty much said the same thing when she'd resigned two days earlier.

*****

If Angela's first day at the newspaper was a disappointment, things did not improve over her two-year tenure. The *Weekly Spectator* was, in her opinion, little more than an advertising rag. She was expected to dig up her own stories, but only after she'd completed Ramona's weekly list of community-friendly features. This included a column called "The Dog Sled Report," an update of the goings-on of the local dog racing community.

Ramona had fended off Angela's objections. "Best way for you to get exposure in this town. Everyone reads it."

Not only did everyone read it, everyone had an opinion about it. The paper was published Thursday morning. By noon, Doreen would have littered Angela's desk with phone messages.

"If I were you, I'd call Mary Tremblay first," Doreen would say. "She wants you to write a personality profile of her lead dog, Henry."

Angela would roll her eyes. "No wonder everyone calls us 'The Yellowknife Weekly *Spectacle*.'"

"Then call Archie Beasley. He has a collection of Native dog blankets you should photograph."

"Hardly sounds newsworthy."

Doreen planted her hands on her hips and struck a pose. "Oh, I forgot. You're the big journalism school grad. Always looking for the investigative angle. I'll have you know Archie's grandmother beaded those blankets. She was a master."

Angela picked up the phone. "I'm going to call the SPCA. Mushers keep their dogs on pretty short chains. Seems cruel."

"Good idea. While you're waiting to get through to the SPCA, think about how you're going to write a weekly column if no one ever talks to you again. Because they won't, even if you could convince Ramona to publish it."

Angela hung up the phone.

The best thing about the column was that her photo ran beside it every week. The worst part was gathering the information in the first place. The smell of the average dog lot was not so bad in the winter, but the cold brought its own challenges. Ink froze at minus thirty, so she had to keep a supply of sharpened pencils in her parka pockets. Taking photos was a feat of coordination and timing—she'd only have a few seconds to whip off her mitts, then frame and shoot a publishable photo, before her fingers became so stiff she could no longer use them. Even that brief exposure meant that she'd have to endure the hot throb and stabbing pain of frostbite as they thawed. As for the dogs themselves—well, really.

Angela's subjects did not return her antipathy; indeed, the dogs couldn't keep themselves away from her. Paw prints covered every one of her jackets, including her designer parka, a pretty crimson number with silver fox fur trimming the hood. Careful as she was, dog hair clung to every garment she owned.

For the first few months, she raced through writing "The Dog Sled Report" so she could get onto better things, but she soon discovered there were no better things. The need to fill blank pages forced her to do a full-page feature on Archie Beasley and his dog blankets, and other stories she preferred not to think about.

The months rolled by and she became depressed by her inability to build up a decent portfolio of news stories. How was she going to parlay her experience into a future in southern Canada if she wasn't getting any experience? And yet, escape was essential. To cheer herself, she'd walk through her apartment, sizing up her belongings and mentally packing her vehicle so she'd be prepared to flee in record time. For two years she waited, and when the call came, it almost came too late.

"I need you here in a week," the man had said. He owned a small television station in southern Manitoba and his news anchor had walked out. "Fourth one I've lost in a year."

Angela was elated. The blue suit—that's what she'd wear for her first broadcast. She'd bought it right before she'd moved north, but it was still in style. And she'd need a haircut.

"I'll leave immediately, no problem."

"You want this job, you'd better. *I'm* reading the suppertime news right now, and no way I'm doing that for more than a week."

"Oh, damn—I'll have to check on the ice road," Angela'd said. "It might be closed."

"Ice road? You mean you can only drive around up there in the winter? What kind of godforsaken place you in?"

"Well may you ask." Angela kept her tone light, but found that the question irked her. What was her problem? After all, she'd been just as surprised to find out about the ice crossing a couple of years earlier. "It's not all our roads—just a patch at the Mackenzie River. If it's closed already, I'll have to wait until the ferry starts running."

"When's that?"

"Mid-May."

"Mid-May! You journalism grads think the world revolves around you and your grand talent. You're here in a week, or not at all. Your résumé wasn't quite at the bottom of the pile."

Angela's vision of her blue suit behind a TV news desk started to slip away. "I'm sure the crossing is still open. I can leave in two days."

*****

"I knew you'd bail as soon as you could." Doreen had walked into Ramona's office as Angela was in the process of resigning.

"I've been here two years!"

Ramona didn't shift her gaze from the page layout she was proofreading. "You'll be back."

"I hardly think so."

Ramona removed her bifocals and looked Angela in the eye. "I've been reading your news copy for two years. Last week you did an 'interview' with Mary Tremblay's lead dog. Not many markets that will tolerate that."

"It was the April Fool's Day issue."

"You're not helping our image as the 'Weekly Spectacle.'" Ramona returned her glasses to her nose and resumed work. "Develop some news sense."

"Need some news to be sensible about," Angela muttered as she went to clean out her desk.

Angela had to pay a month's rent in lieu of notice. True to her word, she was on the road in two days.

*****

"I really liked your photo-feature on Archie Beasley's dog blankets," Marge said.

Between the danger the truck's cracked seat posed to her skirt and the one the hideous dog posed to her jugular, Angela tried to sit as still as possible. This was difficult, considering the poor state of both the road and the truck's shocks. Every time they hit a bump or rut, the dog's head bounced on her shoulder, resulting in a growing patch of drool on her jacket and a boost in the drum solo playing in her head.

"Thanks. They were nice."

"Nice? Those things belong in a museum, with all that beading of Granny Beasley's." Marge looked over at her. "Why are you going south?"

"Greener pastures. Bigger stories."

Marge snorted and popped in a country and western tape. Angela's headache soared and dipped along with the singer's wail of loss and abandonment. She closed her eyes and willed the clouds to come out in the sky, a cold front to sweep down from the North Pole, anything to keep the ice crossing from melting.

They eventually passed the turn-off to Fort Providence and continued toward the Mackenzie River. Just short of the shore, they pulled into the parking lot of a restaurant/service station/motel complex. The ice crossing was farther down the river, out of sight, but Angela was relieved to see a variety of vehicles in the parking lot. Traffic was still coming and going.

"Well, here we are," Marge said. "I'm heading to the coffee shop. Join me when you get a chance."

Angela entered the garage and inhaled the fumes of a full range of petroleum products—gasoline, motor oil, axle grease. No one was around. She stood at the front counter, tapping her nails on the grey Formica surface and looking for a bell to ring for service. There wasn't one. Following the clang of a wrench on metal, she went around the counter and stood at the door of the shop. She stared into the murk.

"Hey! Hello! We need some help out here!"

A guy dressed in greasy coveralls emerged from the gloom and Angela explained her predicament.

"What kind of vehicle?"

"Pontiac Grand Am. '86. You can't miss it—it's cherry red. Underneath the mud, that is. Can you send a tow truck?" Angela held her breath.

"Yep."

"Right away?"

"About an hour or so."

For the first time all day, the pain in Angela's head eased, just a fraction. "Really? And you can fix it? You have the right parts?"

"Pretty sure. Let me check."

Angela returned to the waiting area while the man rattled around in the store room. He appeared with a gas tank, and set it on the counter.

"There you go. I take it you're in a hurry."

"Oh, yes. A HUGE hurry. And I have to tell you, it's a pleasure to finally deal with someone who gets it."

The man shrugged. "No big deal. We can have you on the road to Yellowknife by suppertime."

"I'm heading south."

The man stared for a moment, then shook his head.

"No!" Angela banged a hand on the counter. "No, no, *no*, NO, NO!"

"Ice crossing closed to light traffic an hour ago. That's why it's so quiet in here."

Angela crumpled onto a chair and put her head between her knees. A sour taste rose from her throat and spread through her mouth. She wanted to vomit. Maybe she was concussed, after all.

"Jeez, lady. You okay? Should I take you to the nursing station?"

"No. I'm fine." She rose and headed toward the coffee shop. As she trudged through the parking lot, she passed the muddy blue half-ton. It was shaking, and Angela could hear growls within. The ugly dog had apparently renewed his attack on the upholstery. He took a break to watch her pass, his snout leaving a wet mark on the window.

The restaurant was little more than a glorified cafeteria: institutional tables, black vinyl and chrome chairs, a linoleum floor that was probably beige underneath the muddy footprints. The tables were full, people laughing and chatting over mugs of coffee and plates of sandwiches, burgers, mounds of fries.

Marge waved her over. "Looks like you heard."

A large man wiped his mouth with a paper napkin and got to his feet. "Nice seeing you, Marge. I'll call from Edmonton."

Angela grabbed his sleeve. "You're going? To Edmonton? How?"

"I drive a semi—road's only closed to light traffic."

"Of course. That's it!" Angela stood up. "Take me with you."

"What about your car?" Marge asked.

"I'll sell it. Right here. Right now." She walked among the tables. "'86 Pontiac Grand Am, going cheap. Low mileage. Only driven up this nightmare of a highway once. It's in one piece, more or less." People glanced her way, but kept talking among themselves. She leaned into a table full of men in plaid flannel shirts. "Late Valentine's gift for the missus. Can't go wrong."

The men stopped talking and stared at her. Marge grabbed her by the shoulders and steered her back to the table. "Don't be a nuisance."

"Fine then. I'll leave it where it is," Angela said.

"You can't just leave a car on the highway," Marge said. "It ain't legal."

"Breaking what law?"

Marge's brow creased as she considered the question. "Littering?"

"Littering!" A wave of red anger swept past Angela's eyes. "That is a fine vehicle. A classic."

Marge laughed. "Not for long. Life's hard in the North. Things age before their time."

Angela's rage suddenly let go. She imagined her car abandoned and alone on the highway, covered in mud and dust—the windshield was probably cracked already, and would soon be shattered by rocks thrown up by passing semis. The paint would become pitted, rust would creep through the frame and body. Angela's hand drifted to her wounded face, to the newly discovered lines beside her eyes. Panic replaced anger: cold, white panic that jabbed like icicles through her veins. It was too late for her vehicle, but there was one last way for her to escape.

"You're right, Marge. It's nothing but a piece of trash. Used up. Worn down. Rotting out. Might as well leave it. I'll go back to Yellowknife, buy a plane ticket, and fly out."

"Whoa, whoa, whoa." Marge patted Angela's arm. "I just meant that your car will acquire some northern character. No need to overreact. A bit of TLC, it'll still work for you—just won't be as pretty, is all."

Angela's hands and feet were turning to ice; she jumped out of her chair. "Get me the hell out of here!"

"Way I see it, you got two choices. One, hitch a ride back to Yellowknife right now. Two, overnight here in Fort Providence, have a shower and a good sleep, then catch a ride back in the morning. Lots of time to get a flight south."

Angela plopped back into her chair and assessed her filthy clothes. "A shower might not be a bad idea."

"Forgot to mention that the motel's full. But you can room with Hubcap and me. Hubcap will be delighted."

*****

An hour later, still coated with dirt, Angela was slouched in the passenger seat of a semi heading back to Yellowknife. She lifted a shoulder to ward off the glances the driver kept casting her way and reconsidered the rashness of taking a ride with the first trucker heading north. It had seemed a better bet than spending any more time in close quarters with Hub-cap-the-ugly-dog, but out here alone on the road, she wasn't so sure. She tugged the hem of her skirt toward her knees, and pulled the collar of her jacket toward her chin.

"Aren't you Angela Binnie? The one that writes 'The Dog Sled Report'?"

"Ya."

The trucker wiggled in his seat and twisted toward her. "I love that column. Get the *Spectator* every time I'm in Yellowknife, just so I can read it."

"Do tell."

"You run dogs yourself?"

Angela snorted. "No."

"Because it really sounds like you know what you're talking about. You got good news sense."

Angela unfolded herself and turned toward the trucker. "You think so?"

"Well, *ya*. My family ran dogs out of Fort Nelson for years. Reading your column's just like going back to the good old days. And that's some sense of humour you got. That 'personality profile' of that lady's lead dog just cracked me up. What was his name?"

"Henry."

"You ever freelance for *Alaska Malamute Magazine*, or maybe *Dog Sledding International*? Good circulation, that one."

"International?"

"Well, *ya*. Sledding's a circumpolar sport. But you knew that—you've done interviews with guys after they come back from Alaska, Scandinavia. You ever cover those things in person?"

"Hardly. The *Weekly Spectator*'s not exactly flush with cash."

"You gotta think big, lady. You got a real knack." The driver eyed her again. "You're a good-looking woman. You could do TV. Dog sledding's showing up more and more on those specialty sports channels. Maybe you could do next year's dog derby out on Yellowknife Bay."

Angela's fingers traced the scrapes on her face.

"And those sports channels—they're seen right across the country?"

"Yep."

"So a larger viewership than a small TV station in southern Manitoba?"

The man shrugged. "I suppose."

Angela noticed the trees becoming smaller, increasingly stunted. In the distance, a mud-covered lump materialized by the side of the road. Angela's car. As they approached, she remembered the first time she'd seen it in the showroom. Even before the sleek lines and glowing paint had registered in her conscious mind, there had been a spark of recognition, an understanding that if Angela had been a car, she would be *this* car. They whizzed past, throwing another coat of mud over the vehicle. Angela flinched.

"When we get to Yellowknife, can you take me straight to a garage? I have to send someone out for my car."

As they travelled north, Angela visualized her red designer parka against the white snow, the fur trim of the hood framing her face, hiding any marks from today's mishap. And she'd have to find a better moisturizer to fend off the crow's feet. She tried to block thoughts of the stench of the dog lot and the whine of the animals from her mind. It didn't work, but she assured herself the situation was temporary—a couple more years, and she'd be gone for good. By focusing her vision on the glass of the passenger-side window, she was able to see the vague outline of her reflection.

"From the dog derby trail on Yellowknife Bay, this is Angela Binnie reporting," she whispered.

Publishing History

The Ugly Truck and Dog Contest

Originally published in *Storyteller, Canada's Short Story Magazine*, Winter, 1999

The Yellowknife Yeti

Originally published as "The NWT Yeti" in *Storyteller, Canada's Short Story Magazine*, Spring 2000

The Prospector's Trail

Originally published in *Storyteller, Canada's Short Story Magazine*, Summer 2000
Honourable Mention, Great Canadian Story Contest, 2000
Reprinted in *Imprints 11*, Gage Educational Publishing Co., 2001

Bug Bites

Originally published in *Storyteller, Canada's Short Story Magazine*, Winter 2001

Sand Trap

Originally published in *Storyteller, Canada's Short Story Magazine,* Summer 2003
Honourable Mention, Great Canadian Story Contest, 2003

Baneberries

Originally published in *Winners' Circle 10*, Canadian Authors Association, Toronto Branch, 2003
First Place, Tenth Annual International Short Story and Essay Contest, Canadian Authors Association, Toronto Branch, 2002

Diamond Girl

Originally published in *North by North Wit: An Anthology of Canadian Humour*, Black Moss Press, 2003

Fireweed

Originally published in *Storyteller, Canada's Short Story Magazine*, Spring 2006

MARQUIS
Marquis Book Printing Inc.

Québec, Canada
2009